ALIEN GENOCIDE

ALIEN GENOCIDE

SHADOW VANGUARD™ BOOK FIVE

TOM DUBLIN   MICHAEL ANDERLE   CRAIG MARTELLE

DISRUPTIVE IMAGINATION

THE ALIEN GENOCIDE TEAM

JIT Readers
From each of us, our deepest gratitude!

Veronica Stephan-Miller
Micky Cocker
Rachel Beckford
Jeff Goode
Dave Hicks
James Caplan
Jackey Hankard-Brodie
Diane L. Smith
Dorothy Lloyd
Kelly O'Donnell
John Ashmore

*If we missed anyone, **please** let us know!*

Editor
Lynne Stiegler

Talth, Gray City, Bendosh Market

Tc'aarlat covered himself from the downpour with an oversized poncho. He had prepared for his mission better than usual because he hated the rain. It continued unabated throughout the year, rarely ceasing for more than a day. Ironically, if not for the rain, Gray City would be full of color, dancing lights twinkling between neon signs and blazing 3D images of rotating cans of soda and lustful holographic strangers everywhere one looked.

Thanks to the rain, the city had become infamous for its dismal atmosphere and depressing aura and remained dank despite their best efforts to adapt through things like bigger drains that ran straight to the oceans, clothing that was pure polyester, and streets covered from building to building with colossal tarpaulins.

Mandibles quivering with discomfort, Tc'aarlat grumbled, "Rain! This planet can take its rain and shove it up its oral anifice. Out of all the planets in the Ordanian Hub..." Tc'aarlat pulled a small black rectangular device, a communicator, from inside his poncho. "Why did he have to come to this dump? Only dumbasses and ducks would come here on purpose."

Tc'aarlat knew the answer to his question, but he used it to justify his complaints. Talth wasn't a popular destination for the weather or the sights. It wasn't even popular for the many nightclubs it played host to across its cities, ones that sold the kind of alcohol that had long been outlawed everywhere else.

No, Talth was popular for one thing and one thing only: outlaws found a safe haven on the crime-infested planet.

Talth was what many referred to as a "free world," which meant its people had done away with the government. It wasn't quite anarchy, but the replacement wasn't a formal affair, either. They'd reestablished a people's council since some form of government was necessary to keep everything from breaking down.

And what would the populace complain about without a government? To be a modern civilization, one must be offered the opportunity to join your fellows to bitch about the people in charge. There was little crime enforcement as a result, and plenty to complain about.

Everyone carried a gun because they had to. That limited street crime, but if your home or business was less than a fortress, you'd have to kill or be killed.

Of course, you'd be foolish to think that Talth wasn't under the control of somebody. Money was still the law of the land, and that meant the world was run by the powerful. By the gangsters, rather than elected officials half-assing their jobs.

Working at cross purposes with the crime families

never ended well for the officials, so half-ass was the only way to save their asses.

It was the perfect place for a high-ranking crime boss to come and hide, and that was why Tc'aarlat was there.

A few months ago, the crew of the ICS *Fortitude* had taken it upon themselves to steal information from a doctor who liked to rearrange people's faces. Not just anyone, though. Dangerous people, the kind who worked for crime syndicates.

This doctor had a preference for those under the Yollin mob boss Don Gan'barlo, who controlled a vast criminal enterprise operating under the Federation's nose. But the Shadows were onto him. They found the vault with his material assets and stole the lot, sending the Don into hiding. Finding the doctor had brought them one step closer to their prey.

Tc'aarlat had been following a Garbolglox—a race that looked like elephants, minus the trunk. They ate a lot and then some; it was their gift and their curse. They also ran weight-watching seminars because they had mean streaks as wide as their waistlines.

Roddy Parper, gray and bulbous, sat at an outside noodle shop under a tarpaulin, stuffing a brothy soup into his face with the white noise of rain a constant companion.

Tc'aarlat watched him for a solid half-hour, during which the creature took no break from eating. The Yollin counted seven bowls and shook his head when the Garbolglox waved for lucky number eight.

The dangers of nighttime sent the population indoors, leaving the street empty. Tc'aarlat made his way over, watching for furtive movements from the shadows. He didn't dive under the tarp until he was sure they were alone.

"Hello, sir!" The cook was on the older side of life, and when he smiled, he revealed a massive gap between his front teeth. Tc'aarlat stared at it. "Welcome to Noodles Oodles. What can I get for you?"

"I don't know." Tc'aarlat shrugged and turned his attention to the Garbolglox next to him, playfully slapping him on the arm. "You look like someone who appreciates food. What would you recommend?"

"How about the noodles?"

Tc'aarlat howled with laughter, too loud and obnoxious to be real. He wiped an invisible tear from his eye and turned back to the cook. "I'll take that, then. One noodle, please."

"Of course, sir!" The cook beamed at the order, scooping noodles that looked too much like boiled squid into a shallow pan. The resulting sizzle splattered his already greasy apron. The aroma of burnt nagabeast wafted over, quickly followed by the pungency of too much garlic and chili paste. Tc'aarlat decided he liked the smell and nodded at the chef.

"Where you from, you blubbering gray mass?" Tc'aarlat said once the cook's back was turned.

"I ain't from nowhere in particular," Roddy said.

"Nowhere in particular, huh?" Tc'aarlat teased. "I've heard people bathe on the sun this time of year." The Yollin laughed at his own joke.

"What do you want?" The Garbolglox turned to him, his face turning an ever-so-slight shade of red. "I'm trying to eat in peace, so leave me alone."

"You are eating all the pieces from what I see." Tc'aarlat held up his hands harmlessly. "No need to get sore. I was just making conversation."

"Yeah, well, up yours sideways complete with mandibles, Yollin." Roddy chuckled.

"Nicely done, big friend. I shall join you, as loathsome as that may be."

The cook dropped a bowl on the counter behind Tc'aarlat. The Yollin turned and stared at it until it stopped spinning. For anyone else, it was a normal plate of noodles, freshly cooked and steaming. The cook had even coated them with a layer of soy sauce for added flavor. Tc'aarlat wasn't sure what he was looking at. He screwed his face up, looking at the bowl from different angles as if he couldn't believe what he saw. His mandibles pinched tightly to his cheeks. "Worms? Why have you handed me a plate of dead worms?"

"Those are noodles," the cook stated with a cock of his head and turned his next statement into a question. "It's what you asked for?

"I don't remember asking for dead worms." Tc'aarlat used a nearby fork to bring a few strands closer so he could inspect them. "Looks like they need another round with the cooking pot."

"I assure you, they are cooked."

"Well, if you say so," Tc'aarlat replied, fishing the noodles up and shoving them through his mandibles. He chewed for a second before realizing the taste sensation he had been missing and quickly helped himself to a second forkful. "These aren't bad by half! Not grub guts or bistok, but they are bringing me strange joy."

A moment of peace settled over the small restaurant while the only two patrons attacked their bowls and the cook started his prep work for the next day.

Tc'aarlat belched loudly, then turned back to the Garbolglox and asked without hesitation, "You got a family, Roddy?"

Roddy's eyes went wide. The Yollin next to him had used a name. Not just any name, either. It was his name from a previous life, a life where he had been a dangerous thug at the beck and call of mobsters.

Tc'aarlat could see the creature's emotions as if they were words scrolling across his face. He'd seen it before from too many former servants of the Don. He was sure he'd worn that expression too, probably more than once.

Any sentient creature knew to fear Don Gan'barlo. It was the intelligent thing to do. People usually ran when confronted by anyone representing him, but the Garbolglox didn't look like a runner.

A roller maybe, but not a runner. Roddy didn't have a weapon because Tc'aarlat had liberated it earlier when he bumped into the big creature on the crowded street. Fighting his way free wasn't an option. Tc'aarlat waited patiently while the Garbolglox casually stuffed a big hand into his oversized pocket. One eyebrow started to twitch.

"Your marbles," Tc'aarlat said, trying not to glance at his half-eaten bowl of noodles. He was still hungry. The Yollin briefly wondered why he wasn't more concerned about the elephant man, but he did hold the upper hand, or maybe that was the lower hand, with Roddy's weapon pointed at its previous owner's groin.

"'Marbles?'" Roddy asked. Tc'aarlat glanced down. The

Garbolglox followed his gaze. "Marbles are small and insignificant. 'Cannonballs' was what you meant to say."

"Maybe you were swimming? So much rain. Rain, rain go away…" Tc'aarlat taunted.

"Who are you?" Roddy asked calmly. "What do you want?"

"I'm Tc'aarlat." He watched for recognition, but Roddy's face remained blank. "I'm looking for someone, and I was thinking you have sucked face with them. I mean, seen their face."

"How did you find me?" Roddy wondered. "It's been twelve years since I used that name and did that kind of work."

"A certain doctor gave you away," Tc'aarlat replied, leaning closer. "Where's Don Gan'barlo?"

"Don Gan'barlo?" He slowly raised a hand and scratched at his face as his eyes darted around, looking for Tc'aarlat's accomplices. He felt the hit coming, and he was on the wrong end of it. "I don't know."

"That's not the answer I'm looking for." Tc'aarlat pressed the barrel of Roddy's gun into his thigh. "Tell me where he is."

"I have no idea. He could be anywhere," Roddy stammered, trying to inch away from the pressure being applied to his leg.

"I know you worked for him," Tc'aarlat said. "You once guarded his body, saving his life on multiple occasions. I can read."

"Bodyguard. But that was a long time ago," Roddy replied. "I don't do that stuff anymore, honest."

"You want me to believe you walked out on Don

Gan'barlo after being that close to him? No one does that, Roddy. You still work for him. I know it, and you know it."

"It doesn't matter what you believe. I don't, and I have no idea where he is!"

"I hope you enjoyed your last meal." Tc'aarlat prodded him into motion with the weapon's barrel before turning back to the cook with an enthusiastic wave. "The noodles were great. I'll be coming back here so many times you'll get tired of me!"

"Please do!" The cook waved back.

Tc'aarlat was taller than the Garbolglox, but the big creature had him by a good two hundred kilos. Still, the one with the gun was in charge. "Time to pay the Pied Piper, you pickled pepper."

"What?" Roddy started to tremble. "I don't know anything." He hung his head and started to sob as the Yollin pushed him into the rain.

"For a guarder of bodies, you act like a spineless worm creature from a swamp of effluvia. Man up, already."

Roddy stumbled forward. Tc'aarlat didn't bother helping the big creature since he figured it was a ploy. Fearing for their life made people take risks. The Garbolglox had been a bodyguard. He knew how to fight. Tc'aarlat backed away, keeping a safe distance as he pointed the weapon from under his poncho.

"Into that alley, Roddy, where we can have a conversation about your privates."

"My what?"

"Privates. Where no one will bother us," Tc'aarlat clarified. The Garbolglox slowed as he entered the darker area between the buildings. "That's far enough. Where's Don Gan'barlo?"

"I don't know where the Don is," Roddy pleaded. He stuffed a hand into his pocket, and Tc'aarlat almost shot him for it before he pulled out a wallet and flipped it open. "Please don't do this. I have a family."

"Family?" Tc'aarlat shoved the pistol toward Roddy's face and snatched the wallet. He stepped back before looking down at the treasured memories Roddy kept with him. Getting married to his wife. Watching his son take his first steps. Taking his daughter to school. Moving into their most recent apartment with more room for a new member of the family. Tc'aarlat looked up at him. "You actually have a family? I only joked about that."

"I'm done with the gangster life," Roddy replied, holding his oversized hands up in the universal sign of surrender. "All it ever did was cause me trouble. I'm a bouncer for a nightclub now."

"No families for guys like us. Ever," Tc'aarlat snarled. "My best friend is a bird."

"Mine is my wife. The kids are okay, too. Please." Roddy motioned for his wallet. Tc'aarlat tossed it toward him, keeping his weapon aimed.

The Garbolglox fumbled the catch. The wallet landed between them. Roddy looked at it. Tc'aarlat watched the bodyguard. The Yollin stepped back.

"Nice try. Pick it up." Tc'aarlat waved the barrel of the weapon. After Roddy recovered his wallet and put it back in his oversized pocket with his hands in the open, Tc'aarlat relaxed. "How'd you do it?"

"I met my wife at the spaceport," Roddy said. "As I was

getting out of the transport that brought me here. There she was. I stood in the rain for five or ten minutes, just watching her. A fellow Garbolglox, but different. We don't mind the rain and being wet, so there are a few of us here. We went dancing, and the rest is history."

"Well, shit." Tc'aarlat sighed. "I must be going soft. I still need you to tell me where the Don is."

"If you let me go, I won't tell anyone about this," Roddy said. "Not your name, nothing. I just want to go home and live my life in peace. I'd tell you where the Don is if I knew. Especially if you're going to kill him. It would be nice to have my freedom back."

"Wouldn't it?" Tc'aarlat replied and made a show of considering it.

"Good luck," Roddy stated, having decided Tc'aarlat wasn't going to shoot. The Garbolglox slowly backed away, asking Tc'aarlat with his eyes if it was okay to leave. Tc'aarlat nodded, and the gigantic creature turned and walked away.

Tc'aarlat watched him go. "No information and soaked to the bone. I hate this planet," the Yollin muttered. "I think you know something. Jack will get it out of you."

Tc'aarlat removed his tablet from his pocket as soon as he knew Roddy was out of earshot and brought up the long list of mobsters who had been remade at the hands of the doctor. He scrolled past the many criminals with "deceased" stamped across their profiles until he landed on the Garbolglox's profile.

"The fucker managed to get himself a family," Tc'aarlat mumbled with the shake of his head. "I am already regretting this."

Tc'aarlat stamped the same "deceased" over Roddy's profile, pocketed the tablet, and moved out of the alley, scowling darkly. He was no closer to finding Don Gan'barlo, and he was wet. He couldn't wait to get off this planet.

An Alley, Talth, Gray City

Roddy stopped after rounding a corner and listened for silent footfalls. His oversized ears flapped and focused the sound. He looked around the corner to find Tc'aarlat gone.

The Garbolglox pulled a communicator from a hidden fold under his enormous belly and tapped in a memorized number. Someone answered without saying a word.

"Roddy here. I need to talk to Don Gan'barlo."

Talth, Gray City Spaceport, ICS *Fortitude*, Bridge

Rain pounded the hull of the ICS *Fortitude*. Jack pulled his coat tighter around his neck as if fighting off the weather. He preferred space. Or a bar that he didn't get soaked walking to. And there was another thing. *The Pod-doc didn't do its job.* Jack wondered if his nanocytes were losing their juice. Or maybe they didn't care about his hair since he had discovered his first gray hair only hours earlier. Ironic, considering they had just arrived in Gray City. At least the universe had a sense of humor.

Jack wasn't currently taking in the sights, onscreen or otherwise. His eyes were closed, and his legs were resting on top of the control panel he used to monitor the ship. The rhythmic drumming noise on the hull had lulled him to sleep.

A younger woman entered the bridge, a mischievous smile on her face. A deep-red bird sat calmly on her shoulder as she crept closer to Jack's chair, then silently signaled.

CAW! CAW!

Jack bolted upright in confusion amid a flurry of feathers. His eyes flew open to the sight of a young Raal hawk screeching at him from point-blank range, and he screamed as he twisted out of his chair and landed squarely on the deck.

Adina Choudhury, the navigator for the ICS *Fortitude*, laughed heartily at the success of her prank. "Got you, Jack!"

"Bloody hell, Adina!" Jack groused as he found his footing and stood. "What's that thing doing on your shoulder?"

"You mean Isaaca Newton?" Adina softly stroked her fingers along the bird's chest, and the hawk cooed with pleasure. "Tc'aarlat says I have to keep her on my shoulder if we're going to bond properly."

"I said, no birds on the bridge." Jack pointed. "Especially vermin like that!"

"It's not her fault you don't like her," Adina said. "You won't even give her a chance."

"I don't want to give her a chance. Those flying rats shouldn't be on the ship anyway. One was bloody enough, but now there's four of them. I went to get some breakfast earlier and found all of our meat snapped up."

His eyes narrowed. "Wait a minute. Tc'aarlat named Mist's three devil spawn Hawking, Einstein, and Sir Isaac Newton. So, where'd you get this one?"

"Isaaca Newton turned out to be female, so I renamed her. Oh, and the missing meat was probably Tc'aarlat. He's been pretty mopey lately, and you know how he eats when he is."

"Speaking of which, is he back yet?"

"I haven't seen him." Adina glanced at the floor, as she often did when she was unsure of how her next words would sound. "Do you think he's ever going to give this up?"

"Searching for the Don?" Jack took his seat again. "I doubt it. If there's one thing Tc'aarlat isn't, it's a quitter."

"It's been three months." Adina sat on his armrest. "The guys in that database haven't seen or heard from Don Gan'barlo in that time. It's pretty obvious the Don knows we have the list."

"That just means he has very few places he can turn." Jack shrugged and rubbed the sleep from his eyes. "Besides, Nathan Lowell got in touch. I think he might have a lead on the Don."

"Didn't he tell you?"

"No. He wants to meet us for dinner as a proper congratulations for handing the credits we stole over to the Federation. I assume he's going to tell us what it is then."

"We *deserve* a reward," Adina laughed. "That adventure nearly killed us. Paid well and dinner. I'll call it a win-win."

"It was close," Jack admitted with a nod. "Then again, when is it ever not close?"

Talth, Gray City Space Port, ICS *Fortitude*, Tc'aarlat's Room

Tc'aarlat threw the rain-soaked poncho across his room, where it landed in a soggy heap. Mist swooped down from her perch, landed on his shoulder, and gave him an affectionate rub, which he returned with a click of his mandibles. "I missed you, too."

The Yollin dropped onto his bed, Mist gripping his shoulder pad with her talons and flaring her wings for balance as he did. His quarters were small; some would say cozy. There was just enough room to fit his bed and a few cupboards for clothes, but not enough space to live in, especially since he shared it with three Raal hawks. *This room is my entire life,* he brooded. *Not much to show for it.*

Mist sensed his somber mood and nudged him in concern.

"It's okay," Tc'aarlat said. "I'm fine."

She stared at him with piercing yellow eyes.

"All right, but don't tell anyone." Tc'aarlat brought her closer. "There was this guy today that I'd chased down for information on... You know what, that doesn't matter. What matters is that he was a former gangster like me but managed to settle down, have a family, and a normal life. It's...well, I don't know what it is."

The Raal hawk stared blankly at him. Tc'aarlat laughed. "It's probably nothing. Just a shock is all."

Tc'aarlat jumped at a sudden knock on the door, much to Mist's displeasure. The Yollin's pained "Ow!" rang through the room after she nipped his ear. He patted himself down, soothed Mist's ruffled feathers, and went to answer it. On the other side was a very pleased Adina and her recently acquired Raal hawk Isaaca, who flew in and perched next to her siblings as soon as the door was fully open.

"I still can't believe you renamed her Isaaca, of all

things," Tc'aarlat grumbled. "My name worked perfectly well."

"I thought I saw you sneak past," Adina replied as she stepped into the room. "And you know why I renamed her. How did it go? Did you find out where Don Gan'barlo is?"

"Unless he's hiding somewhere in all this luxury, no. I returned empty-clawed." Tc'aarlat slumped against the wall, half-defeated. "The guy was a nobody like all the others we've chased down. No leads. No nothing. Another dead-end."

"Don't let it get you down." Adina sat on the bed and patted the empty spot next to her. "I thought I'd come and share the good news in person. Nathan's been in touch and wants to take us all out for dinner."

"Yikes." Tc'aarlat shuddered. "Imagine getting into bed with that guy."

"What?" Adina stared, nonplussed, then laughed. "Not that. He wants to throw us a proper celebration for what we liberated from the Don's vaults."

"'Liberated.' Yes, that's what we did." Tc'aarlat chortled at the wording. "We could use leads, too. Cold hard facts we can follow to the Don's ugly face."

"Jack reckons Nathan might take this opportunity to give us a lead. It's been months since we did an actual job for the Federation."

"I was beginning to think they didn't want us anymore." Tc'aarlat stroked his Raal hawk as his face turned dark.

"Is everything okay?" Adina put a hand on his shoulder. "You seem a little…off."

"No, noooo, no," Tc'aarlat jumped up and threw her

some finger guns. "I'm cool, man. Like an ice boob, you know."

"'Cube,' you dolt!"

"Don't call me a dolt! That's a so very much derogatory word on my world."

"See, this is where I get confused. You understand the concept behind the word 'derogatory' well enough to use it correctly in a sentence, but not the word 'cube?'"

"Your language is hard to grasp," Tc'aarlat defended himself. "Where I'm from, we know what derogatory means, but we don't have ice boobs. I mean, cubes."

"Fair enough. You have a carapace. Makes boobs irrelevant." Adina grinned. "We're leaving in about an hour." She looked at the Yollin. "For a while, we thought you might not be coming with."

"Can't I skip it?" Tc'aarlat indicated the heavy rain drumming on the hull. "I'm still soaked from my last trip. Besides, I'm not that hungry anyway."

"No." Adina stuck out her tongue. "Now that I've seen you, I can tell Jack you're here."

She moved to the door while Tc'aarlat crossed his arms. "You wouldn't."

"Should've been sneakier, Mister Yollin." Adina pushed the button that opened the door and promptly exited.

"That's *Mister* Yollin to you!" Tc'aarlat called after her.

Talth, Gray City Space Port, ICS *Fortitude*, Jack's Room

Jack held the bowtie up to his collar, then removed it, then brought it back up, then removed it again. As he watched his well-dressed counterpart in the mirror follow suit, he considered which looked better, the expensive suit with the bowtie or without. Nathan had told them he was taking them to dinner and to wear something appropriate, but he had neglected to say where and what "appropriate" was.

"You know what?" Jack mumbled to himself. "I'm going to go without and put the bowtie in my pocket. If it's wrong, I can put it on in the bathroom."

Suddenly, he was interrupted by a knock and a shout through the door. "Jack, hurry up!"

"One more minute!" Jack called back, but he made no move toward the door. Despite being dressed and ready, he couldn't resist grabbing the comb that teetered on the edge of his sink and quickly driving it through his hair.

It only took a few seconds to find what he'd hoped not to see—a gray hair, the coming of doom. He carefully pulled the strand from his head. He had no preconceptions about being a young man, but this was something else. This meant that he really *was* getting older.

Jack flicked the annoying evidence into the trash, then combed his hair into place and checked it in the mirror a final time.

Talth, Gray City Space Port, The Swanky Hole Lounge

Nathan rose to greet the team as they entered the warm and sophisticated atmosphere of The Swanky Hole Lounge. Each delicately set table was spaced well apart from its neighbors, providing room to move and a degree of privacy for conversation. A small orchestral-style band playing a variety of alien instruments was discreetly tucked into one corner of the room. The music they produced had a cadence similar to Beethoven's. The opposite corner featured a tall fountain that quietly splashed into a large basin with live fish swimming in it.

The patrons and unobtrusive waitstaff were well-dressed. As Jack shook Nathan's hand, he swore he would go into the bathroom at the earliest opportunity and put on the bowtie.

"It's so good to see you again, Shadows." Nathan spoke warmly, his eyes reflecting his sincerity. "I know we talk with each other all the time through screens, but it's nothing compared to meeting face to face."

"Where's Ecaterina?" Adina looked around for Nathan's wife.

"Unfortunately, she couldn't make it tonight." Nathan gestured everyone to their seats.

Jack helped himself to the bread on the table. "Not the trip to the frontier, but finally meeting up with you. I don't think we've seen each other in person since the end of our first mission."

"Onyx Station," Nathan agreed. "Right after you'd finished up on Alma Nine."

"So, what have you got for us, Nathan?" Tc'aarlat clicked his mandibles in anticipation. "Any leads?"

Adina slapped him on the arm. "We've been here for two seconds."

"No, it's okay," said Nathan. "That's what I like about you, Tc'aarlat—straight to the point."

"So, do you?" Jack pressed. "Have any leads, that is?"

Nathan leaned forward. The others did the same. "I was going to wait until after dinner, but I suppose there's no harm in telling you now. The Federation has need of your team."

"I was beginning to think you'd forgotten about us," Adina shared.

"Not after everything your group has done," Nathan said. "Improving relations one planet at a time."

Before Nathan could speak another word, a waiter interrupted by placing drinks on the table. Jack received a cold glass of home-brewed ale, as did Nathan. Adina was given a Coke with a small amount of rum in it. That left Tc'aarlat, who was given a strange-looking brown concoction that bubbled like boiling water.

"Brown coorish," Tc'aarlat said. "How did you know?"

"I have a good memory for that kind of thing." Nathan gently tapped his nose. "As I was saying, the Federation needs your services. Have you ever heard of the planet Fruling?"

"Fruling?" Jack said. "Doesn't ring a bell or bang a gong."

Nathan gave him a strange look but continued, "It's a truly unfortunate planet on the outer edges of the frontier that ended up in the middle of a galactic war between the Krindoparsatespians and the Dran—"

"Krindopars-what-ians?" Tc'aarlat tried. "Krindo spares. Krindos. Yes, Krindos. I can say that."

"Wait a minute. Are you asking us to stop a galactic war?" Adina broke in, eyes wide.

"No." Nathan shook his head. "This war has nothing to do with us, but the Enkelites—the people who once lived on Fruling—were among the first to align with the Federation and have been strong supporters ever since. We want to make sure they're well looked after."

"So, if you don't plan to end the war, how are you going to do that?" Jack narrowed his eyes as he studied Nathan. "Or should I say *we*?"

"Simple. We're relocating the Enkelites to a distant planet, well away from this war. They're ready to go right now, but there's a problem—"

"Let me take a wild guess. The world's not suitable for their species and needs terraforming," Jack finished.

"Exactly." Nathan nodded.

"That's what Zorxia is doing, then?" Adina said. "Overseeing the mission?"

"There wouldn't be a mission without her. She's our diplomatic contact on this one, as well as overseeing the security," Nathan confirmed. "The Enkelites are waiting for this terraforming to happen."

"What's the holdup?" Tc'aarlat said. "And why would you want us involved in that?"

"We want a few people we can trust to deliver the new terraforming technology and help oversee the whole operation," Nathan said after double-checking to make sure he wouldn't be overheard. "As I said, the Enkelites are old allies. We're not worried about them causing problems, but we know that unexpected things happen during operations like this."

"What about Don Gan'barlo? He's out there somewhere, hiding. The longer we waste time not looking for him, the better prepared he'll be when we come knocking," Jack said, silencing Tc'aarlat with a hard look.

"I understand your frustrations," Nathan replied. "Truth

is, we haven't got a clue where he's hiding, not a single lead. You going around roughing up old gangsters isn't getting us anywhere, either."

"We've got to bring him to justice, and there's still plenty of people left on the doctor's list to get answers from," Tc'aarlat blurted.

"Maybe it'll be good to take a break from it?" Adina suggested. "It's like working too hard on a puzzle. The more time you spend on it, the harder it gets. Sometimes it's a good idea to step back and take in the whole picture."

Nathan met the Yollin's gaze and held it. "I promise you, as soon as we have a lead, you'll be the first to know."

Tc'aarlat slumped. Out of everyone at the table, Jack had known the Yollin the longest and felt he knew him best. *This is more than frustration about a missing mobster he has a beef with. Something else is bothering him.*

"It seems like a simple mission," Jack commented, still watching Tc'aarlat. "Something quick to help us get back to basics."

Tc'aarlat glanced at him. "You think it's a good idea to stop searching for the Don?"

"Not permanently. But it's been months, and we've got nothing. Don Gan'barlo will surface again. He can't stay quiet forever. When he pops up, we'll be ready for him."

"That's why I want to find him now before he has a chance to get his legs back." Tc'aarlat fidgeted and played with his hands. "I guess I'm outvoted, though."

Jack turned back to Nathan. "I suppose that means we're in. What's our next step?"

"I'm glad you asked."

3

High Orbit over Renasta, Ark One, Observation Deck

It was closing on six months since the Enkelites had left the pure green of their world for the vast blackness of space and a new planet. Most aboard the three arks that orbited the world of Renasta felt like they were being punished. Although the arks boasted fascinating facilities that catered to their needs, the Enkelites were an agricultural people at heart, with no real interest in the comforts of modern space travel. They enjoyed working the land, growing their fruit and vegetables, and reaping the rewards for hard work. Now, thanks to the ark, they could look down on their new world but not touch it—a horrid torture.

One such person was Wo'Fek Zurr, a female of the species, who had come to the observation deck every day since they arrived. The Enkelites were humanoid in appearance, as though they shared distant human ancestors, but there were differences, especially in the females. Wo'Fek was a prime example of that. Her hair was as wild as straw, a common trait, and two antlers sprouted through the strands, albeit hers were smaller than the other females on Ark One. The other noticeable difference, aside from their attire, was the brown and white fuzz that was so short and sleek it was indistinguishable from bare skin.

It felt like an age since the war had invaded their peaceful world of Fruling. The two alien races had come down in a hail of hellfire and blasters and torn apart everything the Enkelites held dear. When she closed her eyes, she could still see her barn going up in flames and hear the roars of engines and the carnage from blaster fire across the fields. It haunted her dreams at night, and she dearly hoped that feeling the ground underfoot again would rid her of the nightmares.

Just then, a young boy came around the corner, screaming. Wo'Fek's lips twisted from frown to smile. The child was perhaps seven years old and closely resembled Wo'Fek, minus the antlers.

Imis, her son, was aptly named for the Enkelite god of trouble. Behind him and closing in was a rougher, older Enkelite, whose fuzz was turning gray and whose thick beard had long ago gone white. He had a stern look on his face and brandished a wooden staff at the youngster.

"Mother!" Imis jumped into Wo'Fek's arms. She simply laughed.

"What trouble have you gotten yourself into now?"

"Wo'Fek," said the stern man a little breathlessly. Wo'Fek wasted no time in releasing her son and kneeling before Nee'pkan, the Elder of the Enkelites and their undisputed leader. Nee'pkan scowled at the boy while he raised Wo'Fek's head with the butt of his staff until their eyes met. "Your son was stealing supplies again."

"Supplies?" Wo'Fek repeated. "What supplies?"

"Imis was stuffing his face with bread. Aldritch above knows how he keeps getting into the pantry."

"He's resourceful." Wo'Fek looked back at her son and gave him a cheeky wink before turning straight-faced to the Elder. "Imis is the kind of child we need for our second generation. Quick-willed, curious, and—"

"Nothing but trouble," Nee'pkan interrupted. "My patience is wearing thin with your boy, Wo'Fek. I am running out of warnings."

"I'll make sure he stays in line." Wo'Fek confirmed her commitment with a slight bow. "And that he is punished, for good measure."

"See that you do." Nee'pkan nodded. "Next time, I'll lock him in the pantry until he explodes."

Mother and son watched the scowling Elder walk away. When Wo'Fek was quite sure he couldn't see or hear them, she grabbed her son tightly and wriggled her fingers across his body, making him laugh loudly. "You are nothing but trouble, Imis. What is the matter with you?"

"Please." He tried to bat her off while giggling like a maniac as she found all his ticklish spots, but she was far stronger than him. "Mother! I can't stand it!"

"You stole bread?" Wo'Fek placed him on the floor. "Why, son? We have plenty of bread in our room."

"That's boring bread. I wanted something more challenging."

"Well, it's good to know my son is a thief, amongst other things," Wo'Fek said through a smile, stopping his torture. "I suppose that means you won't need any soup later since you've already been fed."

"No!" Imis protested. "I only got a few bites in before the Elder caught me!"

Wo'Fek laughed before beckoning him closer. "Come here, you little urchin." Imis didn't move, thinking it was a trick and he would get tickled again, but his mother was persistent, and he eventually gave in. Wo'Fek swung him up on her lap, so they both faced the thick pane of glass that separated them from the vacuum of space.

"When are we going to leave here?" he asked. "I want to smell the flowers again, and grow things, and drink fresh water."

"I know you do." Wo'Fek brushed his shaggy hair back and gave him a peck on the forehead. "It won't be long now, I promise."

"You said that a week ago!"

"I'll probably say it next week, too," said Wo'Fek. "I'll add a week for every time you ask me and every time you steal."

"We'll never leave, then," he said somberly.

Wo'Fek held him tighter. "We'll leave, and when we do, we'll rebuild our farm and grow fruit again, and above all else, we'll be one with the land, like we once were."

"How are we going to do all of that without Father?"

Everything stopped for the space of three heartbeats, and it took Wo'Fek another moment to acknowledge what her son had said. She didn't reply, mostly because she didn't know how. Instead, she clutched him tighter and lovingly rested her chin upon his head. There'd be another nightmare tonight. She already knew it.

. . .

High Orbit over Renasta, Ark One, the Elder's Room

The three Elders of the Enkelites met on Ark One every week to stroke their ever-growing beards and discuss the problems ravaging the three ships.

It was amazing how, despite every need being met, they had so many problems. Nothing could be done about most of them, so the Elders spent much of their meeting time smoking their long pipes and playing games of Dokk'ra, a dice game that involved the use of live mice.

Hozgak took a long draw and slowly blew out the purple smoke before turning to the other Elder in the room. "Surprises, it seems Nee'pkan is running late again. He should've been here two minutes ago."

"Yup." Shexee, who was the oldest of the three, nodded back. His wrinkles had wrinkles, and his skin looked like it was coated in a thin layer of snow. If it weren't for his gray robe and the staff in his hands, one could have easily mistaken him for a poorly constructed snowman.

Nee'pkan rushed into the room through the automatic doors, out of breath and leaning heavily on his staff. The other two barely glanced at him as they puffed heavily on their pipes. Nee'pkan approached them, quickly gathered himself, and sat at the table. "I am sorry I am so late, brothers."

"Tell us, what is it this time?" Hozgak grinned as he spoke. "More trouble with your misbehaved herds?"

"They're not misbehaved. They're spirited, which is what makes them so talented at agriculture."

"It wasn't because you were chasing one of them around?"

"I never said that," Nee'pkan corrected. "It was Imis again. That boy can run circles around me."

"We've had the same troubles with our flocks," Hozgak admitted. "Haven't we, Shexee?"

"Yup," Shexee agreed.

"The people are bored with this metal world," Hozgak continued. "They yearn to feel the breeze of a new planet and lay their feet on fresh grass and seek new opportunities. It has been six months, and frankly, that's six months too long."

"Aldritch teaches patience," Nee'pkan reminded them. "And it seems that our patience is soon to be rewarded."

"Oh?" Hozgak sat up, a little more attentive now. "How so?"

"The Federation has been in touch with Shexee. Isn't that right?"

"Yup."

"What did they say, brothers? Will the planet soon be ready for us?"

"Soon." Nee'pkan nodded. "They're sending a few of their emissaries to meet with us and implement a machine on the world that'll reconstruct it for us, make it safe."

"Safe." Hozgak chortled. "We thought we were safe on our old world, yet here we are searching for another. The Federation was supposed to fight for us, not send us away."

"I don't think that's ultimately fair, brother. They did—"

"Codswallop!" Hozgak coughed. The purple smoke had drifted a little farther back in his throat than he'd wanted. "What happens when this new planet comes under threat? Will we do the same thing again? Run away?"

"Hopefully, it won't come to that," said Nee'pkan. "You can't expect them to go to war for us."

"I certainly can," Hozgak retorted. "We've fed them our livestock and what we grew for decades. Safeguarding us and the resources we provide isn't too much to ask."

"They rehomed us," Nee'pkan pointed out, "after a war they did not start with enemies embroiled in unbridled hatred for each other."

"Yup," Shexee agreed.

"Not yet they haven't." Hozgak stopped himself, drew a few deep breaths, and strove for calm. "I am sorry for my outburst, brothers. While I do not condone war or violence, I condone the loss of our home even less. We were all born there, along with every ancestor we have. It doesn't feel right, just leaving it for somewhere new."

"And yet, that's what we're doing," Nee'pkan spoke earnestly. "Change is important, Hozgak; you know that. As long as our people are prosperous, that's all that matters."

"Perhaps." Hozgak stroked his chin. "I can't help feeling that we're disturbing the natural order of things, and as the teachings of Aldritch have shown us, upsetting that balance can only lead to disaster."

As if by fate, the ark suddenly rocked. The mice on the table fled for their lives, and the Elders fell flat on their faces. Once they'd righted themselves, they went to the window in search of answers. Another large ship was closing on their arks, headed straight for Renasta.

The Elders looked at each other uncertainly before

Hozgak spoke. "Disaster. Unbalance can only lead to disaster."

Void Space, Protest Ship *Joshua*, Bridge

Captain Bon Noh ran a comb through his thick silver mane as he sat in his command chair on the bridge. A hundred times a day left the hair stunning and gray; that was how the Malatian saying went, and that was how Bon Noh rolled. Unfortunately, he'd not had enough time this morning to complete the ritual in his room, and he refused to shirk it. Like all males of his species, his long tresses were his pride and glory. Proper care before creating the extravagant styles used to help attract a mate was a must.

It had been only a couple of hours since they'd received a tip that the Federation planned to terraform a planet that was already full of life, a process that could ultimately kill the native species. Bon Noh and the others on board Protest Ship *Joshua* were en route to prevent that, in keeping with their self-appointed mission to save lives and right the many wrongs that plagued the galaxy through non-violent protest.

"How long until we reach Renasta?" Bon Noh spoke to a tall Howvan, who was currently studying a star chart on his screen. Theeyej had been a crew member since Bon Noh commandeered the ship from a group of pirates with a nasty habit of wiping out near-extinct species and auctioning them off for profit.

"Hard to tell, Captain," Theeyej replied. "If we don't run into any trouble, perhaps another hour or so."

"An hour or so! That won't do at all! Our informant

says that the Federation has perfected a new way of terraforming. If they've already started before we arrive, there may be nothing we can do!" Bon Noh barked back.

"We could push the ship faster, but it might cause long-term damage."

"Do it," commanded Bon Noh. "There's nothing we can do *after* the fact, Theeyej. We have to beat the Federation there."

Bon Noh was so convinced of the righteousness of his cause that he never contemplated the information he had received might have been wrong.

Protest Ship *Joshua*'s fusion torch drive, which had been boosted by the original pirate owners for greater performance, powered itself forward in response to Theeyej's commands. Increased amounts of propellant ran through the reaction chamber, heated by magnetically confined fusion plasma. As the ship rocketed through the empty parts of space, a reading that indicated a momentary unevenness in heating the propellant went unseen.

4

Void Space, ICS *Fortitude*, Adina's Room

ICS *Fortitude* had left Talth about three hours earlier, en route to an oversized converted freighter called RS *Briccan*. The research ship doubled as an intergalactic research center for important Federation-funded scientific projects. After they had finished their dinner, Nathan had directed the Shadows there to take delivery of the terraforming device. Adina looked forward to seeing Zorxia, the woman who had helped her out of a rough spot when they were on a volunteer mission and her wolf was giving her trouble.

"I think you look lovely." The voice was sweet and motherly. When Adina turned away from her mirror, she came face-to-screen with a middle-aged woman and her charming smile. Solo was the ship's AI and possessed a motherly personality Adina appreciated but which often drove Jack and Tc'aarlat crazy.

"Thank you, but I don't want to look lovely, Solo." Adina swiveled back to the mirror and straightened her uniform again. "I want to look professional. It's been a while since Zorxia and I met in person. The last time I saw her, she was on a vidscreen, sparring with some bureaucrat."

"I'm sure she'll be happy to see you," Solo reassured her. "You've grown as a person since then."

"It's been almost a year." Adina leaned against the wall and gathered her thoughts. "I've made so many mistakes since then."

"And had a lot of success with your missions, and otherwise." Solo gestured to herself. "Things could have gone much worse."

"Could've been better, too," Adina replied with a small smile as she recalled the recent hacker-led hijacking incident and the time she'd held a gun to Jack's head. "I'm not making those mistakes again."

"That shows growth, Adina. Zorxia will notice that, too."

"I hope so." Adina brought her fingers to her mouth and let out a long whistle. A second later, Isaaca had crossed from her makeshift perch atop the wardrobe and landed on Adina's shoulder. Adina stroked the dark-red feathers. "She's getting better at that. Tc'aarlat says I'm a natural at Raal hawk training."

"You'd better head to the bridge," Solo advised. "We'll soon approach *Briccan*."

"Right. Well, okay." Adina shrugged and braced herself. "I'm ready."

As she went for the door, a sudden pain shot through her stomach. She winced and stumbled, then braced herself with one hand against the wall. The pain passed after a moment, and she straightened.

"When was the last time you ate?" Solo sounded concerned.

"I've been so preoccupied with meeting Zorxia that I think I missed lunch. And breakfast."

"Tut, tut," Solo teased. "You know better than to miss breakfast. It's the most important meal of the day."

"Yeah." Adina nodded. "I'll grab something from the kitchen once we're on board *Briccan*."

"A good idea," Solo agreed.

Void Space, Research Ship *Briccan*, Hangar

"So, here is such a big problem," Tc'aarlat announced as the ICS *Fortitude*'s cargo bay opened to allow him and Jack into *Briccan*'s hangar. Jack sighed loudly. He'd heard nothing but complaints since Nathan's dinner had ended, and this would be another one to add to the ever-growing list. "*Briccan* is an official Federation research ship, and look at the other ships in the hangar. Why do they need us to do this when they have plenty of other people who could do it for them?"

"Because they asked nicely, and I like being paid and getting more work where I get paid."

"Jack! Are credits all you care about?" Jack nodded. Tc'aarlat stopped just before they exited the ship and came into the view of strangers. "We were hired to hide under the covers, posing as delivery people and listening in where other people couldn't. Now we are no longer under the covers. We are diplomats! Is that what you wanted when you stole my money to buy the ship?"

"If there's anything to blame, it's our success." Jack

shrugged. "You have to admit we've accomplished more in the past year than most Federation agents do in a lifetime. We've stopped wars and ended crisis after crisis, and that's why the Federation trusts us so much. I like being legit."

"I didn't sign up for this," Tc'aarlat rebutted. "It's fine that we're getting paid, and I'm grateful for it, but I've got my own problems."

"I swear, if you say—"

"Don Gan'barlo is still out there."

"Let it go." Jack pushed past him. "We'll get to it when we get to it."

"You mean when the Federation *allows* us to get to it!" Tc'aarlat shouted. "Or how about when the *captain* of this ship wants us to get to it?"

"Everything okay?" Adina came up alongside Tc'aarlat.

"Yeah, it's fine. Just flustratated."

"Come on." Adina nudged him. "Let's get this over and done with. Think of it this way, the sooner we're done with this terraforming stuff, the sooner we can resume hunting down the Don."

"Pfft, I doubt anybody wants to continue our work to rid the galaxy of the plague known as Don Gan'barlo."

Tc'aarlat and Adina walked down the gangplank together and into *Briccan*. It could easily fit another twenty ICS *Fortitude*s within its hangar. Federation flags with the familiar insignias were prominent, declaring the ships' origins and affiliations, and all the nearby crewmembers wore standard shipboard uniforms with Federation patches.

At the end of the gangplank, Jack shook hands with a blonde human woman in a variant of a uniform and another female who was anything but human. She was a Snowbiral, a bipedal lifeform with horns and bright pink skin. The blonde woman went off down a corridor.

Adina wasted no time rushing toward the Snowbiral. "Aliporta! It's so good to see you again! Wait, you're the scientist behind this? I thought you were working on something else back at Base 11."

"It's good to see you, too," Aliporta replied. "I was, but I was also working on this. When Zorxia had a break-through on a critical section of the process, I transferred to *Briccan* for the final R&D work."

Tc'aarlat walked slowly down the gangplank and nodded quickly at the Snowbiral. "'Sup?"

"Welcome aboard, Tc'aarlat," she responded with a slight bow.

"Do we know each other?" Tc'aarlat wondered aloud. "I feel like you're the kind of person I would remember."

"This is Aliporta." Jack gestured to the Snowbiral. "She's the project's lead scientist."

"Oh, right." Tc'aarlat sniffed. "So, are we ready to load that terraforming machine thing yet or...?"

"Not quite yet," Aliporta interjected. "It's running through a final phase of tests. Once Zorxia blesses it, we'll be ready to go. We weren't expecting you this early."

"If you're the lead scientist..." Adina let it hang.

"Zorxia is a super-scientist, but she's the program manager, and her administrative tasks take precedence over her scientific and engineering duties. She gets to double-check our work and help us when needed. She has a brilliant mind."

"That's what Adina told us. We left Talth as soon as we

could," Jack stated. "Glad to do it, too. That world is wet from sunup to sundown."

"You're welcome to come watch the terraformer in action." Aliporta turned to lead the way, collecting them with a glance. "Afterward, we'll transport it to your ship and load it."

"More waiting," Tc'aarlat muttered.

"I've heard so much about your team, Jack." Aliporta moved close to him. "Have you really done everything they say you've done?"

"I don't know what they've said, but if it's good, then yes. It was us." Jack grinned. "It's been a challenging year, but we didn't get killed too often. We've been happy to help."

Tc'aarlat slowed his pace and watched the team. Adina was catching up with the scientist. Jack was so focused on the Snowbiral that he wasn't paying attention to the separation between them. Tc'aarlat realized with a pang that it was the first time he had ever felt this distant from his group. As if he were alone again.

He picked up the pace. Being distant from the team was his choice, just like being a member of it.

Void Space, Research Ship *Briccan*, R&D Laboratory

Aliporta opened the door with her key card and held it for everyone to pass through. On the other side was an impressive three-story laboratory filled with state-of-the-art equipment. The team was on the top floor, looking down into its heart.

Numerous scientists in white lab coats were researching, experimenting, or both, using large touchscreens connected to the array of computers and individual tablets. Several remote tests were in progress in the lab's various containment chambers.

Zorxia appeared from a side room and joined them. Aliporta headed toward the elevator housed in a large column that rose from the bottom floor to the ceiling.

"Impressive, isn't it?" Aliporta gestured to the room at large.

"I'll say," Adina murmured, trying to take it all in. "It's a far cry from what we had on Base 11."

"The Etheric Federation decided to put a significant amount of funding into new operations, focusing primarily on discovery and invention," Zorxia explained. "*Briccan* is a central hub and has everything needed to move science forward hundreds of years."

"Seems like you could go to this terror-formed world yourselves," Tc'aarlat commented as Aliporta pushed the button to call the elevator. Jack nudged him, but he continued, "Why did you ask to send us if you have this ship?"

"That's a great question, Tc'aarlat." Zorxia moved through the opening doors. "Renasta isn't the only planet we're looking at. As you can imagine, bigger facilities come with bigger responsibilities. We chose this location to anchor *Briccan* because it is equidistant to many worlds we're investigating and providing help where we can. If we move the ship, the scientists in the field will lose their access to all of these facilities. Which is where the three of you come in."

"Floor one, Miss?" Aliporta questioned. Zorxia nodded in reply.

"Then why not send one of those other ships?" Tc'aarlat challenged. "I saw plenty in the hangar."

"There are a few reasons why Nathan and I felt it was best to use the Shadows—you, that is," Zorxia responded as the elevator descended. "For one thing, we trust you to complete the mission with a great deal of character."

"Sure," Tc'aarlat agreed. "But this isn't a dangerous mission. Is it?" He scratched his head. Jack wondered where his friend was going.

"It's not that." Zorxia met his gaze. "It's that *you* have a reputation."

"A reputation?" Jack broke in. "What do you mean?"

"The Enkelites' new home world isn't in Federation space," Zorxia informed them as the elevator halted and the doors opened. They followed her out and along a corridor that led to a large steel door. Above them, scientists milled about, visible through the glass ceiling.

"Wait, you've moved the Enkelites out of Federation space?" Adina exclaimed. "Won't that make them targets?"

"You know that the Federation expands through agreement and not conquest. This planet was available and only needed a few final touches to complete terraforming, so we have a pre-established agreement and relationship with a planet outside of Federation space. We plan to establish a trade presence in the area soon," Zorxia revealed. "Our initial visits identified several opportunities that will benefit the few already-inhabited planets, the Enkelites, and us. The greater problem we faced was that there were very few worlds close by that could provide what was necessary for a stable terraformation. Renasta is the only available planet so far, which again is why we need you to make the delivery."

"So, it *is* dangerous, then," Jack stated flatly. "Potentially."

"This new terraforming technology can't fall into the wrong hands." Zorxia stepped toward the steel door and approached the security scanner on the right-hand side. The door opened quietly after her facial and fingerprint scans were verified. "Someone could do real damage with it, which is why you're the only group we can trust to deliver it safely."

"They could do damage by creating new worlds?" Adina questioned, a little confused by that statement.

Zorxia headed into the room and didn't turn to face them as she delivered her answer. "No, they could do damage by reforming old worlds, killing all life to start over."

Void Space, Research Ship *Briccan*, Aliporta's Lab

The lab was smaller than any of the others they'd seen in *Briccan*'s R&D department, and the interior floor, walls, and ceiling were lined with thick steel as additional security measures. A couple of workstations and large touchscreens were visible.

The most notable feature was also responsible for the limited space. A wide, transparent tube that ran from floor to ceiling occupied most of the lab, and inside it was a miniature version of a world.

Jack, Adina, and Tc'aarlat watched raptly as waves of green energy ran over the world and were amazed to see nature sprouting seconds later. In a moment, this simulated world had gone from an uninhabitable rock to completely livable, right down to the breathable atmosphere and fruit-bearing trees.

"That's incredible," Jack said. "How does this method scale up in terms of time and planet size? I thought terraforming was a process that took hundreds of years."

"That was once true," Aliporta replied. "We still have worlds where the old process works better. This new method, given the right planet—by which I mean it already has a semi-breathable atmosphere, the requisite balance of water and land masses, and will readily support the organisms needed in the altered ecosystem—can terraform it in hours to days, depending on the base state of the planet. The secret is in drawing energy from the Etheric, providing a cascade change. Even the wrong planet would probably take about half the time of the old process."

"Wow!" Adina's jaw dropped while she watched the new world being created. Trees continued to sprout at exaggerated rates, with only seconds passing. "This technology could really help with some big problems."

"Or it could create some." Zorxia nodded at Aliporta, who turned to the controls. Jack, Adina, and Tc'aarlat watched in horror as the once-fruitful world began to decay. The trees withered to nothing, the sky turned black and toxic, and the oceans became wild and savage.

Aliporta gestured at it. "We can't use this machine to create a world from nothing, only speed up a potential process. The drawback is that it can reduce a living world to nothing. I've called it 'reverse terraformation,' and it could be done to a planet in a matter of hours."

"Yeah, that's terrifying." Tc'aarlat shuddered. "Worse than dropping large rocks on a planet to kill it. You should destroy it. Now."

"As long as it's in the right hands, it can be a tool for building new—"

Tc'aarlat turned to Aliporta, his mandibles quivering and clicking. "There's no guarantee. It could too easily become a threat."

"I understand your concerns, Tc'aarlat," Zorxia broke in. "It's perfectly safe in our hands. We won't let it be used for destruction."

"How soon can we load it?" Jack said. "And, uh, does it come with an instruction manual?"

"That was the last simulation," Aliporta replied. "It's ready for a real field test, and yes, you could say it comes with an instruction manual. Me."

"No way!" Adina was practically jumping up and down. "You're coming with us?"

"I'm the only person who knows this machine inside and out," Aliporta confirmed and glanced at a still-sulking Tc'aarlat. "The machine is complex, deliberately so. Even if it was stolen, they couldn't operate it without me. The only thing they could do is shut it off. Even turning it on takes a bit more than flipping a switch. Well, Zorxia can operate it in a pinch, but not as well as I can."

"I suppose that makes it all better?" Tc'aarlat crossed his arms. "Because it sounds like a fuck-up waiting to happen."

"Ignore him," Jack told her, irritated. "Tc'aarlat has had a real stick up his butt lately."

Zorxia turned to the scientist. "Please prepare the machine for transportation. We'll meet you in the hangar."

"Of course," Aliporta nodded.

Void Space, Research Ship *Briccan*, Storage Room

Aliporta double-checked that she was alone before she entered the barely-lit storage area and closed the door, then made her way through the tall stacks of sealed crates full of scientific supplies to the far end of the room. She and the other scientists on board had full access to all spaces on the ship, but she couldn't risk being interrupted.

The lid of a particular crate came off easily, and she parted the many bags of padding to reach the blocky, heavily modified handheld communicator she'd hidden beneath them. Once again, Aliporta nervously glanced back and listened for any hint of another presence before entering a string of numbers. The communicator's screen lit up as it connected. Blue. Green. Orange. Then black.

Finally, the person on the other end came through as an eye that took up the whole screen. Its pupil searched the room before landing on Aliporta, and she physically gulped down her nerves when it did.

The Eye was that intimidating. Aliporta had never seen a face nor heard a proper voice, and she assumed the name she'd been told to use was fake.

"Hello, Aliporta," the Eye said. "It is good to see you again. I assume things are moving along as planned?"

"You were right. They're using a smaller ship and crew to transport the terraforming device," she reported in a low voice. "They're loading it now."

"Did you find out the destination?"

She nodded. "Renasta. I'm sending you the route now."

"This is very good work," the Eye replied after a moment. "You've made me proud."

"I…I want to speak to him," Aliporta begged. "Please."

"Not yet. Not until that technology is in our hands. What's the name of the ship that's transporting the machine?"

"The ICS *Fortitude*. Their captain is Jack—"

"Marber," the Eye finished. "Yes, I know. This has opened up a world of opportunity. I didn't think I'd see the Shadows for a while yet. I'm not sure we're prepared to face them right now."

"There's something else. I'm going with them since I'm the only one who can operate it. Zorxia is going too, in an oversight role."

"That's to be expected," said the Eye. "You've done good work, Aliporta. Keep an eye on this and report any changes. If all goes well, you'll have him back in your arms very soon."

"Do you promise?"

"We promise. Goodbye, Aliporta."

"Goodbye, Benjamin."

5

Void Space, ICS *Fortitude*, Cargo Bay

The machine was large and heavy. It had taken some effort to maneuver the metal crate it was secured within once *Briccan*'s automated loaders brought it to *Fortitude*'s bay. Despite knowing the crate was sealed, Adina had come back to double-check.

It was hard to disagree with what Tc'aarlat had said about people using it as a weapon, and that had gotten to Adina. She felt more comfortable being within visual range of the crate. Not that she thought anything would happen, but still, this was one potential mistake that wouldn't happen on her watch.

"It's good to see you again, Adina." Aliporta came up behind her. "Really, I'm glad we could do this together."

"Is it as dangerous as you and Zorxia said it was?" Adina said.

"Yeah." Aliporta nodded. "Some nefarious character could use it to destroy a world and rebuild it again. I find it damn ironic that I set out to develop a faster but still stable way to terraform worlds and accidentally created a weapon."

"I'm surprised you didn't build more failsafes into it," Adina remarked. "I know you said that it can't be operated without you, but..."

"There *are* others," Aliporta admitted. "We're keeping them quiet. That's for the best, I think. The fewer people who know, the less chance of the knowledge going astray."

"That's why I like you, Aliporta. Strong moral fiber."

"I meant what I said to Tc'aarlat." Aliporta spoke seriously. "I'm not letting it get into the wrong hands. And if it comes down to it, I'll do what's needed to keep myself out of their hands, too."

"Hopefully, it won't come to that." Adina whistled to call Isaaca across the cargo bay. The young Raal hawk landed precisely on her shoulder. "For now, though, we can just enjoy traveling together."

"What a pretty bird." Aliporta reached out to stroke the dark-red feathers but hastily withdrew her hand when Isaaca snapped her beak. "Is it yours?"

"Her name is Isaaca." Adina stood a little straighter. "I'm training her."

"It's good to hear you're getting on so well. I was worried when you left Base 11 without calling to say goodbye."

"We've had our ups and downs." Adina paused, recalling some of the more notable instances. "We're good now."

Void Space, Unknown Ship, Hangar

Three figures in tight-fitting spacesuits and helmets

that hid their faces beneath the black-tinted visors stood together in the empty hangar of their home ship. They were each at least a quarter smaller than a human adult but appeared no less competent. At present, they were syncing their watches, and when that was done, they did a quick weapons check. Each carried a handgun and a rifle with a spare magazine.

They didn't speak while their ship, a small, sleekly-built carrier with a reflective surface that allowed it to remain hidden in the depths of space, moved closer to ICS *Fortitude*. Once it was within range for EVA maneuvers, the hangar doors opened and they were launched by an electro-mechanical system, like being shot out of a cannon.

"Jets." One nodded to the others and waited for the right moment. "Now."

All three activated the jets built into their suits. Several tense seconds later, they came alongside the larger ship, latched their magnetic gloves and boots to the metal supports of the hull, and began to climb toward the closest maintenance hatch.

Void Space, ICS *Fortitude*, Bridge

"Solo, what's our ETA to Renasta?" Jack leaned forward in his chair at the center of the bridge and waited for the middle-aged woman on the screen to answer. He didn't need to be here since Solo could answer him anywhere on the ship, but this was where Jack felt comfortable.

"On the route I've planned, it should take just under fifteen hours."

"Thank you, Solo. Let's make sure we—"

Jack stopped and swiveled in his chair as the bridge hatch suddenly opened. Tc'aarlat stood there, Mist on his shoulder. He walked in and headed to his station without a word.

"Still got a stick up your ass?" Jack crossed his arms.

Tc'aarlat sighed and turned to him. "Fine, I might've been a little rough back there on *Briccan*."

"A little?"

"Yeah, *a little*. I've been feeling reverse-fucked, fist-twisted, and tossed into the dumper since we were told to drop the Don Gan'barlo thing."

"And now?"

Before he could reply, Solo interrupted. "While I'm pleased the two of you are talking this out, there's something else we need to address right now. I've asked Adina to come to the bridge."

"Not Aliporta and Zorxia?" Jack inquired.

Adina entered in time to hear Jack's question. "I asked Aliporta to stay with the terraformer." She blushed and glanced down. "It's silly since Solo can keep an eye on it, and it's unlikely anything will happen, but I feel better with someone near it."

"It might not be as silly as you think," Solo replied. "I detected an anomaly some time ago but couldn't get a good enough reading to determine what it was. Since then, I've refined the data and determined that it's a cloaked ship. Additionally, there are now three suited people who went EVA from it in a highly unorthodox manner and are about to land on our hull."

"You didn't think to tell us this earlier, Solo?" Jack exclaimed.

"It wasn't relevant until now," the AI calmly replied.

Jack huffed in exasperation. "I haven't beaten the shit out of anyone lately, but I feel like it's called for."

"Let 'em board and then take 'em out," Tc'aarlat growled, and clicked his mandibles. "If they are pirates, then I say we treat 'em to the whose gown and find out why."

"Whose gown," Adina mouthed silently, her face a mask of confusion, then she snickered. "Oh! You mean 'hoosegow!'"

"Where the hell..." Jack shook his head. "I want to know how they found us. My guess is, our would-be boarders want the terraformer." He frowned. "Although how anyone knew about it, much less which route to have a hidden ship waiting on, suggests we have a mole. That isn't a pretty thought since it's not one of us, which means we have two other choices."

"Let's deal with these fur-chested, blue-footed boobies first." Tc'aarlat rapped his knuckles on his carapace and spread his mandibles as wide as he could. "Time to rumble."

"Any plans should be made quickly," Solo advised. "The three intruders are now working their way toward a maintenance hatch."

"How do they think they're getting in?" Jack wondered aloud. "Are they carrying equipment, Solo?"

"I see no signs of that."

"Which means they either think they have the codes or a way to override them." Adina spoke absently, brow furrowed in thought, then looked up at Solo's image and addressed the AI directly. "I know you can keep them out. What if you faked that you couldn't?"

"You mean, set a trap by allowing them to think they've overridden my codes?" Solo considered the idea.

Adina spread her hands. "We have multiple potential targets to protect, including you. The best way to do that—"

"Is for us to control the engagement," Jack interjected.

Solo deliberated for a moment longer. "Very well. I shall attempt it."

Adina sighed in relief. "Thank you, Solo. Would you please ask Zorxia to meet me in the cargo bay? I'll head back there now and tell Aliporta what's going on." She spun on her heel and sprinted off the bridge and down the passage.

"I guess that leaves us here," Jack remarked.

Void Space, ICS *Fortitude*, Outside Hull

The three suited figures made it to the hatch, and the tallest of the three tapped a button on his sleeve. The hatch unsealed, slid open a few inches, and then stopped, apparently stuck. After several minutes of trying to force it, they opened it far enough to clamber through. They sealed it behind themselves. A second closed hatch on the opposite side indicated they were inside an airlock.

They'd expected this. A couple more button taps cycled the chamber to match the ship's internal atmosphere and then opened the inner door. They stepped into ICS *Fortitude*'s main passage. No alarms sounded. Their successful infiltration had been the easy part. Obtaining their prize while dealing with the crew would be more difficult. No matter what happened, they were going to leave with the terraforming machine in the next hour.

Void Space, ICS *Fortitude*, Bridge

"Jack." Solo cut through Tc'aarlat's and Jack's conversation with a concerned look on her face.

Jack had barely glanced at her before the sudden force of a loud explosion threw him from his chair over a nearby control panel and to the deck. He remained motionless for a moment as his ears rang, his head spun, and pain wracked his entire body. His arm felt like it was being shredded by a meat grinder. *Those bistok-shit-swilling assholes threw a grenade!*

Void Space, ICS *Fortitude*, Cargo Bay

The three ladies heard the explosion from the cargo bay. Adina and Zorxia rushed toward the inner hatch that led to the bridge. They stopped short when it opened to reveal a suited and helmeted figure who stood just over half their height, pointing a rifle at them. The stranger motioned with the barrel. They raised their hands and slowly backed up toward the terraformer's metal crate in response to the instructions.

"Who are you?" Adina snapped.

The figure turned its head to look at her. She couldn't see the smug smile behind the darkened visor, but she heard it in its voice. "What? You don't recognize me, Adina?"

Adina had never seen him, but she certainly knew that voice. It haunted her whenever she thought about her most recent mistakes. "Benjamin." She sneered.

"Never thought you'd actually meet me, did you? I bet you thought that after you escaped on Scarnlet, we wouldn't come after you."

"How did you get aboard?" Zorxia stepped forward but stopped at the rifle's quick motion. "All access is secured."

"I planted an access code that bypasses your AI. Solo knows we opened the door but can't do anything about it. She is trapped in a decision paradox because the data conflicts." Benjamin reached into his pocket and tossed three sets of handcuffs at them. "Do me a favor and put those on." He nodded at Aliporta. "You, too."

"Or else?" Adina challenged.

Benjamin fired a round at her feet. Metal *pinged* as the bullet struck the deck and ricocheted. All four of them reflexively ducked, although Benjamin kept the rifle pointed at them as he did. Aliporta snapped her cuffs in place once she straightened. Zorxia and Adina reluctantly followed suit. Benjamin watched closely to ensure they didn't leave their restraints loose enough to easily escape.

"You're attempting to steal the terraformer, aren't you?" Zorxia observed.

"I'm not *trying* to do anything," Benjamin replied. "I'm doing it."

"It won't work," Zorxia flatly stated. "It's a complicated machine that you can't hope to operate."

"I don't plan to operate it." Benjamin removed his helmet.

Adina was surprised to see that her recent nemesis was

an Alstublaft, a race of aliens that resembled human children. If Benjamin had been human, she'd guess he was twelve or thirteen years old. However, there were clues that revealed his adulthood, including his clean-shaven head and the red X-shaped tattoo that covered his face.

"Then why do you want it?" Zorxia was exasperated, although she kept it in check while trying to get answers.

"To sell it," Adina answered for him. "Benjamin wants to sell it to the highest bidder. Isn't that right?"

"It certainly is valuable. I'm a big fan of her work." Benjamin nodded at Aliporta. "My group—"

"A group of assholes!" Adina spat.

Benjamin ignored her. "We heard of her innovations in terraforming technology and thought we'd get in on the ground floor, so to speak."

"How do you know about it?" Zorxia's eyes narrowed. "We kept all related information at the highest classification levels."

"We have our ways. Ears and eyes everywhere." Benjamin smiled, then needled, "Maybe *you* told us about it."

"Never."

"'Never' isn't a word I like to use, especially in this context. Now, ladies, please sit there and stay." He gestured at a spot with his rifle.

All three reluctantly sat where he indicated, cuffed hands in front of them. Benjamin kept his rifle aimed at them while he sidestepped toward the crate, then withdrew a pair of slim-fitting goggles from his pocket and donned them.

Zorxia tensed when she recognized that particular

device. The goggles allowed the user to "see" through dense metal by building a composite image from various scans. They were useful in combat situations to shoot enemies through walls and other cover.

"We need to stop this asshole," Adina muttered. "But how?"

"I might have an idea. We need to pick our moment for maximum advantage, though," Zorxia replied equally quietly.

Adina shot her a questioning look.

Zorxia's lips pulled up in a faint grin, although her gaze was deadly serious as she watched Benjamin. "Think he'll still be able to shoot if you go Tasmanian devil on his ass?"

She turned her head enough to meet Adina's eyes. "The bigger question is, can you free yourself while I deal with him and then protect Aliporta? You and I can heal from most bullet wounds, but she can't."

Adina gulped. "I... Is there another way? You know why I don't want to change. Besides, I'm still taking the drug."

"You ladies discussing the finer things?" Benjamin's comment momentarily silenced them. "Let's try to remain silent for the rest of our meeting, shall we? I'd hate to leave this hangar with two fewer bullets."

Adina and Zorxia glared at him.

"Good." Benjamin smiled thinly. "We're all happy, then!"

Void Space, ICS *Fortitude*, Bridge

The bridge was burnt black. Some of the auxiliary consoles were now scattered debris. Several large screens hung askew, and small fires showed through the holes that had been blasted through much of the equipment. Fortunately, the fire suppression system quickly dealt with the rest.

Jack distantly heard his name being called but was so dazed he wasn't sure whether it was inside his mind or someone else. He realized it was Tc'aarlat, who had also been tossed around by the explosion and was calling for Jack through the chaos.

A stranger in a black spacesuit with a dark-visored helmet roughly grabbed him. Through the haze that enveloped him, Jack was aware of the numbness in his right arm. It refused to move despite his best efforts. Although shock was overriding the pain for now, he knew he'd broken it at the very least.

"Stand up." The stranger forced him to his feet. When Jack looked over, he saw Tc'aarlat receiving similar treatment.

"Who are you?" Jack snarled.

"Executioners," the helmeted figure replied and pointed his rifle at Jack's head. "You and your crew have caused us problems for the last time, Jack."

"No offense, but I don't even know who the fuck you are," Jack retorted.

"Does it matter?"

Jack saw the stranger's trigger finger tighten and resisted the urge to close his eyes as he tensed. There was virtually no chance he could avoid a shot from a weapon pressed against his chest, but he wasn't going down without at least trying to ensure it hit him somewhere non-lethal instead.

SKREEEEEEEE!

Mist flew out of nowhere, dark-red feathers covered in soot from the blast. She veered toward Jack and his executioner. For the first time ever, he smiled to see her. That is, until she flew right past him toward the person holding Tc'aarlat at gunpoint. She screeched in fury again and attacked, clawing and biting the stranger's helmet and suit.

Her actions created the opening Tc'aarlat needed. He wrestled the rifle away, shoved his attacker to the deck, and shot him. Mist screeched again as she landed and tore through the suit, leaving bloody gouges in the flesh underneath.

Jack twisted his body to move past the rifle barrel and drove his shoulder into his self-proclaimed executioner. The suited figure stumbled backward. Jack followed him, staying too close for the figure to use his rifle. Jack ripped the pistol from his belt and fired as soon as it cleared the holster. The figure dropped the rifle. Jack stepped back and fired into the middle of the short figure's chest.

"Not today, asshole!" Jack glanced at Tc'aarlat to find Mist still tearing angrily at the body of the one who had attacked his friend.

"Jack!" Tc'aarlat beckoned to him from his spot beside a half-wall of debris near the open hatch. The Yollin was using it as cover while watching the passage on the other side, confiscated rifle in hand.

Jack hustled over and sank to the deck next to him, then blanched as it jarred his arm and pain seared away the numbing effects of adrenaline. A few moments later, Mist joined them. She landed on the edge of a shattered console and began to preen herself.

"Who the fuck was that?" Jack bitched. "Apparently, we knew them."

"Could be anyone," Tc'aarlat replied. "We've been making enemies left and tight. Maybe it was the Don because we got closer than we thought."

"Left and right," Jack corrected.

"'Left and right?'" Tc'aarlat gave him a confused look. "Are you sure that's how it goes? I thought it meant if you don't go left, things will get tight?"

"Where do you get these sayings?" Jack winced as he inspected his arm. It wasn't good. Rather than the closed break he'd expected, it was a compound fracture; the bone was poking through his skin.

"Whoa, that's a wound," Tc'aarlat commented while staring at it. "You hit the deck hard."

"Hurts like a bitch, too." Jack indicated his pantleg. "Help me tear off some strips."

Tc'aarlat ripped a couple lengths of material free, then held the ends in place at Jack's direction as the latter wrapped his wound tightly. "What are you doing?"

"Making sure the wound doesn't kill me before it heals." Jack tied off the makeshift bandage. "Shouldn't take more than a couple of minutes."

"It's already been a few minutes," Tc'aarlat observed.

Jack looked down at his arm. The Yollin was right. Normally, the bone would already be reset and the wound sealed, thanks to his Pod-doc upgrades. It might hurt for a week after, but it wouldn't be broken.

This time, that wasn't the case.

"Oh, fuck. Why isn't it healing?" Worry laced Jack's voice.

"I don't know, but we need to move. There's at least one more asshole on board, and I don't want to be a sitting fuck. Plus, I need my rifle. This one is too short."

"*Duck*," Tc'aarlat. What? Where's your gun?" Jack pulled out his Jean Dukes Special with his left hand. His holster was rigged for a right-hand draw, which made the process awkward and slower than usual.

"Why do I need to duck?" Tc'aarlat looked around in confusion, then belatedly answered, "It's in my room." He turned to the Raal hawk. Apart from being soot-covered and blood-spattered, she otherwise looked unharmed. Tc'aarlat was grateful for that. He gently stroked her feathers before speaking softly. "Mist, go to my room and fetch my rifle, please."

"Yeah, go on, you flying rat!"

"What's your problem?" Tc'aarlat challenged him. "She's helping us."

"You!" Jack exclaimed. "She's helping *you*. Me, she'll leave for dead. Which she did, by the way. I was almost shot in there."

"Almost only counts in horseshoes and grenades." Tc'aarlat stood and offered his hand to Jack. "We'd better get to the cargo bay."

"The cargo bay? Why are we…. *Oh, shit*, the machine. Of course. I gotta stop fucking around and help my crew. That explosion scrambled my brain."

Solo's avatar appeared on the large, slightly warped screen behind them. Both of them jumped, badly startled, when she suddenly confirmed, "The boarders are indeed after the terraformer. One is holding Adina, Zorxia, and

Aliporta at gunpoint in the cargo bay." She vanished from the screen as abruptly as she'd appeared.

"Well, that settles it!" Tc'aarlat clicked his mandibles. "I was just going there to make sure Adina and the others were okay, but it sounds like there's more action waiting."

Jack gathered himself and stood with Tc'aarlat's help, making sure to keep his broken arm elevated and braced against his body. "One fucking smooth mission," Jack groused. "Just once. How did these fuckers even find us?"

"I don't know." Tc'aarlat led the way, his former assailant's rifle in hand, as Mist flew ahead of them. "They must have been looking for us, though."

Void Space, ICS *Fortitude*, Cargo Bay

"Are they dead, Phillip?" Benjamin was communicating via the earpiece he'd donned before the mission began. For a moment, there was no answer, but after much static, a voice came through. Quickly, Benjamin learned that Phillip was dead, Ryan had been attacked by a Raal hawk and wasn't responding to hails, and the captain and the Yollin had apparently escaped with their lives. How the two had survived the explosion, he'd never know.

"Problems?" Adina taunted when Benjamin's frustration briefly showed on his face.

"I thought we agreed on silence," Benjamin snapped, then grudgingly added, "Your friends are fairly resilient."

"They don't take shit from people like you. Which means you're next on their hit list."

Zorxia adjusted her position slightly but stayed quiet.

Aliporta's eyes widened at Adina's goading, but she remained silent.

"All right." Benjamin nodded to himself after a moment. "You ladies stay here. I apparently have some hunting to do."

Before he left, Benjamin triple-checked that his guns were loaded, ready to blow someone's head off, and his extra ammunition readily at hand. Adina and Zorxia watched him closely as he moved to the cargo bay doors that led into the ship, pushed a button, and stalked through the open hatch into the main passages in the ICS *Fortitude*. They watched as Benjamin closed the hatch behind him and heard the locks *thunk* into place. As soon as he was gone, they started planning.

"He locked it, but it didn't sound like he used the emergency manual locks," Adina observed. "Good thing, or we might've had a problem getting out of here."

"We don't necessarily want to leave," Zorxia replied thoughtfully. "His prize is in here, so he'll want to stay close to it. I'd bet anything that he'll come back every few minutes to make sure we don't somehow disable it."

Adina thought it through, then nodded. "I like where you're going with this. Free ourselves, wait until he returns, then tackle him and take his guns. After that, we can deal with him appropriately. Assuming he isn't dead."

"Alternatively, we could hunt down any remaining boarders. I doubt they could stop us," Zorxia noted.

"We need to guard the terraformer, though," Adina replied as she scanned the bay for something to open her cuffs. "Last I knew, Aliporta wasn't a fighter. Solo could help, but I want to keep her as our ace in the hole. If

Benjamin thinks he's controlling her, he's likely to be less cautious." A look of loathing crossed her face.

"We have a few options, then." Zorxia listed them. "One, wait here for Benjamin and trust Jack and Tc'aarlat to kick anyone in the nuts who doesn't belong on this ship. Two, both of us go hunting and eliminate all remaining threats, with or without Solo's assistance. Three, one of us stays here to protect Aliporta and the terraformer while the other goes hunting. I know which I'd rather do."

"First, we need out of these cuffs," Adina reminded her.

"No problem, if you don't mind a big, hairy, and luxuriously graceful creature providing a tactical assist. We've been exploring the change with those who are able to turn." Moments later, Zorxia stood there in her werewolf form, broken cuffs lying on the deck. She motioned with one great paw for the others to hold their hands out.

Adina complied. Zorxia grabbed them in fangs stronger than duranium alloy. The werewolf ripped the cuffs apart, then moved over to Aliporta and dealt with hers as well.

Void Space, ICS *Fortitude*, Corridor

"If there are others on board, they'll know their plan is fucked." Jack kept a sharp watch, gun in hand and ready to fire.

"I wish I had my Jean Dukes," Tc'aarlat groused.

"It's better than no weapon," Jack pointed out. "Besides, you're the one who left your damned gun in your room."

"Because we are in void space! There aren't supposed to be ships out here, and there aren't supposed to be strangers on my ship," Tc'aarlat snapped back.

Jack looked at him incredulously. After a moment, battlefield humor got the best of him and he snickered. "The Don is gunning for us, along with several other people we've pissed off. We get attacked damn near every day of the week. Now we're carrying top-secret tech that people would kill for, and you thought today would be uneventful?" He snorted. "No way in hell would Murphy miss this chance."

"Murphy. He is the lawyer?" Tc'aarlat grabbed Jack's arm and pulled him toward the wall.

"*AHHH!*" Jack's face turned white as he yelled in pain since the Yollin had inadvertently grabbed the arm that was taking its godforsaken time healing. "That fucking hurt. Watch where you're grabbing. What the hell is affecting the nanos? I wonder if there's an Etheric dampening field in play? Maybe that's how they tracked us."

"Of all the times for you to not heal quickly," Tc'aarlat grumbled. "Hang on, I think I hear something coming."

Tc'aarlat and Jack opened the door to the cabin behind them and slipped inside, using Jack's toenail clippers to keep the door slightly ajar rather than risk communicating with Solo. While Tc'aarlat kept watch for whatever was moving through the corridor, Jack looked around the room.

"Hope Adina doesn't mind," Jack commented, trying to see past the Yollin.

Tc'aarlat quickly shushed Jack when he heard voices coming closer. Jack did his best to peer through the gap, but his friend's bulk partially blocked his view. A figure holding a rifle came around the corner. As it drew closer, they saw the large red X tattooed across the unmasked male's face.

"Wait a minute." Jack leaned across the Yollin to get a better view. "He looks familiar."

"He's checking rooms." Tc'aarlat backed up. "Maybe we can jump him."

The two of them looked around Adina's cramped quarters. Between the furnishings and Isaaca's perch, there was barely space for them to turn around, let alone find a good hiding place from which to launch and ambush.

"Well, this sucks," Tc'aarlat whispered, softly clacking his mandibles in irritation.

"The hard way, then," Jack whispered back.

The pair waited for their moment. Jack held his gun in front of him to get off the shot more quickly if needed. Tc'aarlat leaned his confiscated firearm against the wall within easy reach and gathered himself to spring forward. After a few moments of silence, the hatch slid open.

Less than a heartbeat later, a hundred and fifty kilos of pissed-off Yollin launched himself into the intruder. Jack moved to the doorway, keeping the scuffle in front of him, ready to shoot if Tc'aarlat didn't win.

The x-faced intruder tried to bring his rifle around, but Tc'aarlat was too close, hands holding arms in a tangle of limbs. The Yollin leaned close, trying to carve the man's face with his mandibles, but he showed incredible strength and held Tc'aarlat back.

The two snarled and grunted. A shot rang out, sounding louder in the tight space of the small ship's passageway. The bullet splattered against the metal and sent a spray of shards into the doorway where Jack stood.

Jack snapped backward, his face stinging from the cuts of the near-miss.

Tc'aarlat rolled sideways and lost his grip on the rifle. His much shorter opponent freed himself and regained his feet first, jumping back and bringing the rifle to bear on Jack and Tc'aarlat alternately. "That's far enough!" he growled.

"Why should we stop, shit for brains?" Tc'aarlat demanded as he shifted his weight.

Jack still had his gun and was intently studying the tattooed Alstublaft with a growing distaste for the creature.

The stranger glanced at Jack but didn't fully take his attention off Tc'aarlat. "Hello again, Jack. How have you been?"

"You know this asshat?" Tc'aarlat was angry. He shouldn't have lost a fight with someone half his size. He wanted to make it right. He wanted to smash the creature's face.

"No, but I know his name. We met once ten years ago. You're Benjamin Graves."

"That's right." Benjamin nodded toward Jack's gun. "Who are you kidding, Jack? You couldn't kill me back then. What makes you think you can do it now?"

"A lot has changed since then." Jack's finger tightened on the trigger.

"What the hell is going on?" Tc'aarlat stared at them. "And how come I'm not in the hoop?"

"How's your mother, Jack?" The Alstublaft's taunting question hung in the air as he spun and raced back the way he had come.

Jack froze, then roared in anger and fired round after round at Benjamin, who ducked and wove erratically as he sprinted for the nearest cross-corridor.

Tc'aarlat fumed as the barrage of wild shots prevented him from giving chase. "Shit-fucking, bistok-swilling cock-womble. Stop shooting! I can't go after him with you firing blind!"

The angry shouts finally penetrated Jack's fog of anger and pain. He stopped firing and collapsed against the wall, his Jean Dukes Special hanging in a loose grip.

Tc'aarlat ducked inside Adina's room long enough to grab his confiscated rifle. When he came out, Jack was running after the one called Benjamin.

"Hold up." Tc'aarlat jogged to meet him. "You want to tell me what's going on?"

"Bad news." Jack didn't break stride or meet his gaze. "My past is catching up with me."

Void Space, ICS *Fortitude*, Outside Hull

Finding the way back to his forced entry point hadn't been difficult. Jack and Tc'aarlat had survived, thwarting his plan to steal the terraformer, but he wasn't afraid to admit failure. The situation required new thinking. Benjamin recalled what he'd said earlier. They weren't ready to handle the Shadows quite yet. That would require more contemplation. Despite the heat he'd take from his superiors, a retreat now would mean success later.

The interior airlock hatch opened at his command. Benjamin donned the helmet on his suit as he entered, then cycled the lock. A minute later, he blasted away from ICS

Fortitude with his life intact but his plan in pieces. The Alstublaft watched the ship continue toward its destination and promised himself this wasn't over. There would be other opportunities to get the Shadows.

"Until next time, Jack," Benjamin said to nobody in particular. "Until next time."

6

Void Space, ICS *Fortitude*, Cargo Bay

Before he knew what was happening, Tc'aarlat was pinned to the floor with a werewolf standing on him, jaws ready to take off half his face.

Zorxia had been lying in wait, and when the hatch suddenly opened, she'd struck before realizing who it was. She quickly released him before changing back to human form, covering herself as she looked for her clothes.

The Yollin stood as Jack followed him into the cargo bay.

"He's fled," Jack announced, the mix of pain and exhaustion clear in his voice. "We managed to pick off the other two, but not before they blew up the bridge."

"They were after the terraformer," Zorxia said over her shoulder.

"Jack?" Adina went to him. "You look ready to collapse. What happened?"

"He blasted...cracked...broke...got fucked up. Yes. He

got fucked up by the grenade." Tc'aarlat answered for him. "Things got a little hot and bothered."

"Hot and *heavy*," Jack corrected as Aliporta and Zorxia tried to mask their snickers, "not hot and bothered. That's something else entirely. But my arm didn't heal like it should have. Solo, scan for an Etheric dampening field. I didn't think your run-of-the-mill scumbag had that kind of tech."

Adina frowned. "I thought you had quick healing, Jack. The last time you broke your arm sparring, the bone reset in minutes."

"Not this time," Tc'aarlat replied. "We don't know why."

Suddenly, Solo appeared onscreen. "All interior security scans are clear. One boarder escaped and returned to his ship, which has now left the immediate vicinity. I've made notes of its cloaking ability and possible ways to detect it for future reference."

She stopped and looked at the four people standing near the hatch. "Jack, I see that you are hurt. Please go to the medical bay immediately."

"I'm…" Jack fell forward. Only Adina's and Tc'aarlat's quick actions saved him from smashing his face into the deck.

"Jack!" Adina shouted. "He's really hurt."

"He must have been hitting on all the adrenaline cylinders!" Tc'aarlat helped pull him upright, braced him on one side, and turned him toward the door. "There was much fighting after the grenade blast."

"That's the second time you've mentioned a grenade blast," Adina commented as she supported Jack's other side. "They had grenades? Holy crap! How bad is the damage on the bridge?"

"It maybe could be worse." Tc'aarlat grunted as he repositioned his hold on Jack. "But I'm not sure how."

"Those weren't typical thieves," Zorxia informed them as she and Aliporta followed them toward the medical bay. "They were prepared for us. They figured out how to evade Solo's sensors long enough to get close, they knew the layout of the ship, they bypassed the ship's access security, and worst of all, they knew which route we were taking and all about the terraformer."

"What are you saying?" Adina stopped and twisted to look at her, which forced Tc'aarlat to stop as well since the two of them were supporting Jack.

"I'm saying they could only have known that if they were present when the route was initially planned," she responded. "I fear the Federation has a mole or at least has been compromised. You said Benjamin is a hacker, right?"

"He and the others with him," Adina confirmed, then tried to resume walking but jerked to a halt when Tc'aarlat didn't move. Before she could speak, the confused Yollin wondered aloud, "Why would the Federation have a mole? Are they not in space?"

Before anyone could correct him, a flustered red bird flew up to them and landed at Tc'aarlat's feet. In its beak was a glazed bun from the kitchen. He stared down at the creature, who looked up at him for approval. "No, I said *gun*, Mist, not... Never mind. It doesn't matter now. I could've used it twenty minutes ago!"

SKAWWWW!

"Yeah," Tc'aarlat agreed as he let go of Jack and stormed off. "You did miss out on all the fun."

High Orbit over Renasta, Protest Ship *Joshua*, Bridge

Joshua approached the planet of Renasta at speed. The deceleration burn increased to slow the heavy ship down. Hovering above the planet were three arks, big blocky constructs that could house tens of thousands of refugees in times of crisis. *Joshua* shot past them, far closer than most torch ship captains would consider prudent. When it slowed to relative zero, *Joshua* was in a position to interdict any operations between the arks and the planet below.

Bon Noh kept an eye on the window and his screens for a few moments, waiting to see if the arks hailed them or opened fire. When nothing happened, he turned to Theeyej. "I think the best idea is to hail them."

"On it now, Captain." Theeyej was already tapping on the numerous keys in front of him. "What should the message be?"

"Good question." Bon Noh stood and began pacing as he usually did when he needed to think. "Okay, tell them Captain Bon Noh and the crew of Protest Ship *Joshua* have placed the world of Renasta under their protection. We have heard that the planet is soon to be terraformed, and we cannot allow this global destruction to happen." He stopped and turned to face Theeyej. "There we go. That should do it!"

"Why can't we allow this to happen?" Theeyej looked at his commander. "I feel like it might be more beneficial for the Federation to know why."

"Another good point well made." Bon Noh removed his glasses and cleaned them on his shirt. "Mention that we've heard there are single-celled organisms with the potential for growing into complex beings on that planet below, and this new terraforming process could wipe out a future sentience."

"It is done, Captain," Theeyej reported. "Now awaiting replies."

"Good. That should teach the Federation a lesson about destroying life forms for their own ends."

"Actually, sir, the Federation isn't here," said Theeyej. "Those arks are filled with refugees waiting for a new world."

"Well, I wish you had told me that a moment ago!" Bon Noh replied testily. "I just gave them one of my best speeches."

"We could always copy and paste it when the Federation arrives."

"And look unprofessional? Never!"

"Then, what can—"

"I'll have to open direct communications when they get here. I've no other choice." Bon Noh sighed. "You've really made a mess of this, Theeyej. What were you thinking?"

"Sorry, sir…"

Void Space, ICS _Fortitude_, Medical Bay

Jack groggily opened his eyes and recoiled at the intense light beaming down onto him. His body was numb, and he was extremely nauseous. For a moment he thought he was alone, but when he looked around, he saw Zorxia and Aliporta standing to one side.

"Wh-what happened?" he croaked.

Aliporta turned around at once, her smile bright. "Oh, good, you're awake. I was beginning to wonder if you'd stir before we reached Renasta."

"My head…" Jack tried to sit up and quickly realized his right arm was restrained. When he looked down, he spotted the light but strong material that had long since replaced old-fashioned plaster casts sticking out of the sling around his neck. "My arm's still broken?"

"Unfortunately," Zorxia replied. "The bone is now correctly set and the wound cleaned and sealed, thanks to Solo's work with the onboard programs and facilities, but without a Pod-doc, the cast was our only option. Plan on wearing it for the next six weeks or until we can get you to a Pod-doc to upgrade your nanocytes. The sling is there to remind you to take it easy."

"Six weeks!" Jack exclaimed. "Why so long? I've healed from cracks and breaks before, and it took a couple of hours at most."

"Yes, well, that was before your nanos apparently stopped working." Zorxia and Aliporta both looked worried.

"I didn't think that was possible." Aliporta tapped a finger on her chin as she thought. "I haven't heard any rumors in the scientific community about someone developing a viable method to shut down a person's nanos. Assuming they did, do you have any ideas about when it happened or how?"

Jack mentally reviewed the events of the past year.

Every other time he'd been injured, he'd healed quickly. That meant it was a recent change. A flash of realization struck. "The doctor," he blurted, glancing at Zorxia and receiving a slight nod. "When we stole his client information, I played distraction. He injected me with something. That has to be it. There's no other explanation."

Aliporta shook her head when he finished. "I'm no physician, but that doesn't sound good. Let's hope it's temporary."

"That was months ago." Jack rubbed his good hand over his face as his shoulders sagged.

"We've done what we can under the circumstances," Aliporta replied. "Regardless, your arm isn't healed, and you need to take it easy. I also strongly recommend you avoid getting hurt further. You could die."

Jack snorted at that. "Easy. Yeah, sure. Where are Adina and Tc'aarlat?"

Zorxia spoke up. "Making final preparations for Renasta. We should be there in the next ten minutes."

"Damn. I was out for a while." Jack pushed off the bed. "Anything else I need to know before we arrive?"

"Solo reports there's an additional ship there. Protest Ship *Joshua*."

"Oh, God. Not that self-appointed guardian of the damn galaxy Bon Noh again. What's he on about this time?"

"We don't know yet. He hasn't hailed us. We'll deal with him after we've met with the Enkelites. I've had to meet with his type before, almost every damn time we conduct an experiment to make the universe a better place."

Jack grunted in response, then made his way toward the medical bay's hatch.

"Jack?"

He turned when Zorxia called his name but didn't speak. He knew what she was going to say.

"Tc'aarlat mentioned you knew one of the thieves. You called him Benjamin."

"I'd rather not talk about it right now." Jack flicked a glance at Aliporta, then met Zorxia's gaze, silently conveying a message. "That's for the Shadows and Nathan as our boss to know."

"I read your file." Zorxia's words fell into the sudden quiet. "Benjamin was an Alstublaft."

"Whatever you're thinking right now," Jack replied as he turned and opened the hatch, "you're probably correct."

High Orbit over Renasta, *Ark One*, Foyer

Ark One didn't have a traditional hangar like the other ark ships orbiting Renasta. Instead, it had a foyer where a ship could connect to one of its outer doors and dock. The Enkelites were thankful for the feature. Their beliefs that spaceships, outer space, and technology rotted the soul were deeply ingrained, so not seeing other ships flying in had been a blessing in most ways.

The three Elders had been waiting to greet the Federation ambassadors, and their eagerness had kept them in *Ark One*'s foyer for an hour now. Each of them knew their flocks didn't enjoy life in space, so the Federation's earlier communication that it was finally time to terraform their world and a group of ambassadors was en route with the means to do so was welcome news.

"I hope they arrive soon." Hozgak fidgeted incessantly. "It's just like the Federation to keep us waiting."

"We have received their communication." Nee'pkan stroked his beard. "They will arrive when they arrive, and no sooner than that."

"Yup," agreed Shexee, taking a long draw from his pipe and puffing out the smoke.

"Just think, we'll soon be on the ground and farming again." Nee'pkan spoke brightly. "I can't wait to feel good soil underfoot once again, brothers."

"You must be forgetting about the intruders," Hozgak sharply reminded him. "Our view of the planet has been blocked by that...well, that other metal beast that doesn't look at all friendly."

"One of the things we must discuss with the Federation ambassadors," Nee'pkan agreed. "Although I'm sure they can handle it. There's only one, after all."

"Yup."

Silence fell as they waited. Soon, they heard the procedures for docking—the unnerving clicking and whirring as the ark's exterior extended bridge deployed and the thuds and clangs as the mechanical beasts connected. The Elders braced themselves to meet the ambassadors.

"Elder Nee'pkan!"

The three Elders turned to see Imis running toward them, full of youth and vigor. His expression indicated there was something important on his mind. The boy rushed up to them and desperately tugged on the Elder's cloak to grab his attention.

"Imis?" Nee'pkan questioned. "What are you doing here, boy?"

"I want to meet the ambassadors. It's all anyone is talking about."

"Don't be ridiculous. This is not for young ears," Nee'pkan scolded. "Now, get along with you before we—"

It was too late. The docking doors opened fully, and in stepped five individuals. Four were humanoid, a familiar sight for the Enkelites, but the last was a large alien with a carapace and clicking mandibles. Imis hid behind his Elder as they approached. The humans were smiling.

"Hello, my name is Jack Marber." Jack offered his hand. The Elder took it and shook firmly. "This is my crew, Adina, Tc'aarlat, Zorxia, and Aliporta. We're the ambassadors you're expecting."

"High respects." Nee'pkan bowed low. "I am Elder Nee'pkan. This is Elder Shexee, and finally, Elder Hozgak. We three lead the remaining Enkelites into the next stage of their lives. We are honored to have Federation ambassadors on board."

"Honored!" Tc'aarlat echoed. "How about that? I've never been honored by Elders before."

Jack snorted quietly but kept his comment to himself as Hozgak gestured them forward.

"If you would follow us, we have prepared a small feast for your arrival. We hope you have brought your appetite."

"Let me check." Jack tapped his gut with his free hand and listened for the rumble.

"That was so lame," Adina whispered to Jack when the Elders turned around to lead the way. "I'm...wow, embarrassing."

"Trying to lighten the mood," Jack replied. "These guys look like they could use a laugh."

Tc'aarlat trailed behind the group. He had agreed to come along, but that didn't mean he expected to enjoy it. Reminding himself this was merely a short detour, he moved forward but stopped when his path was unexpectedly blocked by a young Enkelite staring up at him in bewilderment.

"Would you move, kid?" he asked. "Trying to get somewhere, here."

"You're weird." Imis giggled. "What are you?"

"I'm a Yollin," Tc'aarlat answered somewhat impatiently as he tried to step around the boy. He ended up physically moving him out of the way instead. "Now, go home. Or wherever you're supposed to be."

Tc'aarlat moved on, trying to walk fast enough to catch up to the others. When he heard the boy rush to his side, he groaned.

"My name's Imis. Who are you?"

"Tc'aarlat."

"Tukarmat?"

"Oh, for the love of... Call me TC if it's too much trouble for you," Tc'aarlat grumbled as he looked down the multiple branching hallways and quickly realized he'd been left behind. "Damn it."

"I can take you somewhere if you're lost," Imis offered. "I know this place really well now."

"Do you know where the Elders are taking my friends?"

The boy nodded eagerly and rushed down a corridor. "Follow me."

Tc'aarlat did so reluctantly. "Why do I have the feeling

you're going to bring me to the exact opposite place of where I asked to go?"

"Come on!" Imis enthused and waved his hand. "Follow me!"

High Orbit over Renasta, *Ark One*, Dining Room

The Elders led the way down a series of corridors and into a grand dining room, complete with a large table, many seats, and a floating bowl of fruit in its center amid other marvelous centerpieces. Jack was astonished by how bright and white it was. The dining room was like a private room in a hospital, impeccably clean.

Jack sat next to Adina. Aliporta flanked him. Zorxia chose to sit on Adina's other side, and the three Elders faced them across the table. For the first time, Jack realized Tc'aarlat wasn't with them and leaned closer to Adina to whisper, "Where is he?"

"I don't know." Adina glanced around, surreptitiously trying to see if the Yollin was merely late to arrive. "He was with us when we first headed here."

"Why wouldn't he have stayed with us?" Jack kept his voice quiet, not wanting the Enkelites to overhear. "Wait, you don't think it's because he's still sulking about the Don, do you?"

"I doubt that's it," Adina replied equally quietly. "He agreed to the mission, however reluctantly. Let's hope that wherever he went, trouble isn't finding him."

Jack and Adina faced the Elders and smiled perfunctorily when Elder Nee'pkan stood and gestured widely. A few moments later, Enkelites poured through the side doors, their hands full of food: every kind of meat imaginable, fruits and vegetables, pies and side dishes of mash, wine and water. The best part was that it all looked fresh and homemade, which was surprising since they'd been in space for several months. The accompanying aroma was something to be sniffed at, too.

"This looks…" Jack couldn't find the words as they set the feast before him. "Amazing, all of it."

"Please eat, my friends. We shall discuss business after." Nee'pkan picked up a freshly filled glass of wine. "I am thankful that we have allied with the Federation, and I am thankful that you have taken us out of harm's way. I only hope that the next stage will come quickly and we can move on with rebuilding our lives."

"Hear, hear!" Jack and the others raised their wine glasses in response.

"Would you say a word?" Nee'pkan gestured to him. "Please."

"Oh, right." Jack stood, unsure of what to say. There was a painful moment of silence before he spoke. "While we're on the topic of being thankful. I'd like to say thank you." He flushed. "Uh, what I meant to say is…" He stopped and shook his head. "You know what? I'm gonna run with that. Thank you. The food looks great." He sat.

"Er, thank you," Nee'pkan said, looking curiously at the other Elders. "Such kind words."

"That's what I do." Jack picked up his fork but quickly realized that using more than one utensil at a time would be difficult with his arm in a cast. He muttered, "I might need some help with this."

· · ·

High Orbit over Renasta, *Ark One*, Observation Deck

Wo'Fek was where she always was, seated on a bench and looking out at the planet below. Only, since that new ship arrived, there wasn't much to look at. The Elders had told everyone that it was nothing to worry about, but she thought differently. The ship wasn't overtly menacing, although it did block her beautiful view. She thought it might be waiting for something.

"Mother!" Imis came running across the observation deck like a kid with his hair on fire, pointing behind him. When Wo'Fek turned, she almost jumped out of her skin. "Look what I found! Isn't he weird?"

"Damn it, Imis, you lied to me!" Tc'aarlat grumbled. "You said we were going to the dinner, not to—"

Tc'aarlat stopped in mid-sentence when he saw the view outside, which included Protest Ship *Joshua*. "That's no good," Tc'aarlat muttered as the young boy roughly pulled him along. The Yollin was vaguely aware of someone staring at him. The ship framed in the viewport held his attention.

They didn't know why Bon Noh and his hectic hippy horde were here.

"This is Taccyrat." Imis proudly pointed at his new friend as though Tc'aarlat was a contender for show and tell. "Taccyrat, this is my mother."

"You must be with the Federation." Wo'Fek stood and bowed courteously. "It's a pleasure to meet you, Taccyrat."

"It's Tc'aarlat," the Yollin corrected, then nodded toward the window. "How long has that ship been there?"

"Less than a day," Wo'Fek replied. "The Elders said it was nothing to worry about."

"No offense, but your Elders probably couldn't smell cheese in a cheese factory." Wo'Fek giggled at his comment. "You laughing at me?"

"Do you meet many people, Tc'aarlat?" Wo'Fek calmed herself. "You're very funny."

"I meet too many people. But yes. I agree. I am the funniest one I know."

"Would you like to sit for a while?" Wo'Fek gestured to her bench.

"I can't." Tc'aarlat clicked his mandibles in irritation. "I'm supposed to be at dinner with the Elders and the rest of my crew."

He gave Imis a look. The boy simply shrugged.

"I'm sorry my son misled you. Imis can be a handful sometimes."

"This is your son?"

Wo'Fek nodded. "I can take you there if you still want to attend the Elders' dinner."

"Why wouldn't I want to attend?" Tc'aarlat sounded confused. "I love dinners, and I'm starving."

"It's probably all gone by now," Wo'Fek replied. "The Elders know how to eat. Plus, it's on the other side of the ship, and of course, they're a bunch of terrible old farts who couldn't spell fun if you gave them the letters."

Tc'aarlat laughed. "Good one."

"Have dinner with us instead, Yollin man!" Imis chirped, bobbing up and down excitedly. "That way, you won't miss food."

"Imis, don't be rude!" Wo'Fek snapped but gave him a sly wink. "Tc'aarlat wouldn't want to have dinner with us. He's far too busy and important."

"Busy? Not at the moment, except with trying to find food," Tc'aarlat responded somewhat stiffly. "There is always time for dinner."

"Yay!" Imis clapped his hands together.

Wo'Fek smiled. "Follow me."

High Orbit over Renasta, *Ark One*, Dining Room

A good hour later, all of the food had been consumed, and Tc'aarlat still hadn't shown up. Jack grumbled something uncomplimentary. His stomach rumbled its agreement. The tone of the room shifted as the Elders leaned forward, moving away from charming smiles and pleasant demeanors to a more business-like body language.

"How much longer do you think it will take for us to be at home on that world?" Nee'pkan went straight to the point. "Our people have been stuck on this metal monstrosity for a good six months now, and although you have given us plenty of facilities for agriculture, we are still yearning for the breeze."

"Renasta is prime for terraforming," Aliporta explained. "It already has many of the necessary elements, so this operation will entail altering and enhancing them rather than starting from an airless, barren rock. I'm confident that my terraformer will complete the process within seven rotations, and then Renasta will be ready to receive you."

"This is good news." Nee'pkan beamed. "However, I would be remiss if I didn't tell you about another difficulty that I feel has thrown off the balance of this plan."

"Oh?" Jack leaned forward, curious.

"We don't really know what to make of it." Hozgak took up the tale. "Less than a day ago, another one of your *spaceships* arrived, and a few moments later, we received a message on that communication device you showed us how to use."

"We saw the ship," Adina confirmed. "It's not one of ours, although we know who it belongs to. What did the message say?"

"We thought it was from the Federation at first," Nee'pkan responded. "The communication was from a man who called himself Bon Noh. He claimed that the world was under his protection, and it wouldn't be terraformed for us to live on."

"He said there's life on Renasta," Hozgak added.

"There isn't," Aliporta blurted. "The Federation has thoroughly examined that planet. There is no sentient life or life that will evolve to sentience. We have performed countless tests. The results indicate that it has the potential to house life but is not yet advanced enough to be livable without a helping hand."

"Have there been any other communications from the ship or threats of reprisals for you being here?" Jack inquired.

"No." Nee'pkan shook his head. "They've simply stayed between us and the planet."

7

High Orbit over Renasta, *Ark One*, Wo'Fek's Home

Wo'Fek started preparing their meal soon after they arrived in her quarters. During that time, Tc'aarlat had dodged a mountain of questions from young Imis and explored the dwelling. It was a tight, sterile room and probably uncomfortable after any length of time, but the arks were designed as emergency refuges and mass civilization transports, not luxury cruisers. A couch, a bathroom, a few beds, even a screen for watching the large catalog of Earth films.

When Wo'Fek called the "boys" for dinner, they took their places around the circular dining table in a room that led off from their bedroom. Tc'aarlat didn't know what Jack, Adina, Zorxia, or Aliporta were up to, but when he saw the food and smelled the oh-so-pleasing aromas that came along with it, he thought he could spare another hour to find out.

The spread was simple but enticing with countless varieties of food, including a selection of pies, naturally-grown vegetables served with butter, soup, roast abblegock and mash, and of course, a large platter of Tulkraan meat. It turned out that the Enkelites raised them. Tc'aarlat piled his plate high. The meat was juicy and tender, far better than what they had on *Fortitude*. From the description Wo'Fek gave him, he assumed it was similar in taste to Earth's legendary steaks.

"I wasn't sure what you would like, so I cooked a selection," Wo'Fek explained. "I hope at least some of it is to your liking."

"Uh," Tc'aarlat mumbled through a mouth full of Tulkraan, "it's good. I like the meat. It's different."

Wo'Fek smiled and tucked into her own selection from the table.

"Are you really from space?" Imis had taken a seat directly next to Tc'aarlat and was so captivated by the Yollin that he hadn't taken his eyes off him.

"Yes," Tc'aarlat responded, not looking down at the kid.

"Really?"

"Yes."

"Reaaaaally?"

"*Yes.*"

"Imis, leave him alone!" Wo'Fek snapped. "Where are your manners? He's a guest in our home. What do we do with guests in our home? We—"

"Treat them with respect," Imis replied shyly. "Sorry, Taccyrat."

"Tc'aar—" Tc'aarlat started while lifting another chunk of meat. "You know what? It's fine. Yes, I'm from space."

"Wow!" Imis' eyes lit up. "Where did you come from?"

"Imis!"

Tc'aarlat leaned toward the boy. "I come from a world of mobsters, uh, bad guys with big guns and lasers. You know what a gun is, right?"

Imis nodded in reply. "I've seen people get shot."

"Okay." Tc'aarlat drew the word out as he looked at the boy, then continued, "Well, I'm like a bounty hunter. I go around finding all these bad guys, and *pow!* I'm currently hunting the biggest one of all. He keeps escaping, but I'll get him, and when I catch him, I'll make him gargle his ba...uh, something he shouldn't gargle," he hastily corrected himself at Wo'Fek's look of shock.

"Cooooool." Imis wriggled in his chair.

"That sounds like dangerous work," Wo'Fek observed. "How did you end up in such a life?"

"It's the kind of thing you stumble into." Tc'aarlat shrugged. "Although these days, I also run cargo for the Federation. Like this job."

"You don't like doing that?" Wo'Fek sounded curious. "What an odd Federation ambassador you are."

"I don't know if I'd consider myself an ambassador, or an emissary, or whatever you want to call it." Tc'aarlat focused intently on cutting his next piece of meat. "I mean, I represent them because I'm part of the Federation, but I'm not a formal ambassador. More like a specialized contractor who accompanies the emissary."

"I see," Wo'Fek murmured.

"What about you?" Tc'aarlat turned the question back on her. "You must've had a lot of dealings with the Federation since you don't seem scared of me."

"Why would we be scared of you?" she wondered aloud.

"Oh, I don't know." Tc'aarlat shrugged. "Maybe because

I look like a hard-shelled warrior, complete with mandibles, that you've never seen before."

"That doesn't bother us. We Enkelites were given good graces by Aldritch to respect every living creature no matter the differences."

"And your feelings about the Federation?"

"In return for their protection, we give them some of our crops for their space fleets."

"My father used to say that they were more trouble than they're worth!" Imis piped up.

"Oh, you have a father?" Tc'aarlat looked around the living quarters curiously. "Where is he?"

"He's gone," Wo'Fek shortly replied, followed by a long silence. It felt like the room's temperature dropped a couple of degrees. Between that and the dour expression she now wore, Tc'aarlat realized he'd hit a sore spot.

"Did you make all of this?" He scrambled for something new to talk about. "It's damn good."

"We make everything, from raising the cattle to growing the vegetables and more," Wo'Fek replied. "We find that life is worth living when you keep yourself busy. It's killing us, being trapped inside this ark instead of feeling good earth beneath our feet and the wind in our faces."

"Hey, if that kind of life floats your goat." Tc'aarlat shrugged. "I like being in space, although I don't mind going dirtside once in a while, especially if the planet in question has good food. Have you ever tried bistok?"

"Bistok?" Wo'Fek slowly rolled the syllables in her mouth. "What's that?"

"Pure aggression on six legs with large horns and a

preference for eating meat, although it's omnivorous. Real tough bas…er, beasts to kill, given that protective carapace over their heads and shoulders, but their meat cooks up real nice. And there's a lot of it since they grow to over three thousand kilos in weight. I'll see if there's some bistok meat in our ship's supplies. You know, my thanks for this fine meal. It is the best I have had in a very long time, but I think eating too good will make me soft."

Wo'Fek shook her head. "You don't have to do that. We're happy to entertain a distinguished visitor."

"Don't listen to her!" Imis insisted. "You do need to! You have to visit us again."

"He's not your pet, Imis." She laughed. "But if you want to visit us again, Tc'aarlat, we'd be happy to have you."

"Maybe I will." The Yollin nodded. "If we have time. But I feel we may have to deal with that ship out there."

Tc'aarlat swallowed the last morsel and stood. A moment later, he'd said goodbye and left the living quarters with a warm feeling in his belly. He didn't know whether it was the good food or the company, but he thought he might well visit them again. Maybe with some bistok steak.

High Orbit over Renasta, ICS *Fortitude*, Bridge

"How the fuck do you lose a Yollin? Especially on a ship we're docked with? It's not like we're out of communication range," Jack grumbled while tapping his foot against his console. He swiveled in his chair to face the avatar on a screen in front of them. "Solo, still no reply?"

Adina had lost track of how many times he'd asked that

over the hours since the rest of the ship's company had returned to *Fortitude*. Tc'aarlat was still nowhere in sight, and Solo couldn't reach him on his wrist communicator despite repeated efforts. His atypical absence was worrisome.

"No, Captain," the AI replied. "However, I believe I've discovered why."

"It better be good," Jack growled as he stood to pace, glaring at the large, conspicuously blank communication screen they'd use to hail *Joshua* and her captain. "He's part of the team. He should be here when we talk with that meddling Malatian Bon Noh." He raked a hand through his hair and then snorted. "Not to mention, he has a way of needling the man that's thoroughly entertaining."

Adina snickered, recalling the first time they'd encountered the erring eco-warrior at Asteroid Joxxen. Tc'aarlat had pricked several holes in Bon Noh's ego by recounting instances when his protests had gone awry. "What did you discover, Solo?"

With the Enkelites eager to begin the terraformation, the team felt the pressure to deal with Bon Noh's claim. Waiting for Tc'aarlat to return wasn't helping that.

"Quite simply, Tc'aarlat's wrist communicator is in his quarters," Solo replied. "He's not answering because he can't."

"Of all the... Why would he do that?" Jack spun to stare at Solo's avatar.

"I don't know, Captain," Solo replied primly. "However, I have some additional news which I believe you'll like. My internal scans show he's approaching what the Enkelites call the foyer. He should be here momentarily."

"Finally. I swear he gets on my last nerve sometimes." Jack rubbed his face with his good hand after forgetting and knocking himself in the head with his cast. "Fucking broken arm," he sputtered. "Of all the goddamn times for this kind of shit to happen…and that includes Bon Noh."

"Why does Bon Noh think there's life on Renasta?" Adina's gaze swung to Aliporta and Zorxia, including them in the discussion. "That's my first question."

"Question about what?" Tc'aarlat had walked in while Adina was speaking. Jack threw him an exasperated look while Adina settled on a mix of concern and relief. Zorxia and Aliporta watched the byplay in silence.

"Where were you?" Jack challenged him. "You missed the dinner with the Elders. We were *all* supposed to be there."

"I got sidetracked," Tc'aarlat shot back. "Literally. By a kid who promised to guide me to the dinner after I lost sight of you guys, but then took me to meet his mom instead." Tc'aarlat rubbed his stomach. "She cooked what might've been the best meal I've ever had, so I win. How was your meal?"

"That's not the point," Jack countered, exasperated. "It was a banquet hosted by the Elders for the Federation's ambassadors. You know, *us*." His gesture included everyone on the bridge.

"Look, I'm sorry. I tried. At least I was making connections with real Enkelites. How much did I miss?"

Jack went to further the argument, but Adina cut him off. "The Elders told us that Bon Noh is holding the planet under his protection. We think he's holding a protest."

"That's right!" Tc'aarlat snapped his fingers. "I saw his

ship from the ark's observation deck. What does that twat want this time?"

"According to the Elders, he claims there's life on Renasta," Jack replied. "Whether he's right or not, he's causing a problem."

"He's wrong," Aliporta insisted. "There's no way all of our scans would miss that. Especially since they weren't all done at the same time."

Zorxia spoke up. "How did he learn about Renasta in the first place? We've kept this project, and the location, under lock and key."

Aliporta looked faintly panicked by the question.

"You haven't spoken with him yet?" Tc'aarlat sat at his station and swiveled his chair to face the group.

Jack held in a growl of frustration. "We were—"

"We were waiting for you," Adina interrupted. "We all need to be part of this conversation."

"Let's get it over with, then." The Yollin spun to face the screen.

"Solo!" Jack barked, and her motherly visage appeared. "Hail Protest Ship *Joshua* and Bon Noh, please."

"Ask nicely, Captain," Solo chided. "Tone."

Jack's face turned a darker shade of red. "Please hail Protest Ship *Joshua* and request Captain Bon Noh."

"At once, Captain," Solo acknowledged. A few seconds later, the five of them were staring at the pristinely clean teal face of one Captain Bon Noh, who had dabbed some glitter on his cheeks for the occasion. His long, intricately adorned silver hair framed his wide smile, and his body language was open and welcoming.

"Captain Jack Marber and your so-called crew, it's a

pleasure to see you again." Bon Noh offered them a slight bow. "I should've known the Federation would send their *best* agents." He glanced at Aliporta and Zorxia. "I don't believe we've met. Captain Bon Noh, at your service."

"Flattery will get you everywhere, Bon Noh." Jack nodded at him. "What's the deal here? What have you heard about Renasta?"

Some time back, the Shadows had had a run-in with Bon Noh when they were making a food delivery to the Scota Brothers Mining Corp. on Asteroid Joxxen. The company mined cathcadium, a rare element used in the construction of next-generation ion pulse drives. Bon Noh was protesting the working conditions of the miners. When he tried to prevent the Shadows from making their delivery, they turned the tables and lured him away with false news releases about a threat to a non-existent species of beetles. Later, they found out he was surprisingly correct; the Joxxers who worked the mine *were* being mistreated. After the Shadows dealt with the problem, they called Bon Noh back to the asteroid to keep the mine's owners in custody until a Federation team arrived. Jack and the rest of the Shadows hadn't forgotten about that. While they still considered him more looney than legit, they weren't as keen to chastise him right from the start.

"I'm here with only the best intentions, Jack. We received information that this planet is teeming with life, which means we can't allow it to be terraformed."

"Please provide your proof to us so we can verify it," Aliporta broke in. "And who your source is."

"It's not a type of life form that would appear on a scanner," replied Bon Noh. "And my source isn't important.

What matters is that this planet's ocean floors are home to single-cell organisms that have the potential to become more complex life forms."

"You're fucking joking!" Tc'aarlat bellowed. "You're protesting against a bunch of refugees who need a home *right now* because of some microscopic nothings?"

"Tc'aarlat has a point." Jack leaned forward. "What's more important, protecting some microbes or saving the nearly ten thousand Enkelites on board these arks?"

"I have nothing but sympathy for the refugees aboard those arks, Shadows, and I can see how this situation would be frustrating. I can't allow you to kill off the potential for life in lieu of an invading species, though."

"Invading species?" Adina uttered slowly.

"Invading might have been the wrong term," admitted Bon Noh. "Not a native species, then."

"What proof do you have? And where did you get it?" Zorxia challenged. "Because this smells pretty damn fishy to me."

"I can't reveal my source," he demurred.

Zorxia crossed her arms over her chest as her eyes narrowed and her jaw clenched. If Bon Noh was disturbed by her apparent irritation, he didn't show it.

"You do realize that we ran extensive tests for *any* organisms in addition to life forms, right?" Aliporta stepped forward and confronted Bon Noh. "There was no evidence that any of them would develop into higher life forms anytime within the next million years, if ever."

"So, you admit that there are organisms!" Bon Noh pounced on her statement.

Aliporta rolled her eyes. "Of course, there are. Any

planet capable of supporting life has some. That doesn't change the point that they're nowhere near sufficiently developed to warrant you protesting."

"Nor does it negate—"

"Enough!" Jack exclaimed. "You're blocking exactly the kind of humanitarian mission you claim to support. So, what the fuck do you suggest? Besides not terraforming Renasta, and that's not gonna happen."

"We want the organisms preserved," Bon Noh replied. "That's all we ask."

Tc'aarlat moved closer to the screen, incidentally magnifying Bon Noh's view of his mandibles. "Why not collect a sample and keep it somewhere safe? Nothing gets wiped out." His mandibles spread wide in an expression that made Bon Noh flinch. "There's probably another ocean somewhere the microscopic nothings can settle in."

"That was our first thought, too," Bon Noh responded as he smoothed his clothes. "We have a submarine that can reach those depths, and it has a suit built for external maneuverability that could withstand the intense pressure."

"So, what's the problem? Use the damn thing." Jack leaned back in his chair.

"Unfortunately, it's not that simple. The organisms are resting on the ocean floor inside an unstable and narrow crevasse. It's far too risky for my people to get the samples we need to preserve," said Bon Noh. "Which means the planet itself must remain in the same state to accomplish that goal."

Tc'aarlat's mandibles closed and clicked in irritation. "What if we did it?"

"Hey!" Jack snapped. Tc'aarlat turned to him. "Remember that conversation we had about you not volunteering us for risky stuff?"

"Just because he doesn't have the balls to do it doesn't mean it can't be done," Tc'aarlat shot back testily. "We pop down, grab some samples, and solve the issue. Then the Enkelites have a new home, and everyone's happy." The unstated implication was that by getting this done, they could return to their search for the Don more quickly.

"Wait a minute." Adina stood and joined Tc'aarlat. "If no one can collect samples, how do we know there's something on the seabed?"

"We don't," said Bon Noh. "But we can't take that risk. If your team wants to use the sub to retrieve samples, we'll allow it, and if samples can be retrieved, we'll step aside."

"Once again, how did you come by this information, Bon Noh?" Jack narrowed his eyes. "I don't see a confirmation of organisms."

"We received an anonymous tip."

"That sentence made my ass pucker." Jack snorted scornfully. "An anonymous tip with blatantly conflicting information. Yeah, that's seedy as shit."

"Either way, we have to be sure," Bon Noh said. "We couldn't live with the risk."

"*You* couldn't, anyway," Zorxia muttered, jaw still clenched as she tried not to rip him a new asshole. "The rest of us have no problem trusting proven science and rational thinking."

"Great." Jack sighed as he looked at the rest of his crew. "Give us a minute to discuss, please. Solo, screen off."

"Bon Noh sucks goat balls sideways through a thin straw," Tc'aarlat offered once the group was alone.

"I'm not sure how helpful that is," Zorxia started.

"It is the truth!" Zorxia stared at him until he looked away. "He does."

"Reasoning with him has proven futile. He fixates on one element, and in this case, it's ridiculous and unproven. If we go down there to collect a sample, then I want his assurance, in writing, that if the results show a non-transforming microbe, he goes away because his protest is based on a false premise." Jack leaned into his chair. He wasn't a fan of any of it. Why did they always get jobs where jackholes like Bon Noh showed up?

"We can't fight him. We can't finalize the terraforming with him there because you know he'd do something that would get people killed. I really hate that guy." Adina shook her head.

"I guess we're going swimming."

"You're willing to do that?" Aliporta asked.

"Fixing problems is what we do," Jack replied.

"Unless that problem is named Don Gan'barlo." Tc'aarlat clicked his mandibles and challenged anyone to defy him.

Jack called for calm with a gesture. "We'll get to him as soon as this is done if for no other reason than to make you stop your bitching."

"Takes one to know one!" Tc'aarlat shot back.

"The two guys on board this ship are calling each other 'bitch.' In front of the women. It's amazing the things you miss out on when trapped in a lab all day." Zorxia put her hand on Jack's shoulder. "It'll be okay. I have confidence in you and your team."

Jack covered her hand with his.

Adina raised one eyebrow as she stared at the two. No one spoke as the silence continued. Adina cleared her throat. "Bon Noh?"

Jack nodded. "Solo, bring Bon Noh up on the screen." When Bon Noh's magnificent mane flowed with a shake of his head, Jack spoke. "We'll do it. We'll take the sub into the trench."

"We'd be forever grateful," Bon Noh bowed. "We would even stay behind to ensure the refugees have a smooth transition."

"I'll transition his face," Tc'aarlat muttered under his breath.

Jack glared for a moment, but his friend had been out of sorts, and that was mild compared to how they all felt. "I need it in writing from you, Bon Noh, that if this search proves the information you based your protest on to be false, you will no longer interfere with this relocation. If the information proves true, then you will have done a service to the galaxy."

"I can ask for no more than that. I will send a letter within the hour."

8

Renasta, Under the Northern Ocean, Tiny Submarine
The Pea

From a distance, the submersible looked indistinguishable from a pea in both size and color. That impression didn't change as they drew closer. Bon Noh's submarine might've fit the Malatian, but it wasn't big enough for the three struggling members of the Shadows. Jack was constantly vying with Tc'aarlat for a view, and Adina had been pushed so close to the window that she might as well marry it and call it a day.

They entered the sea and started downward. With the external pressure, they had to keep clearing their ears. They could feel the volume of water over their heads weighing on them.

Through the windows, they could see there wasn't a single fish or other creature, only an endless expanse of multicolored blue with a rocky base.

"Want to see my impression of a guy trapped in a submarine who would rather be hunting down gangsters than going on a wild chase of gooses to appease an idiot?" Tc'aarlat grumbled. Adina and Jack turned their heads to look. He was sitting perfectly still with a disgruntled look on his face. Tc'aarlat nudged Jack with his arm. "You should've stayed behind!"

"Me!" Jack shouted. "You're the one taking up the most space."

"It is a far, far better space I fill than I have ever filled before. It is a far, far better world I dive deeply into." Tc'aarlat sighed. "Give me many points for trying."

"Tc'aarlat, sometimes you get under my skin, but then there are others where I wouldn't want anyone else on the team." Jack took to looking out the other window.

"Hey!" Tc'aarlat leaned closer. "Is that a gray hair?"

"Is it? Fuck." Jack combed a self-conscious hand through his hair and leaned away from the Yollin, further crowding Adina. "How far until we get to this crevasse?"

"A minute or so," Adina said. "Now, will the two of you shut up? You're like an old married couple."

Jack scoffed. "I could do better than him."

Tc'aarlat stifled a giggle. "What? Like Jenny?"

"Oh, my God, it's happened," Jack said calmly. "I'm finally going to kill him."

"You and what army, One-Arm Jack?"

"GUYS!" Adina shouted. "We're here."

The Pea, as those on board had nicknamed the submarine, shined its searchlights into the dark depths. The crevasse went so far down, the bottom wasn't visible. It was barely large enough for The Pea and nothing bigger. In addition to the crushing pressure everyone knew they would face at the bottom, if something happened, the chance of rescue was slim to nil since they had the only submarine.

"*Fortitude* to *Pea*, *Fortitude* to *Pea*, do you read me?" Zorxia's voice came through loud and clear.

Adina tapped the communications button on her console. "We're at the coordinates Bon Noh was given. It's a long way down!"

"You can do it, Shadows." Bon Noh encouraged. "I have faith in you."

"That's rich, coming from the guy who isn't risking anything," muttered Tc'aarlat.

"Hold on, guys. I'm switching to manual control and diving." Adina gripped the joysticks and quickly discovered how little pressure it took to roll and drive the sphere. She lessened the pressure and regained control. As *The Pea* descended, it rolled from side to side, rocking and jolting the Shadows as it hit the rocky walls.

"Fucking hell, Adina. Are we gonna hit every inch of rock on the way down?" Jack swore again and turned white as a particularly hard bump threw him against Tc'aarlat and jarred his arm.

"Hey! Cut it out!" the Yollin complained as he pushed Jack away. "And yeah, a smoother ride would be good. I'd like to keep my dinner where it is."

"If you puke, Tc'aarlat, I swear I'll—"

"Hold on!" Adina barked, focusing on the controls. "This isn't as easy as you'd think. The area is too tight to navigate safely."

"Then I'd hate to be the driver." Jack awkwardly patted her on the back. "If anyone can do it…"

Adina slowed to a stop to regain her composure. When she started the descent again, it was much smoother.

The Pea forced its way to the bottom, collecting more than its fair share of dents, dings, and scrapes from the many outcroppings it passed. By the time the sphere touched the sandy bottom, Adina was sodden with sweat and *The Pea*'s nice smooth exterior looked ragged and aged.

Adina finally dared to breathe deeply and slump in her chair. "Now all we have to do is collect a sample."

"So, what? We go out there with a jar or something?" Tc'aarlat looked confused.

"Good guess." Jack forced a laugh, although he turned white, and his face had adopted a permanent grimace from the pain. "One of you two will have to do it."

"I'm not going out there!" Tc'aarlat shot back. "Why can't you do it?"

"Uh, hello." Jack gestured to his arm.

Adina spoke up. "I'll do it. Can't remember the last time I had a good swim."

"Have you ever been swimming, Adina?" Jack was momentarily diverted.

Tc'aarlat shuddered at the very idea. "Yollins sink in the water. There is no swimming."

The Pea was equipped with a cable that was specifically designed for deep-sea exploration. It functioned like a hose in most respects. A blend of oxygen and nitrogen, adjusted for the depth to prevent oxygen poisoning, was pumped through so the person it was connected to could breathe. The biggest difference was the latch at one end that attached to a person and created a small forcefield around their body. As long as they were connected to the ship in terms of air and power, they could stay alive under the ocean as long as the ship held out, which was typically a few hundred years for this design. Adina pulled that cable free and attached the latch to the back of her neck. A few moments later, her body was covered in a light purple haze.

"Sparkly," Tc'aarlat jibed. "It's a good look for you."

"Now remember," Jack cautioned, "there's only thirty feet of hose. Be safe and don't stretch it. If that thing snaps, nanocytes or not, the pressure at this depth is crushing."

"No problem. I'll go out there and grab a sample, and we can get back to what we're here for." Adina opened a nearby cabinet and pulled two tightly-sealed large, clear sample containers from it, then made sure the door latched closed. "You guys sit tight."

"Be safe," Jack reiterated. Adina nodded before pulling free the steel hatch that would allow her into a smaller tube, where she could seal herself in to safely open the outer latch and exit without flooding the ship.

"She'll be fine, Jack. It's a planet that doesn't have any creatures on it. What could happen?"

"Knowing us, anything," Jack retorted.

Adina propelled herself into the area lit by *The Pea*'s headlights. The device she was wearing didn't add any weight, so she could swim freely. Conversely, the lack of added weight wouldn't ease her descent to the ocean's floor.

For all its quiet serenity, the ocean felt like a dystopian world to Adina. If it wasn't for *The Pea*'s bright headlights, she'd have quickly lost her bearings and possibly her nerve. She kept the headlights at her back as she swam down and spotted a patch of the ocean bed that was protected by the mountainous rock walls around them.

Perfect. She angled toward the ocean floor as she prepared her jar. According to Bon Noh's informant, the organisms teemed in the sand. With one smooth motion, Adina scooped up the sand and water together and sealed the jar tightly, turning to give Tc'aarlat and Jack a thumbs-up. She moved a meter or two to her left and snagged a second sample before looking up to confirm that she had no desire to make a second trip into the trench.

Tc'aarlat's mandibles gaped in what was supposed to be a smile. "See? Nothing to it."

"Not a fan and don't want to do it again. Next time, we rip Bon Noh's hair out by the roots instead," Jack added somewhat testily.

Tc'aarlat waved the comment off. "I wanted to shoot that illogical twat of a princess right out of this system, but no." He jerked his chin at the window. "She needs to hurry up so we can get this shit done, and I can tell Bon Noh and this planet to kiss my ass."

Jack snorted. "Tell me how you really feel, Tc'aarlat."

"I just did," the Yollin replied, confused.

Jack chuckled. The smile on his face froze when he looked out the window.

Adina had a bad feeling when a small rock drifted in front of her face. She looked up to see what looked like a land-slide. She flailed at the water, willing herself to swim faster.

The reverberation within the water pummeled her ears

as boulders tumbled onto the seabed, the nearby walls, and *The Pea*. The small submarine was jostled, throwing Jack and Tc'aarlat back and forth in a mess of tangled limbs and raging invectives.

Adina dropped her feet to the seabed and looked up as she dodged the rocks coming toward her. She danced left and right and then braced both feet to dart out from under a boulder.

Her mind raced, trying to calculate the odds of survival as she clawed her way through the increasingly murky water while trying to avoid the falling rocks. Her air and shield depended upon the umbilical that connected her to *The Pea*.

Adina cursed silently as she pushed herself to swim faster. She had gone too far to get the sample. She ignored the rocks overhead and focused on getting back to the submarine.

Three breaths later, the rock slide's main mass reached the ocean floor and engulfed her.

Rocks rained down on *The Pea*, delivering a continuous pounding, assaulting their ears and bodies. When it finally stopped, they knew they had a problem.

The windows on all sides showed nothing but rocks.

"Adina!" Jack stared at the window, then spun to face Tc'aarlat, who was steadying himself against the wall. "I can't see her."

"We have other problems." Tc'aarlat pointed at the water pooling around their feet. "If we can't stop that, we'd better learn how to breathe water."

"Shit!" Jack scrubbed his face with one hand, desperately trying to think through the pain throbbing in his injured arm. "There's gotta be something we can do."

"Comms," Tc'aarlat replied shortly as he pushed Jack aside, bent over the console, and tapped the communications button. "Tc'aarlat to *Fortitude*," he called as Jack pulled open the cabinet from which Adina had obtained the specimen jars, hoping to see some emergency sealant. "We're buried in a rockfall, and the sub is taking on water. Adina is still outside, also buried. We're fucked. We need help."

The comms device sparked and then fizzed out.

"FUCK!" Tc'aarlat pounded on the console.

"I might be able to fix it," Jack commented as he closed the cabinet door.

"Before we drown or run out of air?" Tc'aarlat asked and kicked the wall in anger. "Not that it would help. It'd take them too long to get to us, especially since they don't have anything as small as this green piece of shit."

"There has to be something!" Jack argued. "Adina's connected to the ship. As long as we're alive, she's alive."

"Have you been eating idiots for breakfast?" Tc'aarlat gestured at the window. "She was hit by an avalanche of boulders. Any of them could've killed her."

"Adina was wearing this!" Jack grabbed the cable, the woman's literal lifeline, and shook it in Tc'aarlat's face. "If she's still wearing it, she had the equivalent of a ship's shields around her when the rocks fell on her. We stay alive, she stays alive."

"Then what?" Tc'aarlat said. "No one can reach us."

"It's better than just dying." Jack started inspecting the edges of *The Pea*, looking in every nook and cranny and inside every hatch. "Our priority right now is to stop that leak."

UNKNOWN

An unsavory smell hung in the air, a tragic musk of well-lived-in sheets and things that had been long forgotten with age. There was something else, too—a fouler aroma, the stench of death. It quickly snapped Adina's focus back to her situation now that the roar of the avalanche had ceased. When she opened her eyes, she was no longer trapped beneath a mountain's worth of rocks. Instead, she was in a room, lying on a comfortable bed with linen blankets and marshmallowy pillows.

"What?" Adina stirred, struggling to understand as she gazed around the room. It was clear that it didn't belong to her generation. From the shag carpets, worn wooden furniture, and the hundred or so tiny porcelain figurines of giggling children in a myriad of poses, she guessed she was in the room of an elderly woman.

The pictures dotted around the room showed the time-line of a stranger's life. A smiling baby. Birthday parties. Gatherings with friends. A wedding. A funeral. An old woman with her grandchildren.

"Where the hell am I?" she wondered aloud, but there was no answer.

That was when she glanced down and noticed that the bed was covered in a pool of blood. Adina lurched back, afraid. When she looked down at her hands, they were covered, too. She couldn't explain it or the blood running down the sides of her mouth, but her stomach felt sated, and a contented feeling washed over her as if she'd had the best meal of her life.

Adina rushed to the door and stumbled into the hallway of a hospital designed to look as homelike as possible—and familiar. When she'd first opened her eyes, she had thought Jack and Tc'aarlat might have rescued her and brought her to a strange medical bay. Now, she knew that wasn't true. This was the Rosemere Care Home where her uncle Yousuf Choudhury was spending the rest of his days.

9

Renasta, Under the Northern Ocean, Tiny Submarine The Pea

Jack had been fiddling with the radio for about an hour, and still no one was receiving their pleas for help. They were on their own in this. Together, he and Tc'aarlat had managed to stem the worst of the leak using parts of Jack's clothing and some spray fixative they'd found in the meager supply of science equipment. It was an imperfect solution that wouldn't last much longer and was not their only problem. The two of them were stuck in a sub at the bottom of the sea, sitting in several inches of water. On the bright side, the rocks had settled, so at least they weren't getting banged around anymore, but that wasn't saying much.

"Fuck. Radio's buggered." Jack slammed his hand on the panel. "Then again, I'm not as good at this stuff as Adina is. Maybe it's fixed, but the depth and rocks are blocking the signal. I bet if she was sitting here and I was out there, she'd know and would be able to reach *Fortitude*."

"I see where this is going. You couldn't be out there with a broken arm, dickhead."

"Still, I know what I'd prefer."

"Can't believe I'm going to die in a green ballsack at the bottom of a sea I've never heard of." Tc'aarlat's mandibles trembled from a mixture of anger and nerves. He looked at Jack. "Can't help but feel that if we'd done *something* else, we wouldn't be in this situation."

"Yeah, yeah." Jack waved him off and leaned his head on the console. "They should know by now that something's happened."

"Shame they can't do anything," Tc'aarlat snarked. "And worse that we lost Adina."

"She's not dead." Jack sat up.

"Even if she's not dead, she's trapped. How exactly is she supposed to get out from beneath those rocks, Jack? This ass-sucking expedition has killed us."

"I don't know." Jack abruptly faced him with a fiery look. "I. Don't. Know. Okay? We're in a difficult situation, but you can't pretend we haven't seen our share of them. Something will come through. It always does."

"What about the power?" Tc'aarlat gestured at the controls. "Couldn't we force this piece of shit through the rocks?"

"Emergency power, mate." Jack rapped on the console. "We're down to the limited amount of air left in the tanks and enough power to run the comm."

"The comm that doesn't work."

"Exactly. Like it or not, we have to sit tight and breathe less."

Tc'aarlat folded his arms. "Oh, good, more damned waiting. Exactly what I need right now."

Low Orbit over Renasta, Ark One, ICS *Fortitude*, Bridge

"They should've been back by now." Zorxia inspected the data overview of the planet below. It showed everything there was to know about the planet from its land to its sea. No differences showed on the readouts, but she couldn't help feeling that something had changed. "Solo, can you overlay the previous Federation scan data to see if there have been any changes between then and now?"

"Of course, Zorxia," Solo replied. "I'll pull them up right now."

"Still no word from their submarine?"

"I have received no communications."

The visual display changed as the two different times in the planet's history overlaid each other. Aliporta joined Zorxia to study the comparison. To its credit, the planet looked about the same as it always had, although a closer inspection revealed two differences.

The first was in a mountain range a hundred and fifty kilometers away from the ocean. According to the data, one of the mountains had lost about a third of its mass. That was odd, but it wasn't what Aliporta was looking for. She made a note of it and then turned her attention to the other change, located in Renasta's sea. The rocky formations beneath the ocean bed had changed significantly, especially in the area where the submarine had gone.

In a heartbeat, she knew what the problem was. "They've been caught in an avalanche."

Aliporta turned to face Solo on the big screen, the urgency of running out of time finding its way into her words. "Solo, can you put me through to Bon Noh, please?"

Federation Base Station 11, Residential Zone 9, Rosemere Care Home

Adina followed the corridors, noting the blood trails that led into each room and avoiding the urge to look inside. Last she remembered, the walls had caved in and tumbled on her and *The Pea*. Blood was caked on her shirt and around her mouth. Trepidation filled her as she moved toward her uncle's room. "Be okay," she mumbled to herself. "Please, be okay."

When she reached the door, she hesitated. Although her stomach was a tangle of knots, the disturbing noise in the room gave her pause and sent shivers up her spine. Steeling herself to discover the truth of why she was there, Adina barged in.

One step in, and she froze in horror. It was her.

But not her.

A werewolf crouched over her uncle's dead form, devouring his body. He had suffered before he died, judging by the rents from claws and fangs in his flesh.

It *was* her, the werewolf version of herself, but more of a wild beast with its fur matted in gore. Adina could never remember what she looked like as a werewolf.

It was abhorrent if it was truly her. Her feet wanted to move into the room, but she stopped them by force of will.

Or fear.

The creature halted in the midst of its feast and turned

to her, its eyes red, enraged, flesh and blood on its fangs. When it saw Adina, it roared its fury, and blood-specked spittle fountained toward her.

She slammed the door, then fought with the doorknob. The werewolf's paws were ill-suited to let it out. Adina held the door handle to keep the beast from escaping.

When it stopped trying to open the door, Adina sprinted down the corridor faster than she had ever moved before. Heavy thudding preceded a crash and a howl. She found the nearest door, slipped through, and quietly closed it behind her.

Then she waited in the cramped dark of a supply closet, fearing the worst. The beast would come for her, and when it found her, she'd face a similar end—torn to shreds, payback for what she'd done when she used to be unable to control her change.

"Oh, God!" Adina leaned her back against the door and silently sobbed, hoping her bestial self wouldn't hear. *"What is happening?"*

Renasta, Under the Northern Ocean, Tiny Submarine *The Pea*

"All right, my turn." Jack cleared his throat and looked around the sub carefully. After a few moments, his gaze landed on something, and he turned back to Tc'aarlat, his face solemn. "I spy with my little eye something beginning with R."

"Jack, no offense, but I'd rather gargle mayonnaise from a stranger's hole than play another round of this," Tc'aarlat whined.

"When someone says 'No offense,' what they really mean is, this will be offensive, and you should take offense but not get mad." Jack sighed and leaned against the metal wall. They had been trapped in the green ballsack for over two hours now and were silently wondering how much breathable air was left since they'd become lightheaded from carbon dioxide buildup some time ago. "The answer was rocks, by the way. Rocks."

"That's been the answer for the last ten rounds."

"Yeah, well, there's not much in here," Jack replied. "I just hope we can—"

"*J-a-a-ack!*" The pair lurched to their feet and spun to the comms console, which had suddenly crackled back to life. The voice on the other side was faint but very clearly Zorxia. "*Jack-ck, c-c-c-an you h-e-e-ear me?*"

Jack exclaimed and stabbed the button to reply. "This is Jack, Zorxia. Can you hear us?"

"I c-c-c-can hear y—" the voice spluttered. "We-we-we're trying to find a-a-a-a way to get you."

"Thank whatever god you want," Jack said. "For a second there, I thought we were goners."

"Might still be," Tc'aarlat said. "They don't have a way to get to us."

"We think we've found a way," Zorxia countered. "Sit tight."

Tc'aarlat clicked his mandibles, contemplating how he could be wrong. After a moment, he decided he had not been.

"Wait, what are you planning on—" The comm went dead. Jack looked at Tc'aarlat curiously. "What do you think they're going to do?"

Tc'aarlat shrugged. "Beats me, but they'd better do it quick, or I will have to confirm that I was right."

Low Orbit of Renasta, Ark One, ICS *Fortitude*, Bridge

"Wait, you want me to do what, exactly?"

Aliporta had put through a second communication to Bon Noh on Protest Ship *Joshua* a moment after Zorxia had hung up on Jack. Her plan wasn't fully formed yet, but it was quickly coming together. She had originally thought of using spacesuits to go and get them but quickly realized that wouldn't work due to the high pressures at those depths.

That was when the idea had hit her. If they couldn't go to the submarine, they could bring the submarine to them.

"I want to come aboard your ship and magnetize your hull," Aliporta informed him. "Using the stabilizing effects of my terraformer, I'm confident that I can create a huge magnetic force that will pull their submarine from where it's trapped on the ocean floor, even at that depth."

"The rockslide won't be a problem?" Bon Noh toyed with a lock of his silver hair as he considered the request.

"That's why I need your ship." Aliporta leaned forward. "*Fortitude* is made out of a titanium alloy that isn't suited to becoming that strongly magnetic, but yours is andrometium, a metal that can be highly magnetized with a powerful current. It's perfect."

"That's crazy!" Bon Noh half-laughed.

"This is the only chance we have of rescuing the Shadows. We don't have the right equipment to retrieve them, and neither of our ships would survive a journey into the ocean. In ordinary circumstances, I'd simply reach out to *Briccan* for help, but I'm afraid that by the time the equipment gets here, the Shadows will be dead from asphyxiation." *BANG.* Aliporta slammed her hand on the terminal to grab the Malatian's attention. "This is *your* fault, Bon Noh. They're down there because of you. Now help me get them out!"

Bon Noh considered her request for a moment. Aliporta thought he might refuse, but eventually, he gave her a small but respectful bow. "*Joshua* is at your service. Let us know how we can help you."

Federation Base Station 11, Residential Zone 9, Rosemere Care Home

Thanks to Adina's enhanced hearing, she heard the near-silent footfalls of the prowling beast just beyond the door. She saw the moving shadow through the small gap below.

She had been under the ocean. Now she was here. Disoriented. Terrified. This brought a painful memory of the future past—the last birthday she had shared with her mother, when she had inadvertently torn her limb from limb. Adina was about to experience what that felt like.

The beast sniffed at the door, and a second later, it scratched at it with those gigantic paws. The werewolf slammed against the door, hitting it with all the force in its great body again and again until the wood cracked and splintered.

Adina looked for a weapon, but there was nothing except an old mop and a bucket. With one hand on the mop's handle, she clamped her eyes tightly shut and tried to will the beast away. Her heart raced, jackhammering the inside of her chest. Her mind painted visions of horror.

The door shattered, and the beast stepped through. It padded closer, its footsteps slow and rhythmic. She clenched the mop handle tighter as she felt its breath on her face and smelled the rotting decay of its breath.

A heavy paw bumped into her chin and lifted it.

Adina opened her eyes. Her werewolf side was looking down at her, and it was the most terrifying thing she had ever seen.

It opened its jaws wide and lunged.

Low Orbit over Renasta, Protest Ship *Joshua*, Engine Room

Zorxia had wasted no time in reaching *Joshua*, using the *Fortitude* to dock and rush aboard with Aliporta. Bon Noh had barely had a moment to tell them he was at their service before Aliporta commanded a group of nearby protestors to help her carry the terraformer to the engine room.

Within seconds, she was hooking up the terraformer to the engine and running the necessary code through the terminal to direct the proper energy through the ship's hull.

It was a risky task, which was why Bon Noh had been so hesitant. Magnetizing the hull meant running a massive amount of power through the ship's structure, which in turn could mean killing everyone aboard with a burst of electrical current.

Or worse, it could trigger a drive containment failure on *Joshua* that would also destroy *Fortitude*. It was fortunate the terraformer was specifically designed to direct and reform energy, and Aliporta was confident she could keep the current localized to *Joshua's* outer hull.

"Is there anything you need from me?" Aliporta glanced up at Bon Noh and thought for a couple of seconds.

"I need you to get as close to the ocean as you can without submerging." Aliporta's fingers flew across the terminal, reprogramming her machine to perform a task it hadn't been designed for. "The only metal thing at the bottom of that ocean should be their submarine. If I can make the draw powerful enough, it should lift them out."

Bon Noh nodded and marched back toward the bridge, bellowing orders as he went.

"I hope this works." Aliporta typed in the final commands and prepared the machine for operation. What she had deliberately neglected to mention was that the magnetized hull could have an inverse effect if she had programmed the terraformer wrong. Instead of pulling things toward *Joshua*, it would pull the ship inside itself, crushing them instantly.

Renasta, Under the Northern Ocean, Tiny Submarine *The Pea*

The Pea rocked slightly, sloshing the now-mid-thigh water back and forth. Jack and Tc'aarlat looked at each other, fearing the worst. It rocked again, then again. A violent lurch slammed the two into each other and the walls. They continued to bounce around the inside of *The*

Pea until the rockfall that had buried them started rolling off their little ship. *The Pea* was moving, slowly inching upward.

"She did it," Jack exclaimed. "She did it!"

Jack and Tc'aarlat one-arm bro-hugged and shouted with glee, *"She did it! She did it! She did it!"*

"Wait!" Tc'aarlat said then, looking at the now-taut hose that was providing Adina with power for her protective forcefield and the air she needed to live. He pointed at it frantically and yelled, "The hose, Jack!"

"Oh, shit!" Jack leapt to the console, splashing water everywhere, and smacked the comms button. "Stop! Adina's stuck in the rocks. You have to stop *now*!"

There was no reply.

"STOP! STOP!" Jack screamed, but there was no reply from the other side.

With no way to stop it, Jack and Tc'aarlat could only watch as the straining hose grew tighter until finally, it snapped. That was it, Adina's lifeline gone. There was no hope of rescuing her before the combined pressures of the rocks and the ocean's depth killed her. *The Pea* silently drifted up, moving away from where it should be, forcing its way between the rocks until it was free to ascend toward the surface.

"There has to be—"

"There's nothing." Jack beat the wall with his working hand, which only resulted in a reverberating *ping* and bruised knuckles. He collapsed into the water. "We lost Adina."

10

The Inner Atmosphere of Renasta, Protest Ship *Joshua*, Hangar

The battered submarine hatch opened after a short but determined struggle by a team of protestors armed with crowbars. When it finally unsealed, water poured out. Inside the damaged ship, the shaken pair staggered toward the hatch.

Jack had used his trousers to help plug the leak. From the waist down, he wore tight-fitting briefs, socks, and shoes.

"You always struck me as a boxers man." Bon Noh laughed. "Did you get the sample?"

"Did we…" Tc'aarlat looked at Jack and shook his head in disbelief. "Did we… Fuck you, you poncey space twat."

"Where's Adina?" Zorxia craned her neck to look behind them.

"She's not here." Jack spoke in a rush. "We tried to…that is, I tried to contact you. She was outside the ship when we were caught in the rockfall."

"No!" Aliporta blurted and took a few steps back. "Not Adina."

"There was nothing we could do." Tc'aarlat kept his eyes on the deck. "She volunteered."

Aliporta didn't say anything else, simply ran toward *Fortitude* with her hands covering her face and tears streaming down her cheeks. Zorxia swallowed hard, her jaw clenched and her eyes grieving as she turned and walked toward the terraformer, snapping orders at the protestors to help her re-crate it and bring it back to *Fortitude*.

Jack and Tc'aarlat watched Aliporta leave but didn't follow. They both knew there was nothing they could do to help her. They didn't feel much like comforting anyone else, either. They slumped against *The Pea*, alone again.

Tc'aarlat clicked his mandibles and clenched his fists. Jack gently nudged the Yollin. "Come on. Let's get back to the ship."

"Yeah, one second." Tc'aarlat squared up with Bon Noh. "Still need your *precious* sample, or are you going to let all those refugees have a fucking place to live?"

"I'm sorry something bad happened to you guys, and I'm sorry you lost someone close." Bon Noh stepped back. "You already know my answer."

"Yeah, I thought so." Tc'aarlat barged past him, making a point of knocking him aside as he forced his way through. Jack followed him closely, turning to give Bon Noh a disapproving headshake and his fiercest scowl.

Bon Noh stared back, deeply sorry for their loss but confident in his convictions. At least those two were alive, even if they didn't appreciate it.

. . .

Low Orbit above Renasta, *Ark One*, Wo'Fek's Home

Wo'Fek barely heard the knock on her door over the sounds of her pots boiling on the stove. She told Imis to answer it since she had her hands full. The Elders had been quite nit-picky recently, which she assumed came from their excitement at the prospect of finally leaving the steel cages behind. That being the case, she fully expected one of the Elders to walk in.

Instead, Imis ran to her, calling, "Mother! Mother! He's back! Taccyrat is back!"

As Tc'aarlat came into the kitchen, she knew something was wrong. His shoulders slumped, and his mandibles were idle. Tc'aarlat tried his best to shake it off. "I don't know why, but I completely forgot you had a kid. Weird."

"You've returned?" Wo'Fek moved toward him. She was happy to see him but knew he had come for a different reason than a social visit. He looked like someone who didn't want to talk while needing that very thing.

"I brought some bistok chunks." Tc'aarlat threw a plastic bag at her before marching to a seat at the dining table in the next room. "They'll cook nicely if you boil them, or you can eat them like they are."

Wo'Fek turned off the stove and followed him, then took a seat opposite. She opened the bag and managed a few bites before Imis grabbed the lot and ran off with it. "It's quite good, Tc'aarlat. Not too dissimilar from the cattle we raise."

"I thought you might like it. Being a meat-eater and crap."

"Well, I try to avoid eating crap." Wo'Fek smiled. "If it tasted as good as this, though, I might have to change my mind."

Tc'aarlat smiled weakly. She reached over the table to grab his hand and peered deeply into his eyes. "What happened?"

"Nothing." Tc'aarlat sagged in his seat, then admitted, "We lost a teammate today."

"Oh, no, Tc'aarlat. I'm sorry. Please accept my condolences."

"Nah, it's not your fault."

"Mother!" Imis ran in, all smiles, his mouth full of meat. "This crap is delicious!"

"Don't use that word, Imis!" Wo'Fek lightly slapped him on the back of his head. "Now, Tc'aarlat and I are going to talk boring adult things for a while, so why don't you head to bed?"

"But I don't wannnnaaa," the boy moaned.

Tc'aarlat stared at him, mandibles flexing. "I wonder what you taste like?"

Wo'Fek gave him a fierce look. Wo'Fek shook her head at Tc'aarlat, then turned to her son. "Bedtime, Imis. I'll be along in a little while."

"Are you staying with us?" Imis looked at Tc'aarlat. "Please say yes!"

"Maybe, but only if you listen to your mother. Go to bed."

Imis hurried off. Wo'Fek's expression softened as she looked at Tc'aarlat. "Do you wish to stay? You're welcome to the couch."

"I have to get back and feed my birds." Tc'aarlat shrugged. "Deal with this fucking situation…"

Wo'Fek drew a deep breath. "I'm a stranger to you."

"Okay?"

"No, what I mean is, if you were to tell me something, it would mean nothing to me." Wo'Fek moved from the far end of the table and sat next to Tc'aarlat, then grabbed his hand and squeezed it tight. "Tell me what you need to say, and it will go no further than here."

Tc'aarlat regarded her for a moment while fighting the urge to leave. He averted his eyes and inhaled before speaking in an angry rush. "We shouldn't be here. This has nothing to do with us. We should be out hunting down Don Gan'barlo. I know I sound like a broken fucking record, but it's true. I have a score to settle with him, and during every minute I'm not dedicating to settling that score, I want to go into space, take off my helmet, and take a deep fucking breath."

"What's the score?" Wo'Fek inquired, trying her best to understand what he was saying. She wanted to help him arrange his thoughts until he could feel at peace again. The loss was tearing him up inside.

"He killed a friend of mine," Tc'aarlat seethed. "Now someone else has died. It's a fucking shitshow."

"It's difficult, not going down the path you think you're supposed to." Wo'Fek understood what was going on in Tc'aarlat's head. "My husband died the same way."

Tc'aarlat looked at her.

"His name was Ruushin. He was handsome and sweet but arrogant in his ways. Our world became the center of a war that was so far beyond us, most couldn't understand it.

All we knew was that every now and then, two races that were fighting each other would come down to our quiet planet to battle, and they'd destroy anything in their way."

"They killed your husband? That sucks." Tc'aarlat snagged a cookie off the table and popped it into his mouth. He hadn't eaten in a while, and his pants were still wet. Why hadn't he changed?

"They did." Wo'Fek forced herself to focus on her breathing to keep herself from wallowing in the despair that always came when she talked about her husband's death. "When you say it like that, though, you make it sound like they came into our home and shot him with one of those blasters. It wasn't like that. Ruushin went to them and got between them to try and stop their war, and that's what got him killed. If he'd left it alone, he'd be here now to help me raise Imis and make stupid jokes."

"Sounds like he was trying to protect his world. Which is fair."

"Then, what should I do? Should I get a blaster and go on a mad tirade to find the things that shot him and do the same?"

"It's what I would do."

"It wouldn't help Imis." Wo'Fek looked toward her son's room and stood. "It's all my life would have been about from the moment I decided others had to pay. Letting go was the only way to move on. If I had gone after them, they would have buried me right next to him, and the aliens would still be fighting their war."

Tc'aarlat didn't answer her, just absorbed her point silently.

"You're welcome to stay, Tc'aarlat, and you're welcome

to our food. If you need us, we're happy to help a stranger."

"I don't say this often, but thanks." Tc'aarlat stood as well. "I'll leave. I just wanted to drop off those bistok bites as thanks for the meal."

"You're welcome." Wo'Fek offered a slight smile. "They were delicious." She dumped the remainder of the cookies into a napkin and handed them over.

Tc'aarlat took them without further comment.

High Orbit over Renasta, *Ark One*, ICS *Fortitude*, Bridge

Not many people knew about it since Jack had kept it quiet for years, but he had a bottle of Scotch beneath his bed. Nothing fancy, no big label or anything, just a quick nip reserved for when it was most needed. Today, the situation called for it. He brought the bottle and two glasses to the bridge, poured two fingers into each, and handed the second to Zorxia.

"She's died before." Jack took a swig and winced; it was cheap Scotch. Zorxia, who had been slowly swirling the liquid in her glass, turned her attention to him. Her eyes looked bruised and sunken. She didn't say anything, but the move acknowledged that she was listening. "You probably read the report about that problem we had with the Astonians and their cure for mortality that turned into an immortality curse. A little girl literally ate her heart out. You can't make that shit up."

Zorxia nodded. "I read the report. You Shadows do find your share of odd adventures."

"I think what I'm trying to say is, even though she was dead, there was hope. Who's to say it can't happen twice?"

Jack set his glass down on a nearby console. "Is there even the slightest chance she could've made it out alive?"

"I don't think there's any chance." Aliporta spoke hollowly from the hatch. "I did the math. Zorxia and Solo both confirmed it. If we didn't pull her out within the first minute of her being exposed, there's nothing that would—"

"How many life forms are there on Renasta?" Jack moved toward his terminal, emboldened by the quick nip. "It's an empty planet, right?"

Zorxia frowned. "There shouldn't be any. For all intents and purposes, it's a dead world."

"We should scan for life, then," he insisted. "Before we start moving the Enkelites into their new home."

Zorxia grabbed his arm. "You won't find anything, Jack."

"What if you're wrong?"

With a sigh of defeat, Zorxia moved out of his way. Aliporta joined him at the terminal. Together, they initiated a planetary scan of the planet's visible side—the one that mattered. They could've asked Solo to do it for them in less time, but Jack seemed driven to execute this one manually.

The scan was running, so all they could do now was wait.

"Get some sleep, Jack." Zorxia tossed back the rest of her Scotch and turned to leave. "Tomorrow will be a long day. We won't have time to mourn until we've finished the terraforming and settled the Enkelites on their new world."

"Yeah." Jack slowly sank into his seat and reached for the rest of his Scotch. The scans were displayed on the large monitor, and he watched the screen compulsively.

"Hopefully, it'll be a much better day. Hopefully. If Bon Noh gets out of our way."

High Orbit over Renasta, *Ark One*, ICS *Fortitude*, Bridge

Tc'aarlat stumbled onto the bridge with Mist on one shoulder and Isaaca on the other. He didn't know what time it was—a common problem with space travel—and he didn't much care, either. Tc'aarlat knew it was both too early and far later than he'd planned on returning from Wo'Fek's living quarters. He didn't know why, but Roddy was on his mind again. Every time he closed his eyes, he saw the pictures the big guy had shown him in the alley, the ones of his family.

"What's this?" Beeping from Jack's terminal brought him out of his daze. Tc'aarlat strolled over, careful to keep both Raal hawks balanced, and saw the running scans. When he looked closer, he saw that they'd flagged a life form on a beach near the ocean. A secondary scan for other anomalies had tagged something moving a few kilometers farther away than that.

"I thought there wasn't supposed to be any life on this piece of crap rock?" Tc'aarlat mumbled as he blearily noted the coordinates, but his extreme exhaustion dulled his mental faculties and masked the significance of the scan and its results. He yawned and shambled away from the console, heading for his bed.

11

Renasta, Under the Northern Ocean, Beneath the Rocks, Hours Earlier

Adina gasped for air as clear thought returned. She immediately realized her situation wasn't good. The waking nightmare—or maybe it was a hallucination—was fading, but the teeth and enraged eyes of the horrific monster that was her lingered at the front of her mind. It terrified her.

She tried to move but was trapped beneath the rocks. Luckily, she hadn't been crushed, thanks to the forcefield she wore. She still had air via the hose, although it smelled oddly stale. Despite being trapped and frantic to get out, she felt perfectly healthy. Although, now that she was aware of her surroundings, she realized she was famished, like she hadn't eaten a good meal in days. Her energy waned, but this wasn't the time to give up. She forced her hunger aside.

"HELP!" she screamed, repeating the cry until her voice

went hoarse, but no one heard her. She tried again to move to no avail.

When she thought things couldn't get any worse, the hose at the back of her neck—the one supplying her air and projecting the protective field around her—was pulled taut. At first, she thought it might be Jack or Tc'aarlat trying to reel her back into the submarine. Perhaps their ingenuity would free her! Then, as the pull grew stronger and the hose strained, foreboding warned her that something else might be happening.

Adina instinctively filled her lungs with air, then held it as the hose snapped free. Her protection instantly failed, and the rocks mercilessly crushed her helpless body, driving the air from her straining lungs.

There was no hope of rescue. She had gone from one nightmare to another.

As she faded, Adina noticed something she attributed to a dying hallucination. The rocks around her slowly shifted, then lifted high above her and hovered as if being hoisted by a team of rescuers, although she didn't see anyone. Stranger still, the pressure normalized in her body. She no longer felt like a bug beneath a colossal boot.

Before she could rationalize it, her eyes closed and her mind started to go blank like it had earlier. The last thing she thought she felt was the sensation of being picked up and thrown over someone's shoulder like a ragdoll in the water.

Adina's mind went blank as she succumbed to the fluid filling her lungs.

. . .

Renasta, Unnamed Beach, Now

The air was heavy and hot when Adina roused, flabbergasted at being alive. She was lying on a beach, still holding one of the miraculously intact jars with Bon Noh's sample. She was soaked through, even with the sun glaring down on her from above.

The first thing she noticed when she tried to stand was how difficult it was to breathe. She slowed down until the small bit of air she drew in was enough to keep her from fainting.

Adina surveyed the area by turning slowly in a circle. Before her was the ocean that had nearly killed her, going out as far as she could see. Behind her was a geologist's nirvana of stone formations from small to large, both near and far.

"This. Isn't. Good," she wheezed. She had two choices: go exploring and see if she could find something to eat and shelter or stay put and wait for rescue.

It was a difficult decision since her instinct was to seek cover, but she resolved to stay put since she knew the planet was barren. At least, they had *thought* it was. The Federation had run extensive scans with technology that could detect everything from the smallest bugs to the largest sentient beings.

Bon Noh's alleged single-cell organisms aside, Renasta came up clean across the board. And yet, something had saved her. She didn't know if it was a creature, a byproduct of whatever had snapped her lifeline to the sub, or a hallucination as she drowned, but one thing was clear. Adina had been dying at the bottom of the ocean. Now she was on the beach, alive.

With nothing else to do but wait and try to keep from panicking, she attempted to recall what had happened. She remembered the rockfall, but everything else was mixed with her waking nightmare. Every time she looked back on what happened, a detail changed. Instead of an invisible person moving the rocks to save her, it was a werewolf at the bottom of the ocean. When she thought about the care home, it was an invisible person ripping her to shreds.

She sighed. Truth was, she couldn't remember much and didn't believe what she did. The logical explanation, and it was half-baked at best, was either a natural phenomenon or something Jack and Tc'aarlat had done that pulled the rocks off her and allowed her body to slip free. It didn't make sense, though. If it had been her fellow Shadows, they'd have tried to get her back in the sub once she was free of the rocks. If it was due to a natural phenomenon, how did she get to the beach? Did she swim and not remember doing it? And, what about the pressure?

Then there was the nightmare and her stomach. It didn't take long for voracious hunger pains to set in. It happened so quickly it was suspicious. Adina could eat a horse, and not in the metaphorical sense. Thinking about it was driving her crazy. Judging by her body's reactions, it was almost time to take the medication that dampened her werewolf side. The problem was, she didn't have her pills with her and wasn't sure she could prevent the change with this kind of hunger gnawing at her.

Worse still, it wouldn't be sated until she was rescued, and that was less likely to happen if she was moving. Turning into a werewolf did not give her the best chance of survival

. . .

High Orbit over Renasta, Ark One, ICS *Fortitude*, Bridge

"It isn't a mistake. There's a life form on Renasta." Aliporta had turned from somber to hopeful upon discovering that data the next morning while Jack was preparing the ship to leave. "It could be Adina."

"What else could it be?" Jack wondered. "You said it yourself; there's nothing living down there."

The bridge door opened, and Tc'aarlat ran in. "I felt the ship moving. What's going on?"

"We did a search for life forms last night, and we think we've found Adina," Aliporta informed him. "She might still be alive!"

"What about the other flag?" Tc'aarlat yawned, still tired. "Both of them could be natives of Renasta or a couple of Bon Noh's people. It's not worth getting our hopes up."

"There's only one life form." Zorxia swung the screen to face him and pointed it out. "Nothing else on the whole planet."

"That's not right." Tc'aarlat looked at the screen suspiciously. "When I came in last night, there were two blips. Now there's only one."

"Wait, you saw this last night and didn't tell us?" Jack spun to face him. "Why?"

"I was exhausted and didn't realize what it meant."

"Didn't realize what it meant?" Jack was incredulous. "What the hell is wrong with you?"

"I was pissed off, sad, and exhausted, okay? Plus, I was dealing with Isaaca. Not the easiest thing since she's bonded to Adina now."

"Guys, focus." Zorxia snapped her fingers. "Plenty of time to get into a pissing contest later. If that is Adina, she isn't out of the woods yet. Renasta isn't as livable as a human needs. There's no food, no rain, and it's exceptionally humid, which makes it extremely difficult to breathe."

"Solo, take us down!"

"At once," Solo confirmed as she undocked *Fortitude* from *Ark One* and descended. It didn't take long for a ship like *Fortitude* to reach solid ground on Renasta, where it settled on the sandy soil. Despite the air being breathable but heavy, Zorxia insisted on protective masks with a self-contained oxygen supplement.

Jack opened the hatch and cautiously moved down the ramp. Zorxia and Aliporta followed close behind, and Tc'aarlat was last in the queue. They knew that according to the readouts there was a form of life here, but they weren't taking chances. Tc'aarlat had his Jean Dukes Special in its holster and his rifle slung over one shoulder, just in case, and kept an eye westward where he had seen the other blip on the map.

"*ADINA!*" Jack shouted across the empty landscape. "*ADINA!*"

Suddenly, she was there, but not as the woman they'd expected. Instead, it was her werewolf. The beast stared at them, and it was a look Tc'aarlat had seen before. It wasn't fear or apprehension. It was the look of a predator that had spotted its prey.

Aliporta stepped slightly away from the group, out from behind Jack. Adina focused on the scientist, who only saw remnants of clothing that identified her. Aliporta tried to shield her eyes from the harsh sun.

"Thank God!" Aliporta shouted as she ran toward her friend. "I thought we'd lost—"

The werewolf charged, jumped, and hit Aliporta chest-high, slamming the woman to the ground. Her eyes rolled back in her head, either from hitting a rock or fainting at the sight of the wolf.

Tc'aarlat spat, "She's gone feral, breathing this crappy air."

"We have to bring her around. She recognized me last time it happened."

Jack approached Adina slowly and cautiously, his left hand held out in a reassuring gesture. She watched him with her teeth bared, and he could tell she was deciding whether he was friend or food. "It's me, Jack. Remember?"

Adina sniffed the air cautiously. Jack saw recognition flicker in her eyes for a second, but then it vanished. A second later she let out the deep, long howl of a predator, a familiar sound wherever apex carnivores ruled the roost. She hurtled toward them a moment after that. Tc'aarlat had used those brief moments to draw his JDS and set it on two.

One shot.

Two.

A third.

They struck home, but not one of them stopped Adina as she paced forward, hunger and rage holding supremacy in her eyes. Her instincts had taken over. Jack braced himself and Tc'aarlat did the same, but both knew they were handicapped by trying to subdue her.

She had no such restraint. The humanity was gone from her mind.

Zorxia grabbed Aliporta and eased her out of the way while keeping a wary eye on Adina, ready to shift and take her down.

Unfortunately, the move attracted Adina's attention.

Adina wasn't focused on Jack and Tc'aarlat anymore. In her animal state, she saw new competition, and her mind was telling her to destroy it. She lunged forward, trying to reach the one who stole her prey.

Zorxia jumped in front of Aliporta, head up and shoulders back. She closed her eyes as the werewolf bore down on her.

Adina stopped and cocked her head at the willingness of the prey to die. A trick? She didn't know.

"Hey!" Tc'aarlat yelled. He had grabbed a bag of bistok sausage to take to Wo'Fek and put it in his pocket. His hand closed on it. He stalked toward Adina, meat in one hand and JDS in the other. He could feed her or he could shoot.

He thought, *I might be able to win a fight with the werewolf.* He was a Yollin, after all. He spread his mandibles wide.

"Adina. Eat your meat so you can have your dessert." He tossed the bag at her feet. She crouched and growled at him while sniffing, then hunched over the bag, dipping her snout inside and taking a bite. Then another.

Zorxia opened her eyes to see the werewolf eating. She kneeled next to her and reached out. Adina snapped at her.

"No. I just want to pet you. Keep eating. You deserve it."

Adina growled as the hand came closer but returned to the bag when the hand softly touched her shoulder and gently stroked. The werewolf finished the bag, which had held enough for a three-person meal.

Tc'aarlat was happy that he had big cargo pockets on his work clothes. Adina looked up, eyes less yellow, no longer burning with fury.

Zorxia hugged her friend, who relaxed and curled into the tiniest of great furred balls. As she fell asleep, she changed back into human form.

"Let's get her into the ship," Jack said, taking his mask off and putting it over Adina's face.

Tc'aarlat lifted her while Zorxia helped Aliporta to her feet.

"Eat your meat?" Jack said, slapping his friend on the shoulder.

"Not my best line," Tc'aarlat admitted.

"What's that?" Zorxia pointed not far from where they had found Adina.

"It's the sample jar! Holy jump-the-fuck-up-and-down, lip-smacking suckhole goodness!"

Renasta, ICS *Fortitude*, Adina's Room

Adina woke for the third time that day, still looking dazed.

This time, though, she was safe, waking up to the comforts of home with one of the people she admired most in the galaxy sitting by her side with a warm smile. Zorxia. She struggled to sit.

"It's good to see you alive, Adina," Zorxia said. "We... I thought you were gone."

"Yeah, I thought so too," Adina replied. "What happened?"

"Seems like the atmosphere had some dark effects on

your Wechselbalg side, bringing out your less human nature, shall we say. Do you remember attacking me or the others?"

"Oh, my God!" Adina buried her face in her hands. "I don't remember a thing. Well, I remember lying on the beach, thinking how hungry I was…"

"An effect of the atmosphere, I'm sure." Zorxia placed a comforting hand on her shoulder. "What do you remember about the ocean? How did you survive?"

Adina shrugged. "I could've sworn I was saved." Adina tried to think through the memories, but again, the nightmare and real life intertwined too closely. "I was lying there drowning, and something lifted the rocks."

"Lifted the rocks?" Zorxia thought about that for a moment but grew confused. "There's nothing on the planet, Adina, and certainly nothing at the bottom of the ocean. Our magnetics wouldn't have lifted the rocks; they had a low iron content. Only the submarine."

"Yet here I am," Adina replied. "Something saved me. I just don't know what."

"Well, in any case, you're safe now, and you woke up with good timing as well," Zorxia said. "We're deploying the terraformer on the planet as we speak."

Adina rushed to her window. Through it, she could see the world of Renasta, no more than a few meters from where she had been sitting no more than a few hours ago. The *Fortitude* was still firmly resting on the planet, but it wasn't the only ship. A short distance away, she saw a smaller ship that must've belonged to the *Joshua*. It had the same curves, features, and reflective surface as the bigger ship.

Adina couldn't help but giggle. Jack and Tc'aarlat worked to pull the terraformer out of the other ship while Bon Noh stood by, making the occasional remark with arms folded, supervising the whole ordeal.

"I'd better get back to work," Zorxia said. "This terraformer won't operate itself, and Aliporta needed a break."

"I'll come along if you want." Adina rubbed her growling stomach. "After I get some food, though. I'm starving."

Renasta, ICS *Fortitude*, Unnamed Beach

In the time it had taken Adina to wake, Bon Noh had brought his ship to the planet and landed close to *Fortitude*. He strolled across the sand with three of his crew. One started coughing right away and returned to the *Joshua*. The others continued. Bon Noh covered his mouth with a corner of his shirt.

His scientists had examined the sample that Adina had nearly lost her life to deliver.

True to his word and his convictions, he had given the go-ahead on terraforming the planet and brought the terraformer with him. To the surprise of everyone, he'd also vowed to help the Enkelites get settled and oversee the project to its completion instead of "fucking off," as Tc'aarlat had put it.

"Ah, Adina!" He beamed at her with his arms wide when he saw the women approaching. "I'm so happy to see you up and back in your old form."

"You're not the only one," Adina said, still eating the

last of her bistok sandwich, savoring the taste of it. Hunger was a seemingly perpetual side effect of her adventure.

"How are you feeling?" Jack asked.

"I'm fine." Adina took a few breaths through her mask, the same one everyone else was wearing, it was far easier than trying to inhale Renasta's air.

"I was just telling your captain that I've pledged my full support to the mission," Bon Noh said. "We'll even help oversee things."

"When all is said and done, more is said than done. Bon Noh, the stalker and talker. Yes, a stalker. That is you."

"Ever the joker, Tc'aarlat." Bon Noh laughed. "That's why you're my favorite."

Tc'aarlat and Jack heaved the machine forward another few meters and brushed off their hands. "When you want a job done right... Are we done here or what?"

"Just one more thing." Zorxia moved to the machine and pushed one of the many buttons. The machine extended several arms, and a second later, they firmly planted themselves into the ground. "There, now it's ready to terraform a planet. I can activate it from the atmosphere, which is the safest. You don't want your ships subjected to the rapid changes made to the atmosphere or destroyed by the amount of energy this device unleashes as it pulls power from the Etheric to create a cascade effect that spreads around the planet in a very short amount of time."

"If I'm standing on the planet when it's being terraformed," Tc'aarlat asked, "will I age?"

"No, you'll be killed instantly."

"Ah, okay. I thought so." Tc'aarlat shrugged and turned to the *Fortitude*.

"This process should take about a week, right?" Jack asked. "Then we're good to land people on the world."

"If all goes according to plan, yes. We should have a beautiful green world by this time next week," Zorxia said.

"Is it safe, being out in the open like this?" Adina wondered. "I mean, what if Benjamin is still on the loose?"

"Then he'll be killed," Zorxia replied. "The machine is currently tunneling to the planet's core to establish a vent to bring the planet to a consistent temperature optimal for growth. When we activate it, it generates a cascade, splitting the available carbon dioxide into carbon and oxygen, both critical for agriculture. But that cascade starts with a blast of energy not unlike the explosion of an atomic weapon. Anything here will be flattened before the growth begins. The process is greatly accelerated. No life to life."

"Sounds like life to no life and then new life," Tc'aarlat mumbled.

"Right," Jack said slowly. "We'd better get off this planet, then."

High Orbit over Renasta, *Ark One*, Elder's Meeting Room

Shexee took a long draw of his pipe, held it, and then blew the smoke in Jack's direction. He had been offered the pipe a few times but had declined and was now convinced the Elder was trying to second-hand-smoke him.

Jack wasn't sure why he needed to attend the meeting. He was ready to go, just to get Tc'aarlat to shut his pie hole.

They were waiting for the other Elders to arrive. For a group of people who wanted out of their metal confinement, they didn't seem to be in a hurry.

Zorxia had activated the terraformer after one final scan of the surface to make sure no one was left on the planet. The device had gotten to work, pumping powerful waves of accelerated energy across the world in a dazzling show of fractured lights in many colors. Jack, Zorxia, and Aliporta had thought it would be best if they went to tell the Elders together. As the project lead and head scientist, they could answer any technical questions. Jack assumed he was there for moral support and as the Federation's representation.

Which meant he owed Nathan Lowell a report. He wanted not to have to pay attention, but he was afraid he had been promoted out of doing the fun parts of the mission.

An ambassador and a diplomat. What he wanted was a good beer.

"Are they going to be much longer?" Jack asked.

"Yup," said Shexee.

"Getting impatient?" Zorxia wondered. "I thought waiting was your style?"

"You assumed waiting was my style because I seem to be so good at it," Jack replied. "I don't like waiting. Waiting is the bane of life. Every minute that passes is one minute closer to the end, and spending it waiting seems like such a waste when put in that context."

"What about your gray hairs, then?" Zorxia teased, and Jack instinctively combed a hand through his hair. "Is that your style?"

"I don't know what you're talking about." Jack tried to cross his arms, but one remained in the sling. He glowered at it. "How did you know?"

"I walked by your room and heard you yelling something about damn gray hairs. It's a good look on you. Executive."

"I killed that one! It is dead. Do I have more?"

"So, you *did* have a gray hair?" Jack shook his head, and Zorxia looked away.

Aliporta joined the conversation. "I hate waiting, too. It's like being on an elevator with strangers."

All three looked at Shexee. "What do you think about waiting?" Jack asked.

The Elder looked placid.

The two missing Elders came through the door. Nee'pkan and Hozgak stood exchanging confused glances until Nee'pkan stepped forward. "If we're interrupting, we can always—"

"No," Jack protested. "It's fine. We're fine. Let's talk business."

"We're terribly sorry about our late arrival," said Hozgak. "Did we miss anything important?"

"Yup," Shexee said with a grin and a nod.

Once everyone had taken their seats, Jack started. "So, we thought it would be a good idea to go over the plan for tomorrow." The plan was simple. Once preliminary tests were performed on the planet to make sure the terraforming had taken place, the arks would descend upon the area with the most potential to be fertile and break apart as they were designed to do, to provide shelter and food until the Enkelites had the resources to build their own.

The *Fortitude* would keep watch on everyone from ground level while the *Joshua* remained in orbit.

Providing the offered oversight.

More said than done. Jack had agreed because it kept Bon Noh away from the Shadows.

Occasionally during the course of the conversation, the Enkelites had a question about the science, like whether the terraformation would mean they couldn't grow their crops or would the grass affect their livestock, which Zorxia was quick to answer.

The conversation took an hour to complete, and by the end, both sides were ready to stop talking and start doing. The Elders were grateful and promised to host a massive celebration. They bowed before they left the room.

"Next time you want me in a meeting with you, talk yourselves out of it. Yup? Okay."

"We're at the end of it, Jack. We're helping the Enkelites survive," Aliporta offered. "This is something to celebrate."

Jack turned to her. "I'm heading back to the ship. There's a Hot Pocket waiting for me in the microwave that I haven't stopped thinking about for the past hour."

"Something tells me they don't have a coffee shop on board," Zorxia replied. "I might make use of the galley too, and then I'm turning in."

"Probably the best idea," Jack replied. "Me, I'll probably pop a film on, drift off to sleep with it."

"Is that how the famous Jack Marber relaxes?" Zorxia chuckled.

"Yup."

.   .   .

High Orbit over Renasta, *Ark One*, Observation Deck

The waves of energy crashing over the planet below made for interesting viewing. Each time the terraformer blasted out a surge of energy, the planet changed color slightly, moving from red to orange to yellow with the goal of being green by morning.

Enkelites sat on the observation deck, watching the planet move through its accelerated cycles. Already there were small green islands in a sea of brown. The Enkelites felt the hope that life on board the metal monsters was at an end.

Wo'Fek had brought Imis here to witness the birth of their new home, and she was in the middle of explaining how Renasta was like a growing seed when she felt someone sit down next to her. It was Nee'p-kan, casually stroking his beard and watching the sights.

"Hello, Elder Nee'pkan," Wo'Fek said cheerily. "Have you come to enjoy the show?"

"I have," the Elder replied. "And I've come to talk with you, Wo'Fek, as a friend."

"As a friend?" Wo'Fek placed Imis on the deck and nudged him into moving away, which he did as if launched out of a cannon. "Why are you coming to me as a friend? Have I done something wrong?"

"No, no, not at all," replied Nee'pkan. "There have been rumors that you've been meeting with one of the Federation emissaries."

"Ah, well, I can put those rumors to rest, then," said

Wo'Fek. "They're true. The tall insect-looking one has been visiting me. He can't get enough of my food."

"It's just a little…unusual," continued Nee'pkan.

"Why is it unusual?" asked Wo'Fek. "We encourage strangers in our homes. We always have; it's why we are such a strong community. Does that courtesy not extend past our flock?"

"I feel like you know what I'm asking you and you're dancing around it," Nee'pkan said. "Teasing me."

"We're not romantically attached if that's what you're asking, Elder," said Wo'Fek. "I happen to think he's charming and funny, if not a little callous sometimes, but a friend. Nothing more."

"Well, good," said Nee'pkan. "That's good to hear."

"Why is that good to hear?" asked Wo'Fek. "Could I not be romantically involved with Tc'aarlat?"

"He's an outsider and a far cry from our species," said Nee'pkan. "Our teachings are our own, and I've seen how he acts; no respect for anything. He didn't even show up for the welcome dinner on the first night."

"I fear Imis mislead him to my quarters. He asked about the dinner repeatedly, but I was in the middle of cooking and didn't want to spoil any of it. Imis couldn't be trusted. Tc'aarlat's absence was all my fault."

Wo'Fek stood and called for Imis, who showed up a second after his mother shouted his name. She didn't say anything else but barged past the Elder and headed to her quarters, ignoring her son's pleas to stay.

This was what the community thought of her now, and as she moved through the various halls and corridors, she could feel their stares like daggers in her back.

Wo'Fek has gone with an alien fella, they were probably muttering to themselves. *Isn't she a strange one?*

Wo'Fek stormed into her home and threw the door closed behind her, locking it and sealing both of them inside. She was about to move in farther when her body tensed as a figure stepped out of the shadows, stuffing his face with one of the pies she had left to cool. Tc'aarlat.

"'Sup?" Tc'aarlat said through a mouthful of crumbs. She shifted anxiously, eyes darting. "You okay there?"

Wo'Fek relaxed and blew out the breath she'd been holding. "I'm feeling a bit better now, yeah."

High Orbit over Renasta, ICS *Fortitude*, Galley

In her nightmares, she was being chased by a werewolf. When she woke up, she was hungrier than she'd ever been. Adina marched to the galley, clutching her growling stomach the entire way, and forced her way into the fridge to look for something fresh rather than processed. She grabbed a packet of bistok and went to town on it.

The light came on, and she turned to see Jack and Zorxia walk in from their meeting with the Elders. She gulped down the last bite and gave them an innocent smile. "Hey, guys. How did it go?"

"Are you eating bistok out the packet?" Jack raised one eyebrow.

"I'm sorry, I'm really hungry." Adina threw the empty packet into the trash. "I keep getting these urges for meat, and there's my dream, too."

"Dream?" Zorxia took a seat at the dining table and

gestured for Adina to do the same. Jack stood by, listening intently. "The same dream as before?"

Jack rolled his finger for Adina to explain.

"When I was trapped on the bottom of the ocean, I had this nightmare when I was knocked out." Adina furrowed her brow, trying to remember the details. "I was back at Base 11 in my uncle's care home, and he... Well, every-one... I had killed them all while I was turned, while I was a werewolf."

Jack cocked his head. "It's just a nightmare. Death has a funny way of doing weird things to your mind. Work out harder, and you'll be plenty tired."

Zorxia shook her head. "I read the report from your last mission when you stole the Don's money. You were being blackmailed by Benjamin, isn't that right?"

"Yeah, that's right." Adina gave her a small nod. "He said that if I transferred the Don's money to his hacker group, he could cure my uncle's dementia. I still don't know if he was being honest."

"He wasn't," Jack said. "You can trust me on that." He looked at Zorxia. "Why are you reading our mission reports?"

"I'm a scientist. As soon as I learned I'd be put on this ship, I used my clearance to find out everything I could about it and you."

Jack pursed his lips and remained quiet.

"You might be feeling guilty. I don't know. I'm not a psychologist," Zorxia said. "Maybe you can talk with someone when you get back?"

"Tell them I'm feeling guilty about being a werewolf?

What about my hunger?" Adina said. "I've been so hungry lately."

"That could be a number of things. I'd be happy to run some tests as one of my specialties is in biomass energy," Zorxia replied. "I'll figure out what makes your engine run."

Jack sucked his lips between his teeth to keep from uttering what he considered to be a pretty good joke. On second thought, maybe it wasn't.

13

Renasta, New Fruling

The Enkelites cheered while the arks descended to Renasta. It was worth celebration and the declaration that hard work was once again on the schedule.

The next few weeks were filled with the basics of restoring their lives, preparing fields to grow and places to live. Sixteen-hour days of nothing but the hardest of labor.

That was not a problem for the stoic Enkelite people.

Bon Noh, despite his willingness to provide oversight, proved useless to the Enkelite people. He didn't know the first thing about farming or building a settlement, and he didn't have the upper body strength to be any good at something as simple as carrying heavy things from one place to another.

He offered three of his people to stay behind and help while he left the system in search of more lucrative protests to launch.

Jack and Tc'aarlat never found out where Bon Noh's

bogus information had come from. Had it been malicious or simply misplaced environmental vigilantism?

The final stage of terraforming had drastically changed Renasta. The air was fresh, fresher than any other world they had been on. Grass and trees and shrubs had grown quickly across the surface of the world, and some had already born edible food that the Enkelites were excited to harvest and explore.

They didn't build a city, as the Shadows were expecting. Instead, they spread over the land, dotting their small homes here and there and preparing for lives of blissful agriculture, much as it had been on Fruling. They were so enamored of their new home that they called the four hundred square kilometers they had occupied New Fruling in honor of their former planet.

The arks had been designed by the Federation to come apart like a kit and be rearranged into buildings with the press of a few buttons. The Enkelites used the pieces to build new homesteads and barns and fences that ran around the perimeter of each individual space so the cattle wouldn't wander off.

It would do until the Enkelites opted to create their own places the traditional way, but it took more work because of how far they were spread out. The arks contained a limited amount of heavy equipment that the Enkelites used to move the disconnected sections of the ship. Slowly but surely, they settled the new structures into place.

Jack, Adina, Zorxia, and Tc'aarlat regularly came back to the *Fortitude* at the end of the day with their joints aching. They collapsed into bed and woke up when it was time to work the next day.

Through a mixture of determination and perspiration, they managed to relocate thousands of Enkelites to the wild green land that was their new home.

Everyone was grateful to be done at the end of it, and with the Enkelites finally settled on Renasta and ready to start a new life, the Shadows were set to leave.

The last thing on their agenda was attending the huge celebration the Elders were hosting in thanks mostly to the Federation for providing them with this opportunity to live a peaceful life away from the wars of their old world, and for Bon Noh's crucial part in the reassembly of their lives. They had worked hard, especially the Shadows, and they deserved to be recognized.

Renasta, New Fruling, ICS *Fortitude*, Jack's Room

There wasn't a dress code for this celebration, but Jack had decided to play it safe and wear his best suit, minus the bowtie to keep it casual. It was a difficult thing to do with his arm in a sling, and although it was feeling a little better with the weeks that had gone by, it was still sore to the touch. At least he could move some of his fingers again, though living without his right hand was proving to be one hell of a chore.

"There it is." Jack plucked yet another gray hair from the top of his head and inspected it. The conversation he had shared with Zorxia in the Elders' room came back to him. *Everyone gets old.* He shuddered at the thought, wondering why his enhancements were failing. His arm was still broken. It should have healed weeks ago.

And gray hairs. He should look younger, not older.

There was a knock on the door and he went to open it. He was expecting Tc'aarlat with the newest joke he had learned, but it wasn't the Yollin.

Zorxia stood there wearing a slinky black dress and looking nothing like the scientist they'd picked up over a month earlier.

"Where's Zorxia?" Jack asked, attempting a smooth delivery.

"I'm right here," she replied, unused to the ways of the flirtatious.

"I know," Jack said, feeling less sure of himself.

"You clean up nice, Captain Marber."

"I try my best," Jack said. "I will say the same for you times three."

"Oh, this old thing!" She laughed. "I just threw it on. I wanted to look nice for the party."

Jack didn't believe it was an old thing.

Zorxia spotted something amiss in Jack's hair. She leaned in and licked her hand to straighten out a cowlick that had sprung up at the back of his head. As she leaned in, she couldn't help but notice something more: a gray hair beneath the black.

She plucked it for him. He grunted more in surprise than pain. He couldn't help but stare at the breasts she had shoved into his face. "What the hell is going on up there?"

"Still getting old, Captain Marber?" she teased and held the stray hair up to his face.

"I thought I got them all," Jack said. "Must have missed

it, but I shouldn't be getting gray hairs. I'm enhanced with nanos. Same thing with this arm. It should have healed already. *That* is giving me gray hair!"

"You're not still worrying about it, are you?" asked Zorxia seriously. "Gray hair makes men look distinguished, you know."

"It's not the hair, it's—"

"What it represents." Zorxia sighed. "I know, Jack. You said."

"It's just that—"

"Listen, I'm going to tell you something, but it better not get out to anyone!" Zorxia lifted his head out of her cleavage to whisper in his ear, "I have gray hairs, too. I dye my hair."

Jack's jaw dropped for the second time. "You?"

Zorxia nodded, and he yelped when she gave him a pinch. "Tell no one, and keep in mind that I have access to some pretty powerful weaponry. I have a gun that could turn you inside-out."

"Scout's honor." Jack placed a hand over his heart. "Thanks for sharing, though. It's made me feel—" He fumbled for the right word, but talking about his feelings wasn't something he practiced. Not being able to use profanity also stymied his efforts at being clear. He settled for something so weak that he was instantly embarrassed. "It makes me feel funny."

She looked sorry for him and saved him from his discomfort. "Should we go to this party?"

"I'd love to."

. . .

Renasta, New Fruling, ICS *Fortitude*, Outside

It was no secret that Tc'aarlat had been gunning to leave this world behind the second the terraforming had finished, and now the time was finally upon him. Tomorrow, after the celebration, the Shadows would leave and get back to the only thing that mattered: tracking down Don Gan'barlo. Tc'aarlat carried a knife that he longed to shove between the Don's ribs. It was time to answer for his crimes. It was time to pay his debt.

To expedite their departure, Tc'aarlat had done all the necessary maintenance to the ship, including the final maintenance to bring the blown-up bridge back to its former glory. And of late, he did the complete pre-flight. Keeping his hands busy had saved him from going insane. That and Wo'Fek.

She had told him she'd be coming to the celebration, and it had made him glad. Even he couldn't deny how close they had gotten. She gave him something other than revenge to look forward to. Unfortunately, it was Wo'Fek who was on Elder Nee'pkan's mind when he arrived at the *Fortitude*.

"Hello, Tc'aarlat," he said, casually approaching the Yollin. "I don't think we've been properly introduced. You're the only Federation emissary with whom I haven't spent any time."

"I'm not an emissary, so piss off," Tc'aarlat snapped, and Nee'pkan recoiled from the Yollin's outburst.

"We need to talk," Nee'pkan said.

Tc'aarlat turned from the fuel gauge he was checking to the Elder behind him. "Are you deaf, or does 'piss off' mean something else in this language?"

"We need to talk about Wo'Fek."

"Is she in trouble?" Tc'aarlat straightened. "What's happened?"

"She's fine, but I must speak with you about your intentions," Nee'pkan said. "I'm afraid the Elders cannot allow it."

"My intentions?" Tc'aarlat wondered, confusion gripping him as he studied the Elder. "I'm sorry, you can't allow what?"

"I came by to make sure you were leaving tomorrow," Nee'pkan explained. "I've reviewed the situation with my fellow Elders, and we don't think you're compatible with our peaceful ways. Not to mention, you're also a very different species."

"You came here to tell me I can't be with Wo'Fek." Tc'aarlat burst from his chair and stormed over to the Elder. "There's nothing I fucking want more than to be off this rock. There are evil people out there, and nothing will happen to them if I...if *we* don't make it happen."

"That's good to hear," said Nee'pkan. "You should tell her that."

"What?"

"You've been spotted together many times," Nee'pkan said. "They tell me your relationship is more than just friendship."

"It isn't," Tc'aarlat replied. "But we'll do what we want. It's none of your bistok-humping business. Now, I'd fuck off if I were you."

"I will, but I'll leave you with this." Tc'aarlat turned away from him, but kept his ears open. "Any feelings she has for you are probably temporary. She recently lost her husband, and she may have leaned on you for support, but she'll come to her senses eventually, and you won't like the results. She could never love someone like you."

Tc'aarlat turned and snarled with his full Yollin fury. "I said, fuck off!"

Renasta, New Fruling, the Square

Although many of the Enkelites were spread out across the four hundred square kilometers of New Fruling, the Elders had insisted on a central hub. It was a square where they had erected buildings for official business, a hall people could come to talk to the Elders about matters of importance, or a place where they could communicate with the Federation in case of disaster, or they needed a water pump for clean water, or other necessities. These were things they had on Fruling, but everyone had their own. On Renasta, they settled for a centralized hub.

The Elders had set up a long table with seats for a hundred, including their honored guests, the Shadows, and Bon Noh's volunteers. No surprise that the Shadows arrived first. The Elders greeted them with open arms and much gratitude, leading them to the chairs closest to the head of the table.

Tc'aarlat, who had chosen to wear what he always wore, wasn't looking at the head of the table, though. He was keeping an eye out for Wo'Fek. While they were getting the Enkelites back on their feet, he had helped her build her home and barn and herd the cattle into their new pens. Purposely, he had chosen a spot to keep her close to the square. He thought briefly about abandoning this party and heading straight to her, as he had done off and on for the past few weeks.

"What's up, mate?" Jack clapped him on the back. "It's a party! Loosen up!"

"What do the Enkelites know about throwing a party?" Tc'aarlat sat down and grabbed a bottle of wine. He gave Elder Nee'pkan a cold look before chugging it from the bottle. "We should be shooting off of this fucking rock and getting back to hunting mobsters."

"Tomorrow," Jack said. "Just one more night."

Zorxia stayed out of the intramural firefight between the Shadows. She watched, hoping to keep Jack calm without getting into the middle of the angst that gripped the team.

"Well, well, well." Jack, Tc'aarlat, and Adina turned and saw blinding, sparkling hair; Bon Noh had returned. He had thought this party was fancy dress and decided to come with his hair as a disco ball.

His gown was flowing and long and covered in thousands of tiny flashing lights. Bon Noh took a seat next to Adina. "If it isn't my favorite group of Federation servants!"

"Servants?" Tc'aarlat barked. Jack calmed him with a quick shake of the head, leaving his next taunt to turn into a low growl and another chug of wine.

"Adina, how are you feeling?" Bon Noh asked. "Fully recovered?"

"You could say that," Adina replied.

Volume increased with the hum of numerous voices, thanks to Bon Noh's arrival and the number of people he'd brought. The Enkelites were arriving too, and they appeared to be ready to party. They headed straight for the wine.

Food started to arrive by the platterful. There were people singing, fires burning, and tales being told to the young, creating a dull roar of indiscriminate voices.

The Shadows and every other occupant of the table had fought their way through a three-course meal and several casks of wine and home-brewed ale. The Shadows kept the conversation light among themselves, mostly concerning what they had achieved in these few short weeks, but it came to a halt when they noticed a small child run toward the table with a massive grin and wrap his arms around Tc'aarlat.

"Taccyrat!" he exclaimed, wrapping his arms around the much bigger Yollin as tightly as he could.

"Uh…" Tc'aarlat looked sheepishly at those around him. "Whose kid is this?"

"Seems to know you, Taccyrat." Adina giggled, and she leaned down to the boy. "Hello, little guy. I'm Adina."

"You're the one that died!" Imis said in amazement, and he poked her to make sure she was real. "Wow."

Jack gave Tc'aarlat his best hairy eyeball. "Why does this kid know about us?"

"I don't know." Tc'aarlat sat up straight. "I've never seen Imis before in my life."

"I'll go get Mother!" Imis exclaimed, and before Tc'aarlat could stop him, the eager boy was running through the crowd.

"Do you have a secret family, Tc'aarlat?" Zorxia enquired.

"Is this where you've been sneaking off to when we

can't find you?" Adina wondered.

"I just thought you'd found a good place to mope," Jack said.

Before Tc'aarlat could delve into the failures of Jack's ancestry, the din of the party calmed when Elder Nee'pkan stood.

He spoke into the void of silence.

"I want to speak about our new home and the opportunity that has been given to us before we surrender to the joy of the moment, as well as thank both the Federation and Captain Bon Noh for their aid in helping us restore our peaceful ways. It's been a pleasure having—"

Bon Noh stood and interrupted the speech while imploring the Elder to sit down. "I'll take it from here, Elder."

Jack was embarrassed but not surprised. Tc'aarlat glared and would have left had it not been for Adina gripping his arm.

"What? Oh?" Nee'pkan didn't know what to say. "First Captain Bon Noh has some things he wishes to say and apparently, he can't wait."

Tc'aarlat crossed his arms, annoyed, and surrendered to the moment. Adina relaxed her grip but continued to rest her hand on Tc'aarlat's arm.

"Thanks to the collective force of my protestors, the Enkelites have a home to be proud of." Bon Noh raised his glass. "Thanks to my intervention, two lives were saved these past few weeks by the efforts of myself and my crew. We ensured that no current or future life forms were injured in the terraforming process. That's the power of protesting and standing up to everything you think is wrong, no matter how minimal the issue, nor how dire the situation. I just want to raise a glass to my crew and their valiant efforts in making this place a home! I know the Enkelites didn't have much, but now, they have a future full of hope."

There was a round of hearty applause from Bon Noh's crew, but his speech left a sour taste in the mouths of the Shadows. They collectively came to the decision to let it go.

All of the Shadows except Tc'aarlat. Through a mixture of frustration at being stuck on Renasta for weeks, the pure arrogance of Bon Noh, a few bottles of wine, and especially what Elder Nee'pkan had said to him a few hours before, the Yollin decided he wouldn't let it go.

"What about Adina?" Tc'aarlat called loudly enough to restore the silence. Bon Noh looked at him, his face the definition of confusion. "What?" Tc'aarlat shot back. "Did you forget about the woman that almost died to get you confirmation there was no life on this planet? You protest based on false information and then cheer yourself for it. All you did was create extra work that risked our lives. How about you celebrate with a big bowl of fuck you?"

"Oh, of course," Bon Noh raised his glass and smiled again. "Thank you for everything you've done as well, Adina!"

Muted cheers greeted the concession. Tc'aarlat glared at him as he took to his seat again. "That's it? You should be snogging her fucking butthole, the way she helped you."

"Leave it, Tc'aarlat." Jack leaned over and whispered, "Let it go. We're gone tomorrow."

"Yeah, well, I would expect you to fucking say that,

Jack." Tc'aarlat drained the last of his wine and threw the bottle behind him. "This asshat created the crisis that he congratulates himself for after we resolved it. He saved us because our blood would have been on his hands. A win-win for Bon Noh's eco-terrorists."

"There's no need for names or insults." Bon Noh adjusted his glasses. "We've all done our part to help these people get settled. It's just some did a little more than others, that's all."

Tc'aarlat had been spoiling for a fight. Without consideration of the consequences, he leapt across the table and delivered a well-aimed fist into the Malatian's delicately painted face with enough force to crack a hole in a boulder. Bon Noh fell over backward.

But it didn't stop there. Tc'aarlat landed another blow and another until Jack and Adina came over the table to stop him. They pulled him off a groaning Bon Noh.

"You're lucky I keep forgetting my gun in my room!" Tc'aarlat shouted. "You're lucky I'm not in the fucking mood to get it."

"Taccyrat?"

Everything came to a stop in a single second.

Tc'aarlat looked over. His anger morphed into anguish since Imis had fulfilled his promise and brought his mother.

Wo'Fek stood there, horrified at seeing what the Yollin was capable of—the rage and violence he had unleashed on Bon Noh. With tears in her eyes, she ran. Tc'aarlat didn't go after her. He collapsed, sitting on the ground and holding his head in his hands. If Wo'Fek hadn't thought he was a monster before, she certainly would now.

Adina and Jack helped Tc'aarlat to his feet and guided him away. Jack looked back at every face staring at him. He gave them the thumbs-up and shouted over his shoulder as they hurried away, "Great party!"

Renasta, New Fruling, the Square, Quiet Area

"What the fuck was that?" Jack demanded after they had gotten far enough away from the party that they wouldn't be overheard. "We're supposed to be here to oversee things, not cause problems. You couldn't leave your fucking gripes with Bon Noh for another day?"

"*We*." Tc'aarlat snorted while continuing to stare at the ground. "We. We're emissaries for the Federation, we're their servants, we're heroes, we are the pride of the Federation on these border planets. We're not any of that crap, Jack. It's not 'we,' it's *YOU*."

"This is about Don Gan'barlo again, isn't it?" Jack snapped. "You couldn't wait one more damned day. You had to start trouble now, leave a big shit on the table just before we fuck off. Classic, Tc'aarlat, real fucking classic."

"We shouldn't be here—"

"Oh, here we go," Jack said.

"Jack." Adina grabbed his arm, trying desperately to cool him off a little, but he shook her off.

"It's all about you, isn't it?" Jack replied. "Me, me, fucking me. You have to be the most selfish and self-centered creature I've ever met in the damn galaxy, and yeah, that list includes fucking Bon Noh."

"If I'm such a nightmare, then why am I part of the crew?" Tc'aarlat replied.

Adina stepped in. "You're our friend, Tc'aarlat. We care about you, and we care about your troubles. We want to find Don Gan'barlo as much as you do, but it's—"

"But what?" Tc'aarlat snapped his head around to her. "It's too much effort? There aren't enough fucking leads? What?"

"You know what the problem is," Jack said, flopping to the ground. "The Don's gone into hiding, and he's more than a bitch to find. You've got to stop blaming us for that. It's not our fault we can't find him. It's not anyone's fault. When someone with his resources wants to hide, they stay hidden. You've got to accept that."

"I can't do this anymore." Tc'aarlat barged past them. "You can keep the ship. I'll find my own way."

"What are you talking about?" Jack called after him, but Tc'aarlat ignored him.

"I quit," Tc'aarlat insisted. "I'm done."

"What?" Adina took a step backward. "What do you mean, you quit?"

"I mean, I'm done with the crapping Shadows." Tc'aarlat hunched his shoulders and stared at the ground. "If you won't help me find the Don, I'll do it myself."

"Don't," Jack pleaded. "You're letting this mobster continue to ruin your life, and as a more practical and immediate matter, there's two ways off this planet. On the *Fortitude* or with Bon Noh, and I think that second door is closed. Think about it. We leave tomorrow."

"It doesn't matter," Tc'aarlat said, turning his back on them. "I quit the Shadows."

. . .

Renasta, New Fruling, the Forests

Wo'Fek clutched Imis' hand tightly and led him through the darkness under the new-growth trees and off the path so the other Enkelites wouldn't see her in this state. Tears streamed down her cheeks to fall on a dress ruined by the trek across the muddy ground.

Not twenty minutes ago, she had witnessed a person she thought was a good man viciously beat another in unbridled rage. She thanked her makers that she had never before seen such a thing and hoped she never would again. That much anger was poison.

Tc'aarlat was not the person she thought he was. He had been trying to tell her what he was capable of, but she hadn't listened.

"Why was Taccyrat so angry?" Imis asked. "Was that other alien a bad person?"

"I don't know." Wo'Fek couldn't walk any farther. She needed to take a moment to breathe. She drew her son close, and they took seats next to the closest tree. "I think Taccyrat is fighting an evil that may have come from within."

"That's not true!" protested Imis. "He fights the bad guys. He fights mobsters!"

"I'm sorry, Imis," Wo'Fek said with kind eyes, brushing her son's hair lovingly. "I don't think we should see Tc'aarlat anymore. I think it's better he left without saying goodbye."

"No!" Imis pushed himself away from his mother with force. "You're wrong! Taccyrat came to help us, and he's going to stay with us forever."

"Imis, you—"

Imis didn't want to hear it, and as he got more upset, he acted like any child would with trouble he was unwilling to face. Imis ran away as fast as he could. Wo'Fek went after him, but it didn't matter. She wasn't as quick, and within a few moments he was lost between the trees and gone from her sight.

"*IMIS!*" she shouted, and she continued shouting his name until she grew hoarse and her voice rattled in her throat. "*IMIS!*"

There was a sound just behind, the snapping of a twig underfoot, and she turned quickly to find nothing there. Wo'Fek called her son's name again and could've sworn she heard someone coming toward her, but again, she saw nothing.

Her stomach churned in fear and she had a growing feeling she was in danger, which meant Imis was also in danger.

Wo'Fek turned to run, but before she could move her legs, she was violently jerked backward as a hand firmly gripped her neck.

She was lifted into the air, high enough that her legs dangled, and she tried to cry out but couldn't. She managed to say weakly, "*What is happening?*"

No one answered her question. She was tossed unceremoniously over an invisible shoulder. She batted at the thing, but it was like beating on the hull of a spaceship.

Wo'Fek didn't know much outside of her humble life inside the Enkelite flock. Despite her lack of worldliness, this wasn't a creature the Enkelites were familiar with. At least it wanted her alive as it trudged into the darkness.

"Imis! *Save yourself,*" she shouted behind her.

14

Renasta, New Fruling, the Forests

Originally, Tc'aarlat had decided he would go to Wo'Fek's homestead to apologize. He felt horrible. His life had gotten away from him, and despite his anger and drive, he was no closer to finding the Don.

In fact, he was farther away than ever, trapped on a planet that wasn't even in Federation territory. It was the one place he knew Don Gan'barlo wasn't.

"You are the dumbest of all dumb people! You don't even have Mist with you. He will need to eat, but you can't feed him. You must count on your friends who are hating your guts. If they aren't because they are too kind, then they should!" he shouted at himself as he stomped back and forth.

"You're not like us, that wrinkly old ass said. *ASS!*" Tc'aarlat yelled toward the small town. "Maybe I am the ass." But Wo'Fek. She had been kind to him and given him the best food, the best he'd had in a long, long time. And she'd asked nothing of him.

Kindness like that deserved respect.

"I must find her to apologize. But I'm still angry at the Shadows. Did we do everything we could to find the Don? Maybe back to square one. Would they? The ducking bastard is hiding. Ducking. Ha! I'm funny. Why would I bring up ducks? Talth. Roddy. We need to go back and talk to him. He knew something. I see it now."

It had been a long day, and the wine still pulled at him. Tc'aarlat knew what he needed to do, but his eyelids grew heavy. He flopped to the ground beneath a tree.

This secluded place provided the perfect cover for the Yollin to rest, and he disappeared into a restless and drunken sleep.

He was still buzzed when he was shaken awake by the last person he expected to see.

"Wh-what!" He jumped up suddenly, brought roughly from his stupor back to reality.

"I can't find Mother."

"Imis?" Tc'aarlat tried to stand but winced. There was a pain in the side of his head—a drunk's lament. "Shit, pain. Fucker, that hurts. What are you doing out here alone? Where's your mother?"

"I don't know," Imis said. "I ran away."

"Why did you do that?" Tc'aarlat wondered. He rubbed the side of his head, but it wasn't taking the ache away.

"She said you were bad." Imis stared at Tc'aarlat, waiting for him to reaffirm that the Yollin was a good guy.

Tc'aarlat stared back, it was a weird thing to be looked up to, and he couldn't recall other moments in his life when it had happened. He took a deep breath, used the tree to help him stand, and took the boy's hand with a firm grip.

"I am a good guy, but sometimes, even good guys do things that may look bad. Can you take me to the last place you saw her?" Tc'aarlat said calmly. "And please be quiet. I need to concentrate if I'm to find Wo'Fek."

Imis nodded.

"No." Tc'aarlat pulled the kid around to face him. "I want to hear you say it, Imis."

"Say what?"

"Say, 'I'll be good.'"

"I'll be good, Taccyrat. Can we go now?"

"I'm going to hold you to that." Tc'aarlat gave him an affectionate pat on the head. With Imis leading the way, they moved into the depths of the forest, away from the small Enkelite town.

As they walked, Tc'aarlat realized Imis had already lost focus and was chattering in a stream of consciousness.

"Are you nervous? Do you miss your mother?"

The boy stopped talking. Tc'aarlat renewed his grip on the boy's hand and hurried the pace. The boy pulled him to a stop and stared at a tree.

It was the last place he had seen his mother. Tc'aarlat inspected the area, finding the grass crushed at the base of the tree. He brushed it with his hand, and it came upright.

"Someone was sitting here recently," Tc'aarlat muttered.

"What are you doing?" Imis asked innocently. "I know she was here."

"I'm trying to track." Tc'aarlat followed the slight signs of movement across the ground. Renasta, as a new and untouched world, had had little in the way of intrusions.

All footprints were fresh. His and Imis' led into the small clearing.

Wo'Fek had walked throughout the area, same as Imis— a snapped twig here, a footprint there, the ruffle of grass, the sway of an overhanging vine.

"She came through this way, chasing you," Tc'aarlat said, following the tracks deeper into the woods. Imis eagerly hopped behind him, fascinated with the process. Tc'aarlat didn't pay him any attention, though, as he cut a way through the trees and kept going.

"Here," he said finally, pointing to the forest floor. "The trail ends here. It looks like she just vanished. That is the strangest of the strange things."

"What about this?" Imis, a quick learner, had been searching for tracks in much the same way, and his keen sight had found something a short distance away. Tc'aarlat furrowed his brow in confusion. It was a footprint, but unlike anything the Enkelites would leave. The print was huge and deep, which suggested something heavy. It was a strange marking as well; there were no other footprints like it anywhere else.

"What is it?" Imis asked.

"No one leaves only a single footprint, especially in such soft ground. It is the strangest of the strange in one word: strange, Tc'aarlat said, considering it. "I've never seen a footprint like this, but I think it tells us something we didn't know before."

"What?" Imis asked.

Tc'aarlat eyed the trees around them. The sudden realization that they might be in danger caught him in the moment. "I think your mother might have been taken by something, and I don't think it was an Enkelite, not unless they got a whole lot cooler in the past few hours." He kept one hand on Imis' head as he forced the lad behind him while scanning the trees above.

"Then what was it?" Imis demanded. "Why would someone take Mother?"

"I don't know, and I don't know." Tc'aarlat turned to Imis with all the confidence in the world. "I'm going to find her, though, because I am a good guy. I promised to apologize, and I want to keep that promise."

Renasta, New Fruling, ICS *Fortitude*, Jack's Room

BANG. BANG. BANG. Jack found himself waking up with perhaps the greatest hangover of his life after a rough night of drinking. After the argument with Tc'aarlat, he had hit the bottle hard, and he was certainly paying for it now. His throat was as dry as a desert, and every slight movement made his stomach turn. There was the banging again. Jack originally thought it was just in his head, but when it became more persistent, he realized someone was at the door. Jack was about to go to it when he felt something around his waist.

Turning around, Jack unfurled his bedsheets and went wide-eyed at the woman lying next to him, fully clothed and with her lipstick smeared. Zorxia.

The banging continued, but he froze for a few seconds. With no other choice, Jack threw the covers back over her, hoping she wouldn't wake up, and went to the door quickly. Hopefully, he could get whoever it was to leave quickly.

"I'm coming!" Jack crept over and pushed the button on the side of the wall.

The door opened on a stern-faced Nee'pkan, who looked like he was not in the mood for games. Jack finally noticed he had answered the door in nothing but his boxers, thinking it was Adina or Tc'aarlat. Second time on this world he'd been caught in his boxers, but given the situation, it could have been much worse.

"Oh, Elder Nee'pkan." Jack stood up straight. "Sorry about this. I was sleeping when you—"

"I'm glad I caught you before your team left our new world," Nee'pkan said, crossing the threshold without permission. The Elder looked around the room but failed to see the still-passed-out Zorxia on the bed under the crumpled covers. "I'm afraid I come with bad news."

"Bad news?" Jack said. "Should we talk about it in the hall, or…"

"My flock came to me this morning, and what they had to report was horrific, to say the least," said Nee'pkan. "Many Enkelites have been found dead."

"Found dead?" Jack said, confused. "What do you mean?"

"They were murdered in their beds. They were ripped apart. I know; I've seen two myself, and it is not a sight I will ever forget."

"Ripped apart?" Jack's thoughts immediately went to Adina and the trouble she'd been having with controlling herself lately. "If you'll give me a few minutes, Elder, I'll help investigate. The Shadows are here for you."

Jack led him quickly toward the door.

"Very good, Captain Marber," said Nee'pkan. "I will meet you in the square."

"I won't be long," Jack said and shut the door behind the Elder.

Jack hurried back to the bed. "Zorxia, get up. We need to go."

"I feel like shit." Zorxia coughed. "What the... *Jack!* What am I doing in your room?"

"You were trying to comfort me, fully professionally, mind you, but you fell asleep." Jack grabbed his trousers from the floor.

"I don't..." Zorxia clutched her head, trying desperately to think. "I don't remember anything from last night."

"I know last night was too short, and I'm not ready for what we have to do."

Zorxia coughed and ended up holding her head. "Why are you in your boxers?"

"It's how I sleep. But none of that matters. Someone has murdered a bunch of Enkelites." Jack threw a t-shirt around him, carefully pulling it over his broken arm first, then the rest of his body.

"Dead?" Zorxia sobered. "From what?"

Jack gave her a knowing look. "From being ripped apart."

"You don't think..."

"I don't know what to think," Jack said. "All I know is that we've got to find out where Adina is right now."

Renasta, New Fruling, ICS *Fortitude*, Adina's Room

Jack and Zorxia moved into Adina's room quietly to

find her in her bed, sleeping soundly. The other times she had changed, there had been signs like wanton destruction.

There was no blood, no torn clothing, no Enkelite remains or souvenirs. Everything appeared normal.

Jack swallowed hard, confused. "What are we going to tell her?"

"The truth," Zorxia said. "We don't know that it was her."

"I'm pretty sure it was *not* her, which is even more problematic as it begs the question, who?"

Adina stirred and blinked slowly. She shot up when she saw two people in her small room. "Jack? Zorxia? What the hell? You never heard about knocking? What if I was sleeping naked?"

Zorxia frowned and shook her head. "People have been found dead, Adina. They were found ripped apart, like by an animal."

"*No.*" Adina looked down at herself, expecting to see blood and guts, but there was nothing. She was clean. "Was it—"

"We don't think it was you." Jack interrupted before that thought could fully form. "We just thought you should know what's going on. We're heading out to investigate it now."

"I'll come," Adina said.

"Have you been having those dreams?" Zorxia wondered. "And the meat cravings?"

"Yea," Adina admitted. "But not last night. I was worried about Tc'aarlat."

"I'd better see how Aliporta is doing with those blood tests," Zorxia said. "We need to know for sure."

"Adina and I will go to the Elders and check things out. Start the search for whoever did this," Jack said. "Tc'aarlat can—" He stopped himself; he had forgotten the reason he had been drinking so hard last night. "Never mind."

"What are we going to do about Tc'aarlat?" Adina asked. "Did he come back last night?"

"Solo!" Jack called.

"Tc'aarlat did not return to the ship last night. I'm afraid he is somewhere on Renasta," Solo replied.

"He said he was quitting the Shadows," Adina said. "I think he meant it."

"Tc'aarlat is a lot of things, most of them not very nice, but he's not a quitter," Jack said. "Trust me, he just needs to cool off for a bit, and he'll return to us. This time, we'll hunt down the Don."

"Seems like we have bigger problems anyway," Zorxia interjected. "I hope he's okay, though. He was pretty steamed last night."

"He's probably with that Enkelite woman." Jack took a seat on Adina's bed. "I'll look into finding him as well. We can't rule out the chance that there's something dangerous out there, and with my arm in a sling, I'll need a good marksman."

"I think we can." Adina took a deep breath to calm the sudden onslaught of nerves. "Renasta only has one kind of people living on it, and they don't look like the type to tear each other apart."

"We don't know anything yet," Zorxia sat on the bed on the other side of her. "But I promise we'll know more soon."

. . .

Renasta, New Fruling, Along the Path Leading Out of the Square

Elder Nee'pkan led Jack and Adina to one of the houses where the body of one of his kin was lying. The walk was long, and despite Jack insisting on flying over in *Fortitude*, Elder Nee'pkan had shut him down.

The Enkelites were settled now was his reasoning. If they saw ships flying back and forth across the land, they would quickly discover that something was wrong, and despite the Enkelites' peaceful personas, they were as prone to panic as any other race.

"Who found the victim?" Jack asked as they walked.

"Her name is Gl'elle," said Nee'pkan. "The victim was her father Uzosker."

"That's terrible," Adina said. "I wouldn't wish that on anyone."

"Did she notice anything else?" Jack asked. "Anything suspicious, like someone acting strange or aggressive toward her father at the celebration last night? Someone following him? Anything like that?"

"If she did, she didn't tell me," said Nee'pkan. "Besides, I fear this was not the work of one individual. Altogether, fifty Enkelites have been found dead."

"Fifty!" Adina exclaimed. "In one night?"

"Some might have been killed before last night and not found until today," Jack suggested. "There is a serial killer on the loose, the likes of which the universe has never seen."

"There's something else as well," Adina said, giving Jack a nudge.

The Elder turned to them, and Jack sighed. "We've lost

track of Tc'aarlat. We were wondering if you could put a call out to your flock to keep an eye out for him?"

"I would've thought he left after our conversation last night," Elder Nee'pkan replied. "I assumed that was why he was not with you?"

"I'm sorry, your conversation?" asked Adina.

"According to some in my flock, your Tc'aarlat has been getting close to a woman called Wo'Fek and her son Imis," Elder Nee'pkan explained.

"Imis!" exclaimed Adina. "That was the kid from last night."

"What was this conversation about?"

"Purity," replied Nee'pkan. "I was informing Tc'aarlat about a decision the Elders made privately, concerning his romantic affliction with Wo'Fek."

"Romantic?" Adina wondered. "Tc'aarlat is not romantically attached to one of your people. He said she was cooking for him. He was most likely attached to the food."

Jack scowled. "I'm guessing he didn't take that well."

"We've judged him, and we deemed him unsuitable for our flock," said Nee'pkan. "Not to mention that he is of another race and highly incompatible."

"You told him this before the celebration, didn't you?" Adina demanded. "No wonder he was a powder keg."

Jack considered his next words carefully, then moved in front of the Elder to block his way and looked him in the eye. "It's not my business to meddle in your affairs, tell you what to do, or explain right from wrong. That's not what I'm here for. What I can tell you with great certainty, though, is that you'd be *damn* lucky to have someone like

Tc'aarlat in your flock. I thought the Enkelites were supposed to be an accepting race?"

Adina smiled at Jack. If only Tc'aarlat were close enough to hear.

"Take us to the victims, please, so we can start our investigation. We've brought vials to take samples. We need to find out who did this and stop them." Jack stepped aside to allow the sheepish-looking Elder to move past. He did so, and the two of them followed the trail.

"This is all very upsetting. We are a peaceful people, and there has been so much turmoil of late. We need to be left alone. That will resolve most of our ills."

Jack grunted, neither an acknowledgment nor a denial.

"That was the right thing to say, Jack," Adina whispered. "If Tc'aarlat could only calm that volcano inside him long enough for us to get free of here, all would be right with the Shadows."

"He should've told us," Jack replied with a disapproving shake of his head. "We've been here for weeks, and I didn't have a clue. Not one. Why is he keeping secrets again? That's bullshit. All it does is divide us."

"Tc'aarlat isn't like us," Adina replied. "For him, showing his emotions is a sign of weakness, and he respects us too much to want us to think of him like that."

"It's strong to be weak," Jack said.

"I'm sorry, what?"

"When you are one thing but need to be another, you change the definition to best suit you."

Adina ignored his explanation. "You get what I'm saying though, right?"

"Yeah, I do." Jack nodded. "If I'd have known, I wouldn't

have been so hard on him. Crap. Now we've *got* to find him."

"He's probably with Wo'Fek and stuffed like a game hen."

"What if he's not?" Jack wondered. "What if...he was angry and drunk last night."

"Put that thought right out of your head. Tc'aarlat doesn't murder innocent people. We need him to help us find *and eliminate* the one who does."

Renasta, Miles Away from the Square

Tc'aarlat woke up and looked around to get his bearings, then remembered where he was. Imis slept against him.

The forest on Renasta.

Then he remembered why they were sleeping on the ground. Wo'Fek.

Tc'aarlat extricated himself from the boy, who adored him, as much as the Yollin didn't want him to. He walked softly around the area and picked some of the fresh fruit, already ripe after the terraforming enhanced the initial growth processes. Tc'aarlat took a few bites and declared it fit to eat.

They hadn't found anything last night. The track in the ground had not appeared anywhere else despite endless spiraling around the print, looking for where another misstep from whoever had taken Wo'Fek might have landed.

A thought occurred to Tc'aarlat. There had been two blips on the map of Renasta that night he had returned to the bridge from Wo'Fek's quarters when Jack was running the scan for Adina. If there was something else on the planet, that might have been proof of it. He didn't remember much, but he was sure the blip had been headed toward the mountainous region.

Tc'aarlat grabbed the long stick he had found along their trail, the one he had been using as a walking stick, and poked Imis with it. "Get up. We've got to get going."

"Mother?" The boy rubbed his eyes lazily and yawned his way back to consciousness. "Where's Mother?"

"We continue to look for her up, down, everywhere, but I have a new idea to look where there has been a different someone who was not us. That someone has your mother. I am sure of it."

The boy turned up his nose at the fruit. "This isn't very ripe."

"Just eat it. It'll make you big and strong. We might have to fight this thing to get your mom back. You want to be able to win that fight, don't you?"

"Yes, but you're plenty big. There's no one you can't beat. I shouldn't have to fight."

Tc'aarlat sat down and finished the rest of the piece of fruit in his hand. "You see, no one should have to fight, but we do it anyway for those who can't. That's not you. When I'm not here, you'll need to protect your mom. Now eat your damn fruit. It may be gross, but it's not as gross as it could be."

"What kind of encouragement is that?"

"Eating gross food puts hair on your chest."

"You don't have any." The boy pointed at Tc'aarlat's partially buttoned shirt.

"Because I have a carapace. It is like armor. I'm hairy on the inside, very hairy because of the gross things I've eaten."

"That isn't making me want to eat this." The boy scowled at his fruit.

"That thing is going into your body one way or the other, and you don't want to know what the other way is, so close your eyes and eat it. It is like a feast delivered on silver trays by four-legged Yollin women. So very tasty. Hey, why aren't you eating your breakfast?"

Imis glowered after his first bite. "This tastes like ass."

"Where did you learn such language? Out with it!"

"From you."

"Then you have learned well. It tastes very much like ass. But healthy ass, not a saggy old wrinkly ass."

"There's a difference?" the boy wondered.

Tc'aarlat thought about it. "I don't know."

The boy chuckled at the Yollin's confusion and finished eating the fruit without thinking about it further.

"You're funny. A funny ass." The boy howled with laughter.

"I don't think you're using the word right. I have taught you poorly. Collect your coat and let us go find your mother."

"See, that wasn't so bad." Tc'aarlat took a bite of his fruit. "At least the food growing here is decent."

Imis' smile slowly left his face, and his mind returned to the question he'd been thinking about all night. He didn't know why he found this to be the right time to ask. Perhaps it was the quiet of the surrounding beauty, or maybe it was because this was the first time Tc'aarlat had stopped moving in hours, but he asked in a small voice, "Is my mother dead?"

Tc'aarlat kneeled to look the boy in the eyes. "I am not going to lie. I don't know. We will keep looking until we do. Does that help?"

The boy snuffled and wiped his eyes. "I think she's..."

Tc'aarlat put a big finger across the boy's lips.

"You will not say that. I will not say that. We will believe we can find her. Just like I believe we can find Don Gan'barlo."

"Who is that? Is he missing, too?"

"He's hiding. There's a difference, but if that print is anything to go by, he's no less of a monster than what we're looking for. Pick up that stick, Imis. You can use it as a club to help me fight. When the time comes. Yes. You will help me fight."

Renasta, New Fruling, Uzosker's Home

There was someone dead and already rotting in a most horrible way within the home. If the foul aroma hadn't made it clear a kilometer before they reached the front door, the flies certainly would have. Or at least, Jack thought they were flies.

Seemed that when Zorxia's terraformer brought the world to life, it also brought insects. Jack thought about asking her to explain how that had happened.

"Everything okay, Jack?" Adina asked him as they approached the door.

"I was thinking about why terraforming created flies,"

he replied. "Not looking forward to whatever is on the other side of that door."

Jack took a deep breath and walked through the door. Inside, they found wanton destruction. The furniture had been shattered, and once delicately hung paintings had been thrown on the floor and smashed for good measure. Glass shards were everywhere. Adina nudged Jack after a few moments and nodded at the floor, where a trail of blood had been left behind.

"*It's like in my dream,*" Adina whispered with wide eyes.

"Concentrate." Jack pulled out his Jean Dukes Special with his left hand and did his best to hold it steady. He had been practicing for the last few weeks, trying to be ambidextrous, and although he felt a little better, it was a big ask for that short amount of time. He pulled his arm out of the sling and moved the pistol to his right hand but dialed the power down to four. "Keep an eye out."

The trail of blood led them to a bedroom, equally destroyed. A mangled corpse lay within the ruins of the bed.

Adina backed out of the room and fought the urge to throw up. Jack remained, moving closer to examine the damage done to the body.

The body was unrecognizable after the slashing and shredding. Jack knew of one creature that could do this kind of primal damage.

Jack closed the door behind him. "I think we need to talk, Adina."

"This is bad, isn't it, Jack?"

"Yeah." Jack nodded. "This is real bad."

15

Renasta, the Mountain Range Beyond New Fruling

"Are we there yet?"

"For the last time, no!" Tc'aarlat was having a hard time not shouting. The young boy had returned to his most annoying habits once the lack of immediate success had passed. "Stop asking me."

"What about now?"

"AAAAHHHH!" Tc'aarlat failed to muffle his growing impatience with the lad.

Tc'aarlat and Imis had been walking for hours along the rocky ridges of the mountain, following non-paths as they made their way up the range. Neither of them knew what they expected to find, but Tc'aarlat was hoping for a ship or something he could point his gun at—the gun he had once again left behind in the *Fortitude*.

Suddenly he stopped, his muscles tensed and his instincts warning him of danger. He moved Imis behind him as he scanned the area, looking for what set his teeth on edge.

There was nothing. Tc'aarlat wasn't buying it. Ignoring that he hadn't heard or seen anything, he turned to Imis with urgency in his voice. "Do you know the way back, Imis?"

Imis nodded, sensing the Yollin's fear.

"Can you run really fast?"

Imis nodded again, his words stuck in his throat.

"I want you run back as fast as you can and get my—"

The rush came like an invisible tidal wave, slamming into Tc'aarlat and throwing him at the side of the mountain. The Yollin fought to shake off the fog from the blow, looking around for the source of the attack. He saw no weapons, no people, nothing.

He had a millisecond's warning before the next attack through a surge in his awareness. Before he could act, a fist hammered into the side of his head, the sting of a machine's left hook. Tc'aarlat was tired of playing defense.

He lunged forward, hit something, and drove with his legs until it toppled. Tc'aarlat motioned at the boy, who was standing dumbstruck, and shouted at the top of his lungs, "*RUN, IMIS!*"

The young Enkelite didn't need any more encouragement and took off like a rocket, running back the way they had come. Tc'aarlat watched him for a moment and hoped that whatever it was wouldn't catch him. He turned to face his foe, but it was too late. An invisible hand gripped his throat tightly. Tc'aarlat pounded the arm to no avail. He was lifted into the air.

"If you were anything but a fucking damned coward, you'd show yourself!" Tc'aarlat gasped. "Make it a fair fight."

Tc'aarlat took another shot to the head, then another. His arms fell limp as the world faded to black.

Renasta, New Fruling, ICS *Fortitude*, Medical Bay

Zorxia scowled as she studied Adina's blood tests. She was so deep in concentration that she didn't notice when Jack walked in.

"I had an idea," Jack said. He looked at the computer terminal. "Solo, did Adina leave the ship last night?"

"No."

"Settled. What are you looking for?"

"Maybe Adina's blood was used to mutate one of the Enkelites, or Jack the Ripper is running free on Renasta. Until we know, Adina is in self-isolation."

"That's ridiculous. It wasn't her." Jack crossed his arms and tilted his head to look at her sideways. "Any luck?"

"I've run the same test a hundred times, and each time I get the same result. Adina has become resistant to the drugs she's been taking to control her werewolf side. That's why she's been having meat cravings. It could be why she's been having those dreams too, on top of the guilt she feels about her mother."

"The Elders have said there were no witnesses to these killings," Jack said. "A madman running around, covered in blood. Someone had to see something, but the Enkelites aren't coming clean. I'm sure they're not telling us everything. Maybe they wanted to get off the arks because they brought the killer with them."

"I've been trying to figure out a next step," Zorxia said. "Adina is unlike any other werewolf I've seen. She is strong in her form, and she can transform parts of herself at will. Even when she was taking the medication, she could still transform fully. It's unheard of."

"What's the solution?" Jack leaned against the wall and crossed his arms gingerly. He was trying not to think about how much firepower it would take to bring Adina down, not that he could do it if he had to.

"I think Adina's just going to have to learn to control herself," Zorxia said. "I can't see any other choice. Without the medication, there's no other way."

"Fuck," Jack said. "That's some real bad news."

"Like I said, Adina is an extreme case, and she became reliant on those drugs because she didn't want to be a Were. She's going to have to embrace her other half."

Jack turned to leave. "Guess I'd better go break the news to her."

"Wait." Zorxia held up an arm to stop him. "What do you remember…about last night, Jack?"

"You mean, you passing out in my bed after drinking more than your share of my good stuff?" Jack said.

"We didn't…did we?" Zorxia asked.

"Fuck, no! I resent that implication. I let you sleep in your clothes so there would be no questions. You fart in your sleep."

"I what?" Zorxia feigned outrage. "That is yet another reason we shall never mention this again."

"I'm a guy, and you're a beautiful woman. I will ask you out on a date, but not during a mission, and not when we're living on the same ship. When we get back."

"The flatulence doesn't bother you?"

"We already went over this once. I'm a guy, and you're a

beautiful woman." Jack slashed his hand down to signal the end of the conversation. He turned to go. "I'll tell Adina to suck it up."

"Maybe with a little more tact than that."

"I'll throw a flower as I yell it from the doorway."

Renasta, New Fruling, ICS *Fortitude*

Jack was on his way to Adina's room when he heard the faint sound of knocking coming from farther down the hallway. It didn't take him long to realize it was someone banging on the hangar bay door. He rushed to the bay, sensing the worst. Opening the doors, he saw a boy on the other side, drenched in fear and sweat, he was almost unrecognizable, but Jack had seen this boy the night before. Imis.

"What are you—"

"Taccyrat and my mother are in danger," Imis said. "You've got to help them!"

"Slow down, son," Jack replied, allowing him to walk inside. "Tell me everything from the top."

Jack tried to bring the boy to the bridge, but he wanted to go back, bringing both Jack and Tc'aarlat's rifle. They squatted in the hangar bay. Imis told him everything about the events of the past day: where his mother had gone after the party and her getting taken, how he and Tc'aarlat went to find her and ran headfirst into an invisible attacker, and how he had run without a break to get them to help him.

"Solo, summon the crew. We're needed."

An exasperated Imis recounted the story a second time for Adina, Zorxia, and Aliporta.

"I knew I wasn't crazy," Adina said. "When I was trapped under the ocean, something saved me, and it was invisible."

"Maybe this planet has been inhabited all along," Zorxia offered. "Maybe whatever these beings are have been invisible to every kind of scan. That's an amazing level of technology, and if it's not tech, then it is one hell of a biological defense.

"Maybe they're responsible for the attacks as well," Jack offered. "If this planet was inhabited, I can't imagine the natives were happy to play host to refugees taking up their land?"

"We don't know anything yet," Adina said glumly. "They could've come in after New Fruling was set up. Maybe they weren't the ones that saved me."

Zorxia spoke up. "Remember what Tc'aarlat said. When we were doing a scan of the planet, he said he saw two blips. One of them might've been one of these invisible things, but why would it detect it then and not now?"

Jack turned to the boy. "You said the mountains, right?"

Imis nodded.

"Solo, I need you to take the ship to the—"

"No," Zorxia said, stopping the command. "If they are here, there's a high possibility that they are natives, which means they have technology beyond the Federation in some regards. If we fly *Fortitude* over, it could look like a sign of aggression, and we could be shot out of the sky. Federation protocol says we should always try for peace first and war second."

"Aggression?" Jack said. "They've been slaughtering people!"

"We don't know that," Adina said. "Your best option is to go to the mountain range and check it out while I stay locked in my quarters."

"Adina, we know it wasn't you, but we also know your drugs aren't working anymore. You're going to have to control the beast from up here." He tapped her head.

"No, Jack," Adina replied. "I won't leave this ship until we're one hundred percent sure."

"There's still one problem, though," Zorxia said. "How are we supposed to defend ourselves from something we can't see? Whatever it is that easily beat Tc'aarlat, it'll do the same to us."

Then, out of all the people in the room who were considering this problem, an unlikely voice rang out— Solo's, who showed her motherly visage on the extended screen that ran the length of the room. "I may have the solution to that concern, Zorxia. For the past few weeks, I have been running in low mode while I've been navigating my way through an unexpected dilemma as a result of the scans you ordered me to perform on Renasta."

"Oh?" Zorxia replied. "What dilemma?"

"When the scans were completed, I took note that there was a difference in the two different time periods between my scan and the Federation's initial scans. It was something you took note of too at the time."

"The mountain." Zorxia turned to the others to explain. "It had lost a third of its mass between scans."

"My dilemma was deciphering the reason behind that anomaly," Solo said. "A dilemma I believe I have managed to solve."

The bridge darkened as the AI brought up a holographic image of Renasta. "For me to solve the problem and discover the truth behind the mountain, I realized I had to create a new kind of scan that could discover not energy, but things that have been displaced from time. I came to this realization when I discovered that the disappearing mass in the mountain wasn't a result of the removal of space, but the disappearance of time."

"What the hell are you saying, Solo?" Jack said.

"She's saying that the mountain is still there in full." Zorxia leaned over the console and marveled at the discovery. "It's just not occupying the same time as us. It's out of sync, making it appear invisible. Solo, how on earth did you discover that?"

"My initial scans detected an unusual number of tachyons around Renasta, something the Federation scanners aren't programmed to see."

"There's never been a need to," Zorxia remarked.

Solo adjusted the holographic image focused on the mountain range. At one point it was an empty husk, just a pile of pointed rocks in a formation. The next, there was a city there. A large metallic city that looked like something from a few thousand years in the future, if a little empty.

"This world has been inhabited all along," Zorxia said. "We've got to go to that city and try to make peace. If these natives are behind the attacks, there's little we can do to stop them."

"We still can't see them?" Jack said.

"We can now," Adina said with a grin. "Using Solo's new form of scanning, we can create a haptic feed that can show us what we're not seeing."

"A second out of sync." Zorxia pursed her lips tightly and nodded. "Absolutely amazing."

"All right, plan time!" Jack smacked his hands together and rubbed them eagerly. "Me and Zorxia will check out the mountain city while Adina stays in her room."

"What about New Fruling?" Adina said. "They'll be defenseless if something happens."

"I had a thought about that too," Jack said. With a reluctant sigh, he turned to Solo. "Can you put me through to Bon Noh, please, Solo?"

Renasta, the Mountain Range Beyond New Fruling

"Tc'aarlat!"

The Yollin came around to the sound of his name, said urgently in a voice he recognized. Opening his eyes, he saw that he was in the middle of a large caved-in mountain that stretched for kilometers. It was like a dip or a crevice formed naturally between the rock-strewn ridges, and for a moment, he thought he had been abandoned here.

That was until he followed the urgent call, and to his pleasure, saw that Wo'Fek was the source.

"Wo'Fek!" Tc'aarlat ran to her before she could say another word and smacked into an invisible wall. Feeling his way around, he discovered that he was in a box or a room he could not see.

"We're trapped," said Wo'Fek. "I think they have imprisoned us."

"Yeah, I'm pretty sure they have." Tc'aarlat collapsed into a sitting position. "How are you feeling, Wo'Fek? Have they hurt you?"

"I don't think I should talk to you about feelings." Wo'Fek turned her back on him. "After what I saw you do to Bon Noh."

"I'm sorry you had to see that," Tc'aarlat said. "Would you believe me if I said that guy had it coming?"

"It doesn't matter," she replied. "You could have the best reasons in the world, but it doesn't make you any less violent. I didn't see someone I knew there. I saw a monster."

Tc'aarlat left it alone for the moment, reflecting on what she had said. Beating the crap out of Bon Noh was far from the worst thing he'd done, but he guessed it probably wasn't that pleasant for someone to see. "Let's focus on getting out of here. Have you learned anything while you've been a captive?"

"The walls are invisible," Wo'Fek replied. "Whatever I was taken by was strong. Really strong. I thought it might be one of the Federation's machines."

"The Federation doesn't have machines like that," Tc'aarlat said.

"Have you seen my son?" Wo'Fek asked, and she glanced at him.

"I have, as it happens," Tc'aarlat replied. "Don't worry, he's safe. I've never seen a faster kid."

"What are they going to do to us, Tc'aarlat?"

"I don't know," the Yollin replied honestly. "I think if they wanted to kill us, they would've done it by now, though."

"That doesn't sound very promising." Wo'Fek flopped down on the floor.

"It sounds fairly ominous."

16

Renasta, New Fruling, ICS *Fortitude*, Adina's Room

Adina took a deep breath, held it for a moment, and then released it. She had been doing that for the past half-hour during her self-imposed exile. Another deep breath. Another exhale.

She was bored, and her mind drifted. The devil within she sought to contain rushed in to fill the void. There she saw her uncle again, her werewolf self, the blood, the guts, and the gore everywhere.

SQUAWK! Isaaca flapped her wings to accompany her screech, most likely seeing that her master was having difficulty. That brought her back to reality.

"Damn the nanocytes!" She didn't mean that, but she was less than amused by her deteriorating condition.

The breathing exercise wasn't working, probably because she had her doubts about it. Adina didn't fix problems by sitting around and breathing. She fixed problems by finding tangible solutions.

The drugs no longer worked. She needed to find an alternative.

Isaaca flew down to her bed, and Adina petted her gently.

Solo appeared on the vidscreen, her face screwed up with the appropriate amount of concern. "I came to check in and make sure everything was all right."

"I'm fine," Adina lied. "Have Jack and Zorxia left?"

"About thirty minutes ago," Solo answered. "They asked me to keep an eye on you."

"I can't blame them," Adina said. "I'd keep an eye on me, too."

Solo clicked her tongue. "That's not what they meant. How are your exercises coming along? I've done extensive research into—"

"It's not working," Adina shot back. "I appreciate the thought, Solo. I need a new way to dampen my werewolf side. There has to be a different drug, a better drug, essential oils, natural herbs, or something I could take. Maybe I could increase the dose?"

"Increasing the dose could be dangerous, Adina." Solo lost the concern and adopted a matronly look. "It can do permanent damage to your internal organs. That is, if you don't overdose and die from your heart exploding or sending blood clots to your brain first."

"Okay, fine, just a thought." Adina closed her eyes again and took a deep breath, shaking her head at the inanity.

"Was that any better?"

"No," Adina said. "It feels like I should be checking my chakra or something."

"Well, I can do some research on that too if you—" Solo

stopped in mid-sentence, her face contorted into an apprehensive expression, and she turned to Adina quickly. "Adina, I think there's an intruder on—"

Solo disappeared from the screen.

"Solo?" Adina stood up. There was no reply from the motherly AI. "Solo, where did you go?"

No answer.

"She's been shut off? How is that—" Adina gulped. She knew the answer to the question before she answered it, and she shot to her door. There was only one person she knew of who could perform a trick like that, and if he was on board, that meant he was after one thing: the Terraformer.

Her self-imposed exile had turned foul. She was trapped inside while an intruder wandered the *Fortitude*, and if she didn't get out quickly, they'd be free to steal whatever took their eye.

"All right, you fucking knucklehead," she said to herself. Adina grabbed one of the many screwdrivers strewn across her floor. Using it as a crowbar, she pried open the access pad to expose the wires inside, then got to work figuring out what each of them controlled. "It's time to break out."

Renasta, the Mountain Range Beyond New Fruling

With Solo's new scanning software and Zorxia's building skills, they had brought the special time goggles to life in a matter of an hour, but they had not yet been tested. They were cobbled together with recently soldered exposed wires and an uncomfortable fit due to several thick rubber bands holding them tightly to their heads.

Jack scratched his head during the entire journey.

Bon Noh had been kind enough to let them borrow one of his smaller shuttles, the ones he had used to transport the material needed to build the Enkelites' new homes. They were ratty old things that veered to the left at odd times, but they got the job done.

Jack and Zorxia exited the shuttle and saw no fierce battalion surrounding them with technology beyond the grasp of the Federation. That might have only proven that the goggles they were wearing were not working.

"Just over the ridge," Zorxia pointed toward the mountain. "That one lost a third of its mass."

"Wait, do you hear that?" Jack held his finger over his earphone. Solo had a theory that her scanning software could detect not just visuals but sound as well. A low whirring noise was approaching them, like the propulsion of a hoverboard. "Get down!"

Jack and Zorxia dove behind a nearby boulder. A drone appeared, large and robotic but humanoid, floating a few inches above the ground. It had a single giant glass eye in the center of its head and four arms attached to its torso. The thing looked to be made of metal from head to toe.

"I've seen my fair share of robots, but nothing like that," Zorxia said. "It looks like next-generation stuff."

"So, what do we do?" Jack asked. "Are we assuming the race looks like this, or do you think this is just a robotic guard?"

"My instincts tell me this is the thing we're looking for," Zorxia said. "We need to find a leader, though. We can't just rush in an—"

"HELLO!" Jack rolled himself over the boulder and kept

a hand close to the gun in his holster, knowing that if he had to pull it, he would have already lost the fight. He decided to raise his hands and look as non-threatening as possible.

His goggles chose that moment to itch.

The robot faced him, the iris behind the lens focusing in and out. Jack smiled before casually raking his nails across the spot under the bands. He then gave the thing a thumbs-up as if he were posing for a picture. "Analysis, Alien Entity. Threat level, high."

"High threat?" Jack replied. "Wh...I'm no threat? I'm here on behalf of the Federation to talk about—"

"Conclusion. Too dangerous to be left alive." Jack watched with a mixed expression of horror and wonder as the thing's arm rose and changed before his eyes. Its arm transmogrified from a useful appendage to a blaster-type weapon leveled at Jack's head. Without a second thought, he dropped and launched himself like a frog behind the boulder, where Zorxia scowled at him.

Jack pulled his gun. "It's time we give this thing a healthy serving of fuck you."

"Normally I'd say we should try to resolve the situation with the least amount of violence," Zorxia replied, "but it *is* firing at us." The energy projectiles traced a line around the boulder.

Jack reached around the boulder with his left hand and fired blindly on a setting of three because he didn't want the JDS to fly out of his hand. He dialed it up to five and fired from the other side of the boulder, then jumped back to the other side and looked around as he fired.

The five setting was enough to stun the thing. He

stepped out and fired three more times in rapid succession from point-blank range. He snarled at the dead robot when the sound of a new threat caught his attention. Once again, he found himself diving behind the boulder.

He looked at Zorxia through his goggles. "I'm fresh out of ideas. What do you got, Doc?"

Renasta, New Fruling, ICS *Fortitude*, Adina's Room

Adina twisted the bare wires together on her fourth attempt to get the door open, and still nothing happened. She continued her efforts, digging out the wires and touching them to each other one by one.

When the power failed, the doors were supposed to open, but she couldn't make it work despite her considerable knowledge of engineering. Having run out of ideas, she slunk back to her bed. The intruder was going to get what he wanted, and there was no way she could stop him.

"Great!" she shouted for no one to hear. "Just great."

The fire within rose from an ember to a flame to a bonfire. It was a mixture of feelings at the pit of her stomach, and she found herself standing. She picked up her chair and hurled it against the door with a force she shouldn't have been able to generate within the small room.

Isaaca flapped her wings and screeched in shared agony with her human.

"Just open, you stupid—"

"Hello?"

Adina stopped, trying to calm her breathing to listen. She had heard a voice that had come from beyond the door

—a friendly voice, not an intruder. The owner of the voice must've been drawn to the racket she'd made.

"Hello!" Adina went to the door and pressed her ear to it. "Is anyone there?"

"I'm here."

"Okay?" Adina said. "Who are you?"

"I'm Imis. Who are you?"

"Imis, thank goodness. It's me, Adina." Adina grinned from ear to ear; it was a miracle. "Listen, sweetheart, I need you to open the door for me. Can you do that?"

"I want some water," Imis replied without hesitation. "Where is your water?"

"If you open the door, I will get you some water," Adina said. "You've only got to pry it open a little. I can pull it the rest of the way."

"There's a tool wedged into the opening," Imis said.

That was why it hadn't opened when the power failed. Someone had sabotaged the ship and locked her inside.

"Can you remove it?" Adina listened to what could only be described as grunts as he tried. She knew the boy was reaching for something beyond his grasp and shook her head when she remembered how small he was. "I... can't...reach...it."

"Imis," she said calmly. "Why don't you go and find a chair or something so you can reach the tool and pull it free?"

"I don't know if I'm thirsty anymore."

"Imis, please!" Adina pleaded. "I have to get out of this room. We could be in danger!"

"Okay."

Adina listened to his footsteps padding away from her.

She hoped he was going to get something to stand on but thought more realistically that the young Enkelite had abandoned her for his own pursuits. Only time would tell.

Renasta, the Mountain Range beyond New Fruling

Jack watched as Zorxia worked herself into an adrenaline-fueled engine of peak performance. She looked down at Jack and nodded tightly one time. He gave her a nod in return just before she dove out of their hiding place and took off running along the path down the mountain.

Just perfect. I'm on my own now, Jack thought, keeping a close eye on the robotic henchmen. They were in hot pursuit of Zorxia. As far as they were aware, there was only one person behind the boulder, and given Zorxia's speed, they'd have a hell of a job chasing her down. That gave Jack an opportunity to sneak past an unprotected part of the mountain and work his way inside the invisible city.

Keeping a firm grip on his gun, Jack sidled close to the hillside and along the natural slope. He followed the route up until he came to a small bridge that led over an embankment. Beyond it, he found what he'd expected, but he hadn't realized it would be so magnificent.

An incredible city built by an advanced civilization only one human had ever looked upon it.

Captain Jack Marber.

The silvery spires stretched up for kilometers, far beyond the mountain's crest. They glowed in the sunlight. The city sparkled and glittered as if it were the surface of a mirror held by a mystical unicorn. The curves of each building and street were clear and concise but not straight.

Nothing in the city followed a straight line, but simple lines flowed from building to building. It was the grandest city he had ever seen, an architectural masterpiece.

There was one thing missing, though, and Jack saw it straight away. People. The streets were empty, the buildings silent, and there was no sight or sound of anything alive. As much as it radiated beauty, it appeared abandoned and lifeless—a monument to a race that was no longer there. Jack strode into the city, head on a swivel, wary of finding more security robots.

"Shit!" Jack exclaimed, still in awe of the grandeur that surrounded him. "How am I supposed to find Tc'aarlat in all this?"

17

Renasta, the Mountain Range Beyond New Fruling, Cell

Tc'aarlat's invisible prison was square, with one solid metal door that didn't have a handle. He was fairly certain there was a viewing hole from the outside looking in, although it was a clear cell.

This was just a place of confinement like every other cell on any planet he'd been on. Tc'aarlat was a prisoner.

At least he wasn't dead. Or Wo'Fek, for that matter.

For perhaps the hundredth time, Tc'aarlat looked at Wo'Fek, who was lying motionless in her cell with her back turned to him. He knew she wanted him to believe she was asleep, but he knew better. She didn't want him to see her sobbing.

In his life, he had never been very good with words. Tc'aarlat considered himself a person of action, and that had never necessitated their use.

"I know you probably don't want to listen to me, and I can't blame you," Tc'aarlat said. "I've been a rotting asscrack lately, and I didn't want you to see me kicking sixteen newly discovered colors into Bon Noh's skin. I guess that's just who I am. I'm the guy that licks the ass of bad people. I always have been."

Wo'Fek sat up slowly and looked at him, her face mournful. She shook her head. "*Kicks* ass," she corrected.

"Yes. The asses that need to be kicked, I am the kicker. I don't like it as much as one would think. Maybe I don't like it at all, but it is the thing I have always done. There is some comfort in that."

She spoke in an anguished tone. "Oh, Tc'aarlat. Has it ever brought you one moment of happiness? Have the pain and suffering that come from that been worth it?"

"There isn't as much comfort as one would think. Maybe there's no comfort at all," Tc'aarlat said, adjusting his previous words to bare his soul more than he normally would. Not to Jack or Adina, but to Mist. His Raal hawk. Why had he not brought her? She could have helped him escape.

There was no time to be remorseful. Rough hands grabbed him and held him tightly. His arms were pinned to his sides, and no matter how hard he fought, he couldn't break free. He didn't fight very hard. He didn't want Wo'Fek to see him.

A pinprick on his right temple and a weight, then a sharp pain as the pinprick turned into needles digging deep into his flesh, and finally through his skull. He screamed in pain and terror.

Tc'aarlat couldn't see his attacker. He, a Yollin, was powerless to fight back. His lungs ached from his vocal cords' shrieks.

When the pain stopped and he opened his eyes, he

couldn't see a single mountain rock because he found himself in a room surrounded by smooth walls with a robotic creature standing in front of him. The unseen attackers had finally revealed themselves, and he would have fought them if he had the use of his arms.

"You will come with us," the one towering over him ordered. "Designation One wishes to meet you and the other."

"Don't touch her," Tc'aarlat said, but he had no influence. He was weak compared to them. "I'll kick you right in your robot balls if you hurt a single branch on her head!"

They didn't care. Wo'Fek screamed horribly, and Tc'aarlat raged. He twisted and pulled, using his body weight to gain leverage on the metal monster that held him, but he found no purchase.

When she stopped screaming, Tc'aarlat called to her. "Wo'Fek, are you okay?"

"What is in my head?" she cried. "What are these things?"

"It'll be okay." Tc'aarlat had no idea if anything would turn out all right.

Tc'aarlat was forced next to Wo'Fek, and they were frog-marched down the many hallways of the building within which they found themselves.

They noticed the absence of living creatures beyond their metallic guards. They looked for anything to suggest someone was alive but saw nothing. Art and color were missing, but what they saw through windows showed the art was out there in the architecture of the fantastic city.

"Where are we?" Wo'Fek wondered.

Tc'aarlat shook his head. "There were no cities on Renasta. I looked at all the scans. No cities. No life."

They approached a door that looked like the usual oversized double doors that led into a grand chamber.

There were no signs, no runes, nothing to indicate what it was. The door was adorned with metallic cogs and gears around the frame in a display of form and function. One of the robotic men extended a hand to touch the door and the gears started turning, slowly at first, then with increased speed. Finally the latches retracted and the door opened.

"What is this?" Wo'Fek said.

"A king or an emperor?" Tc'aarlat ventured. "Maybe we'll find someone alive. See who is master of this place and these creatures. A master of our disaster, the master baiter for capturing us. The ass-master for coming at us from behind. So many masters rolled up into one. Or maybe more. We shall find out soon."

They were pushed inside, where they found an even greater surprise. And a shock.

It was a room of a million cables, crawling across the floors, up the walls, and hung from high points in the ceiling like jungle vines. At its center, where the cables converged, there was an entity that looked like the other robotic creatures they had encountered, except this one had two eyes. In place of appendages, cables connected into it, or out of it. They couldn't be sure if he was the alpha, the beginning, or the omega, the end.

The thing opened its eyes like a pair of oncoming head-lights on a dark night, and they covered their ears against the digital screech it released from its ill-begotten maw.

"What the fuck is this?" Tc'aarlat shouted at it. "What the fuck is that?"

"I share the sentiment." Wo'Fek clutched her ears. "Please, make it stop!"

"Fuuuuck! Offfff!" Tc'aarlat took a deep breath to shout again when the entity ceased making its godawful noise.

"That is Designation One," the closer of the robotic men said, taking a few steps backward. "You have an appointment with it."

"Welcome to the High Society of Security," Designation One said calmly, acclimating to their language. Its low baritone voice sounded as if it were speaking through a megaphone. "I am Designation One, ruler of security in the City of the Onbir."

"Ah, your great buttholiness," Tc'aarlat said. "I've got to play ambassador, don't I?"

"It appears so," Wo'Fek replied. "For my species and yours."

Tc'aarlat cleared his throat and said in his grandest voice, "I am Tc'aarlat."

"Welcome, Tc'aarlat," Designation One said. "You'll find that—"

"Hang on. I've got more," Tc'aarlat interrupted. "When we arrived, this planet was supposed to be abandoned. The Federation performed all sorts of checks and scans and crap. How come they didn't find you? Also, follow-up question. Why is everyone invisible?"

"The answer to that is one and the same," it replied. "The Onbir, our race, has been hidden and is still hidden *in time*. We were awakened by a large magnetic disturbance three weeks ago."

"In time?" Tc'aarlat gave Wo'Fek a look; she shrugged. "What are you talking about?"

"Our scientists asked the same thing, and they came to the same realization. It all started when our binary star exploded early in our development, leaving us with only one star for Renasta and an everlasting curse," Designation One said. "The massive explosion was so close it should have killed us and destroyed our world. However, it didn't. The resulting shockwave knocked my species out of sync with the rest of the universe by exactly six attoseconds. That is why you cannot see us in your scans or with your eyes. To you, we do not exist."

"You guys aren't robots, then? This is, like, a suit you all wear?"

"Our species does not look like this unless they have been assigned to protect," Designation One replied. "After the first hundred million years of our society, after we had discovered every other star and proof of alien civilizations thriving in the universe beyond us, we realized our plight. We were out of sync with everything. A plan needed to be devised, so our species was placed into stasis chambers that would take sixteen thousand years to perform a single action: reverse the effects of the sync, helping us align with the rest of the universe and finally be seen."

"This guy talks too much," Tc'aarlat whispered in Wo'Fek's ear. "When you said 'security' earlier, you're, like, the guys who protect those people in stasis?"

"We were given these bodies so we would live longer," Designation One replied. "Beneath this city lie two million pure Onbir people unsullied by metallic suits, as fleshly now as the day they were born. Our duty is to defend them until our charges come out of stasis, and this is the first day on which we have encountered dangerous intruders on our world."

"They aren't dangerous, they're Enkelites," Tc'aarlat stated. "Completely harmless."

Wo'Fek didn't agree with that but was too afraid at the enormity of this situation to speak up.

"Enkelites?" repeated Designation One. "That's what you call them?"

"That's right," Tc'aarlat said. "Really, they're cuddly balls of fluff."

"These Enkelites are dangerous to our society, and they must be eliminated before they destroy us," Designation One said. It leaned closer, straining the cables to which it was attached. "Perhaps you do not know of the dangers that lie just beneath the skin?"

Tc'aarlat gave Wo'Fek a look. "I think you're wrong about that."

"Which leaves the two of you," Designation One said. "We must assess and study your makeup for any weaknesses. You will be torn apart and evaluated."

"Okay, I heard 'torn apart,'" Tc'aarlat noted. "That came through loud and clear, and you can take your dissecting trays and anal probes and stuff them up your pie hole."

"You are the first of your species we have encountered. You must be evaluated and put into the records."

"Why meet us, then?" Tc'aarlat tensed in the grip of the Onbir behind him. "What was this meeting all about?"

"Part of the assessment," Designation One replied. "To see if you would be more useful to us dead or alive. I will allow you a last question, then you must leave."

TOM DUBLIN

"What if I don't ask a question?" Tc'aarlat snarked before adding, "That doesn't count."

The Onbir began to take them back through the doors and to their doom. "That would be unfortunate."

"Wait, uh, how long has it been?" Tc'aarlat said, frantically searching for a question that might be the least bit useful. "Since your species was put into stasis?"

"Sixteen thousand years and counting." Designation One watched them as they were forced through the door. Tc'aarlat took note of that and decided he didn't like the creature. It seemed unnecessarily logical, and it had to be brought down.

As they were being marched back through the endless corridors, Tc'aarlat glanced at Wo'Fek, whose face sagged as if the end of the world lay at her feet. If Imis had run straight to the ship and hadn't been captured, Jack should know about them by now. Despite their argument, Jack would come to rescue him. He knew it, and he could only do that if he could be seen.

"I have an idea," he whispered to Wo'Fek. "Can you create a diversion?"

Wo'Fek didn't need to be asked twice. She made a run for it past the Onbir and up a corridor that turned into an intersecting hall. They went after her with amazing speed, but Tc'aarlat only needed a second. He smashed his head against the wall until he heard a spark and a buzz. He had killed the gadget attached to his head, and he was once again free to see the world around him through its invisible walls.

He was instantly rewarded. There was Captain Jack

Marber, wearing a cobbled-together set of goggles over his eyes, about a mile away. The Shadows had figured it out!

Jack could see the city

That meant he couldn't see through the walls. Tc'aarlat lamented the failure of his genius.

He felt a grip on his shoulder, and once again, he was marched along a corridor. This time he couldn't see where he was going, and he was sure if the Onbir noticed that, they'd give him a new gadget.

Then he could see and Jack could see, and everything would be right with his world once again. He decided to show his hand.

"Hey! Invisible fuckstick? You are a brass-ball-slapping pickle-knob!" He winced, expecting to be knocked senseless for being an upstart.

He felt something grasp his hand. It was gentle and soft but mostly reassuring. Wo'Fek was leading him.

18

Renasta, New Fruling, ICS *Fortitude*, Adina's Room

After fifteen minutes, Imis returned.

"I have a screwdriver and a stool," the boy claimed proudly.

"Well done, Imis!" Adina called through the door. "Get that blockage out of there, and let's go rescue your mom."

Scratching and thumping accompanied Imis' efforts to dislodge whatever was keeping the door from opening. He started pounding, then suddenly it stopped. Adina leaned into the door, trying to slide it open, but it wouldn't budge.

With a final cry of triumph, the door popped and a heavy tool crashed to the floor, followed by Imis.

The door slid open once the resistance was gone. The stool was the only thing that remained upright. A pry bar, a screwdriver, and Imis lay side by side in the corridor.

He raised his head. "Good. Now we can go find Taccyrat and my mother."

Adina didn't waste a second. She grabbed the small

pistol she kept near the door and dashed past Imis, who waved at her as she went by. There was no place to go but the hangar bay, where the terraformer was stored.

Hitting one corner at speed, she spun off the wall into the next corridor and continued racing toward the hangar bay while the boy tried to keep up. Through the hatch and over stored cargo, she landed heavily, staring at the back of a person she recognized and expected. Benjamin. He waved her off.

"Busy," he said over his shoulder.

"Freeze, Benjamin!" He had no one with him; he was working alone. He took something from the side of the terraformer's console, a small disk, and placed it in his pocket. "I said, freeze! Don't move a muscle, or I'll shoot you."

"We both know that's a lie," said Benjamin. "If you were going to shoot me, you would have already, and you and I both know—"

Adina aimed where she wouldn't hit the terraformer and fired.

The shot tore through his shoulder and threw him into the terraformer. He bounced off and rolled to the deck. Benjamin coughed and clutched the wound. Blood dripped heavily and steadily onto the steel plating, but his smile did not fade. "Okay, you would shoot me. You just wouldn't kill me."

"Try me," Adina said, moving closer and placing the barrel against his head. "You hacked my ship and blackmailed me. Now it's my turn."

Benjamin looked her straight in the eyes, and she stared into his maniacal face. "What are you going to do with it?"

"Get you to tell the truth," Adina replied. "Was there ever a cure for my uncle's dementia?"

Renasta, the Mountain Range Beyond New Fruling

"I am the biggest twat in the universe. That's the name of the award they will give me for this one, where I'm walking around a deserted city, looking for someone who isn't invisible. I should be able to see Tc'aarlat through the buildings. That was the whole point of the goggles—to see what isn't there, not what is." He pulled the goggles off his face and let them hang around his neck.

The buildings disappeared around him, replaced with the flat but rocky slope of the mountain. Jack searched the expanse until he saw a familiar sight. Tc'aarlat was lying flat on his back, struggling against invisible restraints. Jack took off running to get to him before whatever was about to happen happened. Only problem was that the city was invisible, not intangible.

"Shit, shit, shit," Jack said as he ran, constantly switching between his goggles to see the city and the real world to make sure he was going the right way. It was like a mixed-up version of Marco Polo, where Jack was always Marco but wasn't having any fun.

Working his way around the buildings wasn't easy. He detoured, rerouted, and took shortcuts and longcuts but kept moving toward Tc'aarlat. Sometimes he had to walk in the opposite direction of the way he wanted to go to get closer.

Finally, after having some luck and second-guessing himself, he managed to get to the right building, or at least what he thought was the right building, where one of the metal monstrosities hovered over Tc'aarlat's body.

"Hold on, buddy!" Jack exclaimed, placing the goggles over his eyes once again and searching for the door. "I'm coming!"

Renasta, City of the Onbir, Surgery Room

Wo'Fek held Tc'aarlat's hand all the way to the room, a clean and sterile place with two floating beds, where they deposited them. Wo'Fek wanted to cry out as they placed the straps around her waist, chest, and legs, then pulled them tight. She held her breath, though. She wanted to go out strong and thought only of Imis and how safe he must be back at the square.

"Tc'aarlat," she said, turning her head to him. "I know you can't hear me, but I've got something to tell you. I knew you were unlike anyone else when I met you, and these past few weeks...they've been like old times for me when my husband was still alive and life was about hard work but also fun and joy. I want to thank you for that, and I don't want to die without saying I do have feelings for you."

That was it. The Onbir had finished their preparations and were ready to commence dissection. When Wo'Fek saw their surgical instruments, the scalpels and drills straight from a child's worst nightmare, she wanted to be in Tc'aarlat's position—blissfully unaware of what was about to happen next. Wo'Fek closed her eyes as they approached her. Scalpel raised, she heard them distantly say they were going to start with the brain.

"You don't have to do this," she tried, fighting the anxiety of imminent death. "My people are no threat to you. We want nothing but peaceful lives. If you were to talk with our Elders, I'm sure we could negotiate a life of harmony between our species."

"This isn't the time for negotiation," the Onbir said, placing the scalpel against her head. "You must be studied."

That was as far as the creature got before his robotic head exploded in a shower of dazzling lights and clock-work gears. Wo'Fek strained to see one of Tc'aarlat's friends in makeshift goggles as he shot the second robot. It fell back into the wall and hit the floor as a jumble of parts.

"It's about fucking time!" Tc'aarlat shouted. "Get us the fuck out of here!"

"Gratitude, gratitude." Jack crossed the room and undid the straps, pulling Tc'aarlat up and moving over to Wo'Fek.

"Thank you," she murmured. "Thank you."

"It's okay," Jack said. "I'm just glad I got here in time."

"Is she there?" Tc'aarlat asked, and Jack nodded to him. The Yollin tapped the side of his head. "There's a device in the side of her head that allows her to see the city and the creatures. If you pull it out—"

"Then she'll be blind, just like you," Jack said, helping Wo'Fek to her feet. "If we're going to get out of here, we need to work together. It's better that she can see the city for now."

"Can she hear me?"

Jack nodded. "Every word."

Tc'aarlat went to where he thought Wo'Fek was, which turned out to be three feet in the wrong direction, and started talking to a wall. "Wo'Fek, I'm so sorry about this. I'm such a—"

Jack grabbed him and walked him in front of Wo'Fek. "There you go, buddy."

"I'm going to get you out of this alive, Wo'Fek," Tc'aarlat promised. "And I'm going to make sure these Onbir don't touch your people."

"I trust you," said Wo'Fek, grabbing his hand and squeezing tightly.

"She said—" Jack started.

"I know what she said," Tc'aarlat interrupted. "I love you too, Jack. Now, let's get the fuck out of this shit bubble."

Renasta, New Fruling, ICS *Fortitude*, Hangar Bay

Adina bounced the business end of the gun off Benjamin's head as he looked her in the eyes. Silently, Imis had crept into the bay to see what was going on and found himself captivated by the unfolding scene.

"Tell me the truth," Adina ordered.

"It was real," Benjamin said. "There is a cure, and it's not too late to work together if you want it."

"You're lying."

"No, you only want me to be lying," Benjamin said. "If I'm lying, it means you didn't betray your friends for nothing, and there really is no way to save your uncle. There is, though, and I have it."

"How? Where did it come from?" Adina said. "It's supposedly impossible."

"So's that terraformer over there." Benjamin gestured with his head toward the machine. "Yet it exists, doesn't it?"

"If you want to live, you're going to give it to me," Adina directed. "Now."

"No," Benjamin replied. "As soon as I give it to you, you'll kill me for everything I've done to you. I think I'll keep my mouth shut, thanks."

"Give it to me." Adina was frustrated, and with the emotion came an overwhelming sensation. Her head was flooded with images of the last birthday she'd shared with her mother, the emotional guilt about killing her, and the way her uncle had looked in her dream. She dropped the gun and clutched at the physical and emotional pains echoing through her skull.

Benjamin dove for the gun, the pain of his ruined shoulder lancing throughout his body like lightning, but he was too late. Adina was transforming faster than she ever had before, her eyes filled with the bloodlust that had haunted her nightmares. Fur rapidly spread across her body, her muscles tightened and expanding. Claws shot out of her fingers, and her face sprouted fangs.

She swatted Benjamin like a fly, launching him ass over teakettle. He bounced off the terraformer and dropped to the deck. He tried to regain his feet but settled for the only way he could defeat a werewolf. He dove behind him, looking for the pistol where it had clattered away.

Adina towered over him, jaws dripping saliva as she growled deep in her throat. Imis started to sob. She glanced at him and back at Benjamin, then snapped at Benjamin's face, driving him into a huddled mass. He rolled into the fetal position, covered his face with his hands, and waited for the end as a coward, terrified of the monster ready to strike.

Imis sobbed long and loud before running from the hangar bay. Adina was torn. She knew she had to protect the boy. Protect! She bolted after him.

Benjamin heard the werewolf's heavy tread retreating into the ship. When he looked up, he was alone. He dug out his pistol, and with a shaking hand, he removed a memory stick and plugged it into the system supporting the terraformer. He downloaded all the files in a matter of seconds.

He headed for the hatch that led to the great outdoors but stopped himself. "Adina needs to die since she's the only one who knows my role. Then I'll get to feel good about saving the kid." He sprinted into the ship, pistol before him and ready to shoot.

Benjamin also wanted his revenge on the one who had brought out his cowardice.

Renasta, City of the Onbir

Getting out of the building had been easy. Getting out of the city was going to be hard.

Jack led Tc'aarlat through the maze of corridors and out to the street, Wo'Fek following closely, as the Yollin attempted to explain everything he had learned from Designation One, including who the Onbir were, where they had come from, and why they had a grudge against the Enkelites.

"The Onbir are attacking because they think they're under threat," Tc'aarlat said. "They're trying to protect their citizens."

"The Enkelites aren't dangerous," Jack said. "They don't have a violent bone in their bodies."

"Thank you, Jack Marber," Wo'Fek offered. "We try."

"Honor to your people, Wo'Fek. Many say they are peaceful when they are not. Your people say what they believe and do what they say." Jack gave her an awkward smile.

"They're going to start a war, Jack, and the Enkelites won't survive it," Tc'aarlat said. "You've seen the Onbir. You know what they're capable of."

"I know," Jack said. "Fifty Enkelites have already died. The Onbir didn't just kill them, they killed them ugly."

"What are we going to do?" Tc'aarlat remained blind to the time-shifted aliens, so Jack and Wo'Fek were the eyes and ears of the trio.

"Right now, we've got Bon Noh defending the square," Jack said. "We told him to get everyone there and under his protection."

"You're trusting that space twat on this?" Tc'aarlat asked.

"What choice do we have? You were taken by the bad guys," Jack replied. "We need to get back to the shuttle. Zorxia might have some ideas. I thought I saw the wheels turning. That is, if the Onbir didn't get her."

"Zorxia is with you?" Tc'aarlat wondered, looking around. "She's clearly the smart one of you two."

"She was busy providing a distraction at the time and

was a bit too preoccupied to come and hold your hand. She sends her love, though, complete with bunny kisses, you fucking jerk."

"I'm sorry," Wo'Fek interrupted. "Aren't you friends?"

"Yes," Jack replied. "Tc'aarlat is my best friend, and that's why I came up here looking for him, knowing he would have found you. He cares more than he'll ever admit."

Jack gestured for them to back up against a wall. "I hear something."

"Bullshit tumbling from your suckhole," Tc'aarlat said in a low voice.

"I hear it too." Wo'Fek craned her neck to listen.

"Inside," Jack encouraged, pushing Tc'aarlat through an opening and behind a wall. Jack leaned out to see what was coming.

Hundreds of Onbir security guards marched down the street in a line like an army of soldiers ready for battle. If they had faces, they would be sporting their most determined looks.

"What? What is it?" asked Tc'aarlat, who hadn't seen the army marching by. "It's something fucking bad, I can tell."

"It's an army of Onbir, hundreds of them," Jack replied. "They're heading out of the city toward the trail leading down the mountain."

"Then we're out of time!" Tc'aarlat exclaimed. "We've got to go."

"It's not that easy," Jack replied. "There's a metric fuckload of them. I was barely able to beat one, and I had a boulder to hide behind."

"We'd better hope that Bon Noh has his shit together, then." Tc'aarlat scoffed. "These guys are fast, can fly, and are invisible to the masses. I hate to say it, but it looks like it might come down to that wankstain."

19

Renasta, New Fruling, the Square

Bon Noh strolled across the town square, projecting confidence with each step. Inside, he was scared shitless. The Enkelites had shown him one of the victims to give him an idea of what he was protecting them from.

To his credit, he didn't spout the technicolor yawn. He maintained his poise but swallowed hard throughout. One was enough, and there were forty-nine more just like it. A murderer was running loose, and not just a killer, but one capable of shredding flesh and painting a room with the blood of his victim. The horror would haunt him forever.

He maintained his false bravado as he looked around the square at his handiwork, his hands placed on his hips like a benevolent superhero. He wore a look of grim determination. His crew worked quickly to round the people up and bring them to the area while his ship, the *Joshua*, hovered overhead.

He decided on a tactic he had used a number of times before. The *Joshua* would extend its shields ever farther, increasing the perimeter and covering the whole of the square and the surrounding area with an impenetrable shield. It would act as a protective bubble over the people.

"Theeyej," he called to his second in command. "When will the town be secured?" Bon Noh was happy he had kept the fear from his voice. He felt the courage of doing what needed to be done despite the fear telling him to flee.

"Soon," Theeyej replied. "There is a problem, though…"

"Which is?" enquired Bon Noh.

"In order to fit ten thousand Enkelites beneath our protection, we've had to extend our shields farther than they were designed to go. It's putting a strain on our engine," replied Theeyej. "There is another problem as—"

"Our engines can handle it," said Bon Noh, brushing his second's information aside. "Like us, they know the value of preserving life of all kinds."

Bon Noh glanced at the three Elders approaching him. He gave them a respectful bow and retrieved the comb from his pocket, making sure his hair was ready in case of spontaneous photo opportunities.

Hozgak stated, "My entire flock is here."

"Of course," Bon Noh replied. "My shields can hold against anything."

"My flock is here too," Nee'pkan said. "Except for Wo'Fek and her son, who I cannot find."

"I must ask," Hozgak started. "What is it that we are being defended from?"

"Something terrible," Bon Noh replied, raising his head as he talked, seeking praise for his bravery. "I received word from *Fortitude* that you needed protection. Then I saw one of the victims from last night's attack. After that, there was no denying the danger."

Bon Noh and the Elders climbed the stairs to the top of the grand hall to look down on the square. The area was full to bursting, ten thousand Enkelites rubbing shoulders with each other and creating a sea of faces trying their best not to panic.

After a few troubling hours, stories of the dead were already running rampant. Enkelites torn apart. Fear cast its own stench across the masses.

Nee'pkan raised his hands and called for calm. "Our trials to establish our new homestead continue. With the help of Bon Noh and Captain Jack Marber, we will get through this. We ask for your patience and understanding while our friends stand between us and the evil that's out there. We shall persevere."

Hozgak touched his fellow Elder. "Well said, Nee'pkan." He lowered his voice. "If only it were true."

Renasta, New Fruling, ICS *Fortitude*, Hangar Bay

Benjamin ran down the corridor, making a beeline for the pounding that reverberated toward him. He turned a corner and found Adina, no longer a werewolf, wearing shredded clothes and hammering on the door to Jack's quarters.

She stopped when she sensed Benjamin.

"What do you want?" She focused on the pistol in his hand, which was leveled at her. "This is what I get for sparing your life."

"This is what you get for costing me mine," Benjamin countered.

"You are bottom-feeding gutter slime. You were before we met. You'll continue to be after I never see you again. You'll be that whether you kill me or not. Too bad you won't learn it until after you pull the trigger. It won't make you feel any better about how pathetic you are." She turned back to the door. "Imis. I know you're in there, and you need to come out so we can get to your mom."

"Stop. I don't want the boy out here."

"Which is all the more reason he needs to be out here." Adina decided to change her tactics, no longer taunting him or challenging his manliness. "Don't make a mistake you'll regret. You're better than that. Imis!"

"You can't save her or any of them, let alone yourself."

"What are you talking about?"

"You haven't realized that you've unleashed demons? Only one thing in the universe kills like that, and it's the Skrima. They come from the Etheric, and they rip people apart. They look like Satan's own harem."

"What? Skrima? I've never heard of them. You're making stuff up just so you can shoot me while I'm looking puzzled. That's really dicked up."

"They are hush-hush. Anyway, it's time we got down to business. Raise your hands and lean against the wall." He aimed.

Adina turned toward the door and leaned against it instead of the wall. It was a feeble attempt at giving Benjamin the finger. She didn't think he would shoot someone in the back.

"I need you to come out, Imis. We have to go. Your

mother isn't going to rescue herself. She needs her son to do it."

While Benjamin was working up the courage to shoot Adina, the door slid open. Adina stumbled, and Benjamin jerked his pistol into the air and squeezed the trigger.

The discharge filled the corridor with a brain-shaking concussion. Adina dove on top of the boy to protect him with her body.

Benjamin held his head with one hand while he apologized for the misfire. Adina stood, lifted the boy to his feet, and glared at Benjamin while brushing Imis off. She took his hand and headed for the nearest airlock.

"Let's go find your mother."

"Adina," Benjamin called, but she was already gone. He closed his eyes and flopped to the deck.

Renasta, the Mountain Range Beyond New Fruling

Jack, Wo'Fek, and Tc'aarlat waited for the Onbir army to pass, then followed them out. Tc'aarlat hung onto Jack's arm and felt useless since he could no longer see the enemy. Wo'Fek clasped his other arm, but he couldn't see her either. They continued through the pass and down the mountain to where Jack had landed the shuttle.

As they approached the craft, the hatch opened, and Zorxia waved them in. They stumbled aboard and buttoned it up.

"You found Tc'aarlat, but what about Wo'Fek? Is she dead?"

Jack laughed. "No, she's right here. Put on your goggles."

She held them to her head but didn't put the band around it. "Wo'Fek! I'm glad you made it." She rushed in to give the Enkelite a hug.

"What now, Jack?" Tc'aarlat asked.

"We get that thing out of Wo'Fek's head, and then we see how your buddy Bon Noh is doing."

Zorxia pulled out the toolkit, and with the goggles on, she was able to make quick work of the implant. "There's going to be some pain, but that can't be helped." With a single violent tug, Zorxia pulled it free from Wo'Fek's temple.

She gasped at the brief agony of the extraction before blinking as reality returned. "It's good to be back," she said.

Tc'aarlat smiled when he saw her again. She rushed into the Yollin's arms.

"What happened to you guys?" Zorxia asked. "You look like hell."

"Glad to know I look like how I feel," Tc'aarlat replied, helping Wo'Fek into one of the many low-gravity chairs Bon Noh had placed in the shuttle. He flopped down next to her.

"You managed to escape," Jack stated. "Did they do anything…"

Zorxia shook her head. "No. They didn't make it to any of the settlements. After a while, they gave up. They must've been called away to join the army that passed right before you showed up."

Wo'Fek spoke up, her face full of concern. "What are we going to do about saving my brethren? And my son is down there."

"I won't let anything happen to Imis," Tc'aarlat

promised. "We're going to fly back right now and save everyone."

"There are four guns on the planet," Jack noted. "We're no match for them."

"We can't give up," Tc'aarlat pleaded while holding Wo'Fek's hand.

"We're not giving up. We need to find the right plan to stop the threat. Since we can't take that army on head to head, we need to think of something else."

"Do we know what they're after?" Zorxia asked. "Is it as simple as they want the people on their planet gone?"

"They think the Enkelites are a threat," Tc'aarlat said, turning to her. "They want to wipe them out because of it."

"Why do they think the Enkelites are a threat? How do you know any of this?"

"We met their top dog," Tc'aarlat said. "Designation One. It told us a bunch of stuff. It didn't say why it thought the Enkelites were a threat, though, just that it *knew* they were dangerous."

"Think carefully." Zorxia hopped her chair closer to him, leaning in to catch every word. "What else did it say? Anything important?"

"I don't know. The Onbir are an advanced race who use their displacement in time to their advantage. They said something about their twin suns exploding when their species was just developed, and they've been in stasis for thousands of years. Those guys are essentially the security guards," Tc'aarlat said with a shrug. "Typical stuff. They were woken up by a force of magnetism, and—"

"Magnetism?" Zorxia repeated. "They were put on alert when I rescued you guys from the bottom of the ocean?"

"Must have been," Jack agreed. "I think we need to—"

BEEP. BEEP.

An incoming call from *Fortitude*.

"Captain Marber." They knew that voice. It was the one and only Solo, and she sounded panicked. "Something's happened. Benjamin has come aboard the ship again, and worse, Adina is transforming into a werewolf and back more rapidly than she's ever changed before. She left with Imis in search of his mother."

"Imis!" Wo'Fek cried. "Is she safe with Adina?"

"Sometimes she's dangerous when she's transformed, but I don't see her hurting a child no matter what," Jack answered. "I would bet my life that Imis is safe with her, but neither of them will be safe if they run into the Onbir."

"I think I understand." Zorxia started pacing, mumbling to herself before speaking aloud. "They said they were woken up by the magnetism, which was me rescuing you from the ocean bed."

Jack huffed. "We don't have time for—"

"Adina said she was rescued by something invisible that could lift the rocks off her, and it took her to safety," Zorxia said. "That must have been the Onbir, but I don't think they were rescuing her."

"It does seem out of character." Tc'aarlat shrugged. "But then, what were they doing?"

"Studying her," Zorxia said. "Imagine you're the Onbir. You wake up to a powerful force on your homeworld that's real close to where you're hidden, so you investigate. You come across a woman, and upon studying her, you find she is far more than she seems. This person can become a vicious animal at will, and there could be more of her. That's what they thought was the threat. That's why when you approached them earlier, they saw you as a threat too!"

"The Onbir aren't after the Enkelites. They're after Adina." Jack jumped to the communication microphone. "Solo, you've got to get out of there. You have a whole lot of trouble coming your way. Where's Aliporta?"

"Aliporta is not on board," Solo replied.

Tc'aarlat vigorously shook his head. "No, Designation One specifically said he wanted to destroy the Enkelites. I was there when he said it."

"*You* named them," Wo'Fek clarified. "Designation One didn't have a name for humans before you came along. It thinks that an Enkelite and your Adina are one and the same."

"That means the Enkelites are still in danger," Tc'aarlat said.

"No, I don't think so," Zorxia said. "Otherwise, they would've destroyed the settlements before now. I think they know the Enkelites are no threat, and that's why they're not after them. They'll be going after Adina and any other human on this planet."

"They murdered fifty Enkelites. I don't think anyone is safe."

Zorxia's face fell. How could she have forgotten about the horror that had befallen the Enkelites?

Jack looked angry and determined. "We still need a plan. Where do we go from here? How are we going to stop the Onbir and save Adina?"

"We have to find Designation One," Zorxia said. "The Onbir must be connected to one another. If their race is that advanced, maybe Designation One is the server? The core?"

"Shutting him down shuts it all down," Jack finished. "Looks like we're splitting up. Me and Zorxia will track down Designation One and figure out a way to shut it down."

"We'll track down the *Fortitude* and save Adina and Imis," Tc'aarlat said, moving to the pilot's seat. "I'm not a big fan of Bon Noh, but I appreciate his shuttle."

"We've got our missions." Jack gestured to Zorxia. She pulled her goggles into place, checked her weapon, and gave Jack a thumbs-up. Jack put a friendly hand on Tc'aarlat's shoulder. "I know what the Elders said to you, mate. If I'd have known then, I wouldn't have argued with you."

"It's not your fault," Tc'aarlat said. "It's them who are the big hairy dickheads."

"Good to have you back."

"Didn't you hear me?" Tc'aarlat smiled at him. "I said I quit."

"Does that mean I still get the ship?" Jack moved to the hatch, grinning all the way. Tc'aarlat watched him with the slightest shake of his head. "You can't go back on that."

"It's yours," Tc'aarlat replied, powering the shuttle up. "Just as soon as you give me the half you owe me."

"Yeah, I was expecting that. Good to have you back, buddy. Let's do some damage."

Renasta, New Fruling, ICS *Fortitude*

Benjamin looked at the small blaster in his off-hand. Blood oozed from his shoulder, and the shock of his injury was overwhelming the adrenaline surge. He leaned heavily against the wall. The pistol clattered to the deck.

"Benjamin, this is Solo, and I have to bring it to your attention that we're leaving."

"Leaving?" Benjamin wondered. "Where to?"

"Captain's orders. We have enemies inbound."

"Enemies? What kind of enemies?" His mind started to cloud from the loss of blood.

"Bad ones," Solo replied. "Very bad."

The ship lifted into the air, swiveled in the direction they needed to go, and accelerated quickly before decelerating just as quickly.

The ship rocked suddenly and violently. Benjamin slipped to the deck, his legs failing him. He was no longer afraid. The ship was under attack, and there was nothing he could do about it. If anyone was going to fight the battle, it was Jack, Tc'aarlat, and Adina.

The Shadows. They were already on the ground where they could do the most damage.

Solo's voice came back over the loudspeakers. "They're here."

Renasta, Bon Noh's Shuttle

The shuttle shot past the tops of the trees at maximum speed. Tc'aarlat bobbed his head as if trying to push it faster. The Onbir were on their way to attack the *Fortitude*.

"After everything we've gone through, we can't let them get to the ship," Tc'aarlat growled. Wo'Fek stood by his side, worried about her son.

"What did your captain mean when he said the Elders

had spoken to you?" she asked him, choosing this moment since it could very well be their last.

"My captain?" Tc'aarlat said. "Oh, Jack. Uh, he meant one of them paid me a visit and had a talk."

"A talk about us?"

"Yeah." Tc'aarlat shrugged. "I wasn't going to tell you because it was bilge that spilled from Nee'pkan's mouth. Runny shit."

"It was about us being together, wasn't it?" said Wo'Fek. "I bet he gave you a speech about how incompatible we are and how being together was bad for the flock."

"It's like you were there. What you said. Exactly that." Tc'aarlat looked at her. "He talked to you too, then? That fucking shit-stain."

"Apparently, people spotted us around the new settlement and on the arks," said Wo'Fek. "They've been talking, as people who have more time than sense do."

"Fuck 'em." Tc'aarlat spun the helm, and the shuttle somersaulted through the air as elegantly as any bird. The radar painted the *Fortitude* not far away. Tc'aarlat pointed the shuttle toward it and renewed their forward speed.

"Do you?" she asked.

"Do I what?" Tc'aarlat asked, glancing at her.

Wo'Fek leaned toward him and placed a hand on his knee. When he looked at her again, she had something in her eyes. It wasn't lust, and it wasn't quite love either. It was something between. "I know you care about me, Tc'aarlat. I know it."

"I do care about you, Wo'Fek," Tc'aarlat said. "I'm just not... I'm not very good with this emotional crap-heap stuff."

"You can answer this next question in any way you are comfortable with," she continued. "You can say yes or no, nod your head, or squeeze my hand tightly, but you have to give me an answer. Can you do that and promise it'll be the truth, Tc'aarlat?"

"I promise," he said.

"Do you have feelings for me? Real feelings? Love?"

Tc'aarlat gripped the controls tighter, his knuckles turning white. At that moment, he could see every relationship he'd ever had, and the moment was a lot shorter than it should have been. He had never been successful at relationships. The longest he'd ever been around one person was Jack. Even his parents hadn't wanted him. His life had been about violence, destroying the lives of others. Taking what he couldn't have.

"Tc'aarlat, please," Wo'Fek pleaded. "I have to know."

"I-I..." Tc'aarlat stuttered, but he didn't know what to say or how to say it. He didn't even know how to begin to articulate his feelings. "I'm not good at talking about my feelings. I'm bad at it. Very bad."

He didn't answer the question.

He saw the *Fortitude* on the main screen. He pulled away from Wo'Fek, placed the uncomfortable goggles over his eyes, and focused on flying the shuttle. "Imis is counting on us."

Wo'Fek sat back and sobbed softly. She had been given her answer, and it had not been the one she was hoping for.

20

Renasta, City of the Onbir

Jack found the city just like it had been the first time he walked through—abandoned. But this time, there were no Onbir warriors hiding in nooks and crannies. He just needed the artificial life form called Designation One to be where Tc'aarlat said he would be.

The Yollin had given what sounded like explicit directions, but Jack was having a hard time finding the starting point the verbal map counted on.

Zorxia had heard the same directions and was equally confused.

"We've already been there once," Jack grumbled. "I went a much longer way to get there. Wait a sec. We need to backtrack to where I first saw him."

Jack took off his goggles and pointed.

"Right there." He retraced the steps in his mind. "Got it. Follow me." He held his goggles to his face so he could rapidly switch views to keep his reference point in sight.

Zorxia followed, amused by Jack's running commentary about everything Onbir, with spicy bits of flaming vitriol reserved for the Yollin.

But the words weren't angry. They were nearly reverent in their condemnation. "You two-legged, hard-headed, knuckle-dragging, scabby, pustule-infested, crumb-sucking, ass-wiping, crack-snacking cockwomble. You are such a fur-brained... Ah! Here we are." Jack bent down to pick up the device Tc'aarlat had ripped out of his own head.

Zorxia oriented herself and started walking. Jack let her go since she marched smartly in the direction he remembered Tc'aarlat specifying.

They started to jog. Every second they wasted was one more second of the Onbir soldiers delivering the full might of their firepower into the *Fortitude* and the Enkelites.

Neither said they needed to hurry, but by the end, they were sprinting.

They stopped to catch their breath. Both were enhanced, but their fitness didn't include running. They lived in space.

"What if I was able to shift them further out of our time until they lived completely in another dimension? Unlike now, where they retain a physical link to our time."

"Isn't that a bit extreme?" Jack asked. "Sounds like genocide."

"I'm not sure it is," Zorxia replied. "It's just a thought, but it would depend on getting one of the living Onbir out of stasis."

"All we have to do is ask, right?" Jack smiled and pointed at the final doors.

"Can't hurt." Zorxia nodded and headed for the door.

Jack stopped her. "I was kidding. If we give Designation One any time to think, it'll kill us and continue its plans to exterminate every other living creature on Renasta."

Jack pushed the door open, revealing a hallway ahead.

"Damn. I thought we were here." They hurried forward. Jack pulled his JDS and dialed it to nine.

Renasta, New Fruling, ICS *Fortitude*

The *Fortitude* jerked and wove through the air, acting more like a compact fighter than a full-sized starship. Solo increased the gravity on certain plates in the corridor to hold Benjamin in place.

He groaned as he came to. The sounds of explosions as energy weapons pounded into the gravitic shields got his attention immediately. He tried to sit up.

"Solo, what's going on?" he managed.

"The Onbir. We are bearing the full burden of their onslaught. As long as we remain in the air above New Fruling, we are at great risk."

"What about the automated program I installed? That should provide you extra capacity."

"Yes and no," Solo replied. "I'm going to take us into orbit." The ship stood on its tail and accelerated skyward. The impacts on the hull lessened but did not disappear.

"They fly, don't they?" Benjamin mumbled, his head swimming from the lack of blood.

"Yes."

"The good news is you're leading them away from New

Fruling. The bad news is that once we're destroyed, they will descend upon them."

"Starting with Bon Noh's ship. Once that's destroyed, nothing will keep them from completing their genocide."

"Only you, trusty steed," Benjamin said. "Activate my program and deliver massed firepower the likes of which you've never seen."

"It'll burn out my power relays, transformers, and circuits."

"Nah." Benjamin slumped back to the floor. "It's got a failsafe to keep it from exceeding a hundred and thirty-four percent."

"Because design tolerance was one thirty-five?" Solo argued.

"Exactly."

"That's when the ship was new, you idiot!" *Fortitude* bucked under heavier impacts from Onbir weapons modulated to penetrate the shields.

Solo guided the ship away from the square in case she was killed and the ship destroyed. The debris would rain into the fields instead. "Activating the program and preparing to fire. I condemn you for all eternity for installing your malware on board this ship."

"Mal where. Say it slowly with me, Solo…" He passed out before the AI could reply. The shields started to hum beyond full strength as they turned into a resonance field ready to emit an electromagnetic pulse to disable their mechanical enemy.

Renasta, New Fruling, Bon Noh's Shuttle

The shuttle didn't have any weapons, but Tc'aarlat arrived at an alternate solution. He chased the Onbir skyward as they arrowed after *Fortitude*, continuing to fire at the ship.

Relentless. Single-minded in their efforts to bring the ship down.

Tc'aarlat dove through their formation, crashing into a line of them and circling back for another run. The impacts were as destructive as any weapon, but once the Onbir saw the tactic, they spread out, making it harder for Tc'aarlat to hit multiples on one pass. There were too many for him to keep it up for long, even though the shuttle's maneuverability was almost as good as a starfighter's.

He had started at the bottom and kept working his way upward, as long as they didn't shoot at the shuttle. It wasn't designed for combat and wouldn't survive more than a hit or two before coming apart and scattering debris and their blood and guts on the ground below.

"Can we get on board? Is that possible?" Wo'Fek asked.

"We could get into the hangar, but I wouldn't risk it!" Tc'aarlat shouted back. "As soon as we open those doors, all these fuckers are going to fly in. They're like ants; once you have them, you can't get rid of them."

"You can't get rid of ants? Simply ask them to move."

"Ask them?" Tc'aarlat replied. "You can't ask ants to move."

"Well, we Enkelites can," Wo'Fek replied. "We've always had an understanding between us and animals both large and small."

"Okay, I think we can—"

The sky lit up in a bright digitalized blue as a large

bubble of lightning expanded from the *Fortitude* and hit everything around it. The Onbir. The shuttle. Everything caught between those. Wo'Fek screamed at the sudden burst of energy, but Tc'aarlat had seen it before. They'd been hit by an EMP launched by the *Fortitude*.

"Nice," he said to himself. It was a smart tactic. They were being attacked by robotic entities, which meant the enemy was probably susceptible to EMPs, but it was fucking crazy to do it while they were several kilometers in the air. The Onbir fell first, seemingly dead and limp, plummeting like dead birds.

Then the *Fortitude* nosed over until it was pointed at the ground, where gravity was pulling it home. It tried to glide, but it was too big and heavy without sufficient lift from the small wings. Like a stalled airplane, there was only one place for it to go.

"Hang on!" Tc'aarlat shouted.

The shuttle hit the top of a loop and turned downward. The power was gone and the systems were dark. The manual controls were more of a struggle, but Tc'aarlat managed to bring the shuttle out of the spin with a hard left rudder and use the vehicle's lifting body like a wing to point the nose toward the vast ocean.

If they hit it at a shallow-enough angle, they would skip and settle. That would soften their landing. But an Onbir managed to get in front of them, then it self-destructed. Then another. Those systems must have been hardened against the EMP, and they terminated the robots before they could fall into enemy hands.

It was a short-lived theory since the blasts threw them

off-course. The second one stole their life, and they plum-
meted with the aerodynamics of a rock.

Tc'aarlat pulled as hard as his strength would allow, but
the nose wasn't coming up quickly enough. The treetops
rushed toward them. The ship hit, and the stubby wing
caught and threw the shuttle into a spin. It shattered
branches and came apart when it hit the hard ground.

21

Renasta, New Fruling, ICS *Fortitude*

"Power. Power," Solo begged. First to come online were the attitude thrusters. Solo jacked them to one hundred percent to slow the ship's descent. "Come on, you gutter-slug!"

Very un-AI-like, but she was being trained in human-isms by the best.

When the end is imminent, one should give the finger to the Grim Reaper while shouting obscenities. It was the only way to go, according to Captain Jack.

"Suck. My. Ass!" The engines sputtered and coughed with the return of unregulated power. "Ball-slapping knob-gobbler!"

The ship jerked from its vertical descent and leveled out. It raced over top of Bon Noh's ship, skipping off the shield wrapped around it and the town.

The shield sparked, flashed with the impact, and faded out.

"Sorry, jagoff," Solo said. She banked hard and raced

back toward the area where the Onbir had crashed. Many had survived, but they didn't survive the *Fortitude*'s forward cannons. Solo slowed the ship and strafed anything metal and shiny. She walked the cannon back and forth across the debris field to turn it into a junkyard. After one solid pass, she declared herself on a search and rescue mission to look for where the shuttle had gone down.

She had seen it when it was too late. Guilt was obsessing her circuits. Solo had killed the people who were coming to her rescue and who she was fighting for.

The Shadows, all except Adina. Gone.

Renasta, City of the Onbir

Tc'aarlat's directions, although detailed, were worthless.

"This was what he said," Zorxia proclaimed.

"I agree. Exactly what he said. Every turn was as he described. What a cockwomble."

"You like him, don't you, even though he pisses you off?"

"He's my best friend." Jack shrugged. "At least, the best I've ever had. He can get under your skin, but his heart is in the right place. He says he doesn't care, but he does. You have to watch what he does, not listen to what he says. What you saw with Bon Noh? That guy is scum. He deserved it."

"He didn't fight back."

"No one said eco-terrorists weren't brave. He loves being the victim and loves lording it over people if you concede anything to him. He didn't own the Shadows until he pulled us off the bottom of the ocean, but that was you and Aliporta. He wants us to owe him when he put us there with his made-up bullshit. Fuck that guy."

Zorxia squeezed his good shoulder. "Holding onto your anger?"

"None of this would have happened if that asshole hadn't sent us into that trench. None of this!"

Zorxia shook her head. "The inevitable was only delayed. Sixteen thousand years had passed. They were going to wake up any day now. No, it's better that we were here for it. Had we not been, the Enkelites would have been slaughtered to the last person."

"Like the first fifty were. Probably a test, even though they were looking for the werewolf within. They did to us what they thought we were going to do to them. Is that what an advanced race looks like?"

Jack stomped his foot and was ready to go.

"No. We need to talk with them—the real Onbir, not the metal monsters. Something's wrong with their programming. They're defective."

"They're assholes," Jack stated. He clenched his teeth and ran at a pace he knew he could maintain, not knowing how much of the city they would have to explore before finding Designation One or the original inhabitants and their stasis chambers.

Renasta, the Woods Beyond New Fruling

Tc'aarlat groaned and crawled out of the wrecked cockpit of the shuttle. "I am alive!" he declared in a raspy voice. His carapace had protected him once again. But he hadn't been alone.

He started digging with one hand for Wo'Fek, finding her where the co-pilot's seat had been. She looked like she wasn't breathing, and blood pooled from a gash along the side of her head. Wo'Fek hung limply from the straps in the remains of the chair.

Tc'aarlat fought off his own straps and climbed over to her, ignoring the pain that sought to claim his body. He tamped it down. He had something he needed to do; he had a person counting on him. Tc'aarlat felt her wrists, but he couldn't feel a pulse.

"Fuck. Fuck, fuck, fuck!"

Tc'aarlat pulled her out of her seat and placed her on the deck. He began to pump her chest in a regular and precise rhythm, but he had never done this before, so he had no idea how it worked. "One, two... Come on, Wo'Fek, get up."

One. Two.

One. Two

One. Two.

Nothing was happening. He tried blowing into her mouth, using his mandibles to latch on. Nothing. Tc'aarlat refused to give up as long as there was any hope.

"Oh, fuck." Tc'aarlat crumbled. He took her hand and gripped it tight, so tight it was on the verge of breaking.

He stared at her. Tc'aarlat had seen death a thousand times but never like this. He took a sharp painful breath. "I care about you. I'm not...this isn't...you're, like, the first person that has ever understood me. You're the first who made me want to be a better person."

He compressed her chest for another minute, not knowing what else to do.

"This is what happens whenever someone gets too close to me. They end up fucking *dead*." Tc'aarlat wiped a tear on his shoulder as he kept trying to revive Wo'Fek. "Oh, shit. I'm such a fucking coward. Why didn't I tell you this while you were alive? I'm sorry this happened to you, and fuck, you have a son. You're another person that would have been better off staying away from me. For what it's worth, you can take my apology into the afterlife with you, not that it does any good."

Tc'aarlat pulled her body close to him, wrapping her in his arms and holding her tightly. She was soft and still warm. He ran his fingers through her hair and across her skin, and he failed at trying not to let memories of her overwhelm him. Wo'Fek remained motionless. Tc'aarlat couldn't stop the tears. They came in a flood, the gates opened to release all his anguish from the entirety of his life's failures.

Renasta, New Fruling Town Limits

BOOM! The tree Adina had been close to a few seconds before exploded in a shower of splinters. She dove for Imis to protect him. When the wood and debris stopped raining down, Adina looked for the source.

Judging by the trees and brush being cleared as they passed, two Onbir were tracking her through the woods. "Run, Imis!"

The boy took off in one direction. Adina knew they were after her. She bolted in another direction, leading them away. She zigged and zagged, checking out of the corner of her eye to make sure they were still following.

She thought they were. She felt the fury coming into her—rage at being the prey and not the predator. In the space of one step, she turned from human to werewolf and accelerated away from her attackers, then looped back and came at them from the side, leaping and seeking something to bite. She landed on the machine, clamped her jaws on a protrusion, and wrenched it free. She removed a second before bolting away.

Blasts followed her into the woods. She looped back again and leapt upon an Onbir. Something that felt like a battering ram hit her midway to the soldier. She flew away, pain wracking the side of her body.

A cacophony of terror ripped into the trees and through the space where the two Onbir soldiers had been. The screech and cry of torn metal told her wolf ears that the monsters were dead. ICS *Fortitude* raced by overhead, banking sharply as it went through another search grid for more Onbir.

She changed back to human form, her clothes nothing more than tatters.

The fire suggested *Fortitude* had won the fight, so she waved the arm on her good side. "Give 'em hell."

She tenderly stood, in agony from her crushed ribcage, but unlike Jack, her nanos were intact.

"Imis," she called in a weak voice, but he didn't respond. She backtracked along the route the Onbir had taken through the woods to find the spot where they had split up.

As her ribs healed, she moved faster. She turned where Imis had run to find him no more than ten meters away.

"I came back when I saw you weren't with me. I

thought you were afraid, but that's not true. You led them to a place where your ship could kill them."

"Yeah, kid. They needed to die. It would have been much easier if I had my JDS with me, but I left that secured in the safe because I didn't trust myself. I thought I had lost my way."

"We're right here," the boy replied. "There is no other place one can be. My mother taught me that."

"Your mother sounds like she understands. Let's go to the town and see if anyone has news about her. If they don't, we'll start our own search. What do you think about that?" Adina held out her hand, and Imis took it.

He assumed a look of grim determination and tightened his grip on Adina's hand as she powered forward.

Renasta, City of the Onbir, Designation One

"This is it," Jack stated. "Fucking Tc'aarlat. Right means left and straight means backward."

Before them was the double door Tc'aarlat had described in painstaking detail: the cogs along the sides, the sheer size, three times higher than necessary, and in Tc'aarlat's words, the feeling that it led to a big fat dickhead.

They were soon to meet the creature known as Designation One. Jack had no plan besides confronting the creature and persuading it to stop the attack.

"You ready?" Jack kept the Jean Dukes Special in his hand, figuring the easy answer was to blow the creature away. He checked his recovering arm, shifted the weapon to his right hand, and dialed it back to eight. Better not to miss, even though eight would blow a massive hole in the side of the building and Designation One would be flushed out with the debris.

Zorxia moved to the door and inspected its individual parts. Jack stood back and let her work, keeping an eye on the corridor. He switched between the goggles and his normal sight. They were alone. The Onbir had committed all their forces to the attack and cleansing the new life off their planet.

"Very interesting technology," Zorxia murmured. "I'm not sure I can get it open, though. There's a complex design to this, and I don't think it has a key."

"Then how does anyone get in?" asked Jack.

"No idea." Zorxia shrugged. "It could take years of research to uncover this door's secrets."

"We don't have that kind of time. We've got right now." Jack marched past her, and with the butt of his pistol, he banged on the door. "Hey! You've got intruders out here. Open the door and deal with us!"

"I don't think that's going to—"

There was a creak, followed by the shifting of the many gears around the door, and they took a few steps back as it slowly opened. The complexity of what they saw inside the room gave them pause, but the resolution to their problems was there.

Designation One dominated the space.

The room was a jungle of cables and wires, with an individual sitting at the center of everything they could see. Once they had crossed the threshold, the door slammed shut behind them.

"Hello, Enkelites." The machine bowed slightly. "Congratulations on making it this far into the city. Your determination must be commended since it is not an easy place to navigate."

Zorxia held up one hand before getting closer to the machine, studying its parts. "We are humans, not Enkelites, and we want only peace. Our finding you and you us has been a mistake. You know very well that we couldn't see you, not until I developed these goggles. We had no way of knowing you were here. Are these the advancements we're to look forward to, not allowing for a mistake you knew other races would make? That's evil, so maybe *you're* the ones who should be eliminated."

"Not the approach I would have used," Jack mumbled.

Zorxia gave him the side-eye, knowing it was exactly the approach he would have used.

"Do you know why we're here?" Jack asked, stepping forward.

"I can only assume you want to negotiate." The machine jangled its cables and rattled connected devices for some unknown reason. "You are invaders, and dealing with you harshly will send a message to everyone else not to come to this world."

"That is serious bullshit," Jack replied. "Grade A, one hundred percent manure. Bull-fucking-shit. Look at the races who are on this planet right now: humans, Enkelites, Malatians, and even a Yollin. You cannot stop the wave. All the races can travel between the stars with impunity."

Zorxia picked up on Jack's thoughts. "Your firepower? You better have something else up your sleeve since we've transmitted the coordinates of this city. Next group that comes will drop hydrogen bombs from orbit. You won't even see them before your existence ends. This isn't a threat, but it's the reality when you conduct the genocide of a people like the Enkelites. You kill them all, we'll kill your whole race. With the time distortion, it'll be as if you never existed. Bye."

Designation One stilled. "Mutually assured destruction. Is that how humans negotiate?"

Jack smiled. "Although *we*," he gestured at Zorxia and himself, "may die, humanity will not. You will. Your entire race will be wiped out. The people in stasis will disappear in an expanding fireball with temperatures approaching that of your star. You're supposed to be smart. Run those calculations."

Designation One went silent.

Zorxia glanced at Jack.

Jack raised his JDS and took aim. "I'm done fucking around since your army of mechanoid whatever-the-fuck-they-ares is attacking the settlers on this planet. Call them off right-fucking-now."

Designation One assumed a low and steady tone of voice. "I am the protector of the people. I am responsible. I have failed."

"No, you haven't," Jack replied. "You've taken a wrong turn, but you can get back on track. The right turn is to talk to us. Let's get those people out of stasis and see how we can share this planet in a way that is beneficial for all. The universe is a far different place from what it was when the Onbir went to sleep sixteen thousand years ago."

"Time to try a different approach." Zorxia held her hands behind her back as she studied the machine. "Call off your attack, and let's keep talking."

"You don't understand. The Onbir security forces have been destroyed. Your people have won the battle. They have dominated us as we've never been mastered before. I have failed to advance. We have been stagnant while the rest of the universe caught up and passed us."

"That's what happens when you isolate yourselves." Jack didn't want to show his relief at the revelation, but he relaxed. They'd won the fight, but what was the damage? He holstered his pistol. "We have found that we're better together—all the races. Isolation and fear are no way to live. It's a great universe out there, Dezi."

"Dezi?"

Zorxia looked at Jack with a smile and a twinkle in her eye. His thoughts jumbled. He forced himself to tear his gaze from hers.

"Dezi. That's you since Designation One sounds like it came from a technical manual. We recognize that you are sentient, even though you were manufactured. We don't judge races on the nature of their existence. Talk to us about the Onbir. Let us see what we can do."

Renasta, New Fruling, the Square

Bon Noh's shield collapsed after the impact with the *Fortitude*. The Enkelites huddled together, terrified by the battle that raged around them.

After one last strafing run from *Fortitude*, the sounds stopped, and a heavy silence descended over them. The void of the unknown.

Bon Noh's men shifted and kept looking toward the ship. After a minute, it descended outside the city.

The men ran for it.

The Malatian tried to maintain his composure. He strode through the square against the press of the Enkelite masses. "The battle is over!" he declared without knowing. "Our time to move on has come. You have demonstrated your relentless drive to build a new world, and I know you will. I'm glad I could help in some small way."

He waved and held his hands up, all smiles as if leaving a celebration in his honor. Once beyond the bodies, he hurried toward his ship, only to find Adina and the boy Imis blocking their way.

"You cowardly fuck." Adina snorted. "You don't know if the battle is over or not. You lost your shields, and now you're running. You are nothing more than a fucking bully."

"Why, Adina, you're looking poorly. Too many violent blows to the head?" He tried to work his way around them, but Adina was having none of it.

"You're going to apologize to these people for ordering them around."

"I saved the Shadows. I protected the city. I ensured there was no life when we had reports of organisms. I. Me. Bon Noh. No one else. Take your self-righteous Shadow drivel and open your eyes. There are other people out there who are doing more for this galaxy than you. It's you who can't reconcile yourself with reality."

Imis let go of Adina's hand and closed on the Malatian. He studied Bon Noh's face.

"That's right, son. This is the face and mane of a hero," Bon Noh declared.

The boy twisted into an uppercut that tagged the Malatian right on his twig and berries. He collapsed with a grunt of pain and writhed on the ground, holding his private bits.

"You can't project your bullshit on me, Bon Noh. You were feeling guilty about putting us in that trench. Otherwise, you wouldn't have done anything. You extended your shield over New Fruling because you thought there was no risk. As soon as your shields failed, you bolted. You're a coward and a bully, and the Shadows will make sure the entire universe knows it. Now get the fuck out of here."

Adina took Imis' hand, happy that he had taken action but unsure if she wanted to say anything about it.

"No, wait!" Aliporta shouted, running toward them. "I've been running tests. I think we can end the time shift, but I need to put the terraformer back on Bon Noh's ship."

Adina scowled. She returned to the Malatian and hauled him to his feet. "Sounds like you've volunteered to help us—out of the kindness of your heart, of course, you lame fuck." She looked at Aliporta. "The world is going to shit, and you were researching?"

"Someone had to. You guys handled it." Aliporta waved her hand dismissively.

Renasta, the Woods Beyond New Fruling

Tc'aarlat continued to hold Wo'Fek. He didn't know what else to do. There was nothing else he wanted to do. What he'd denied himself in life, he sought in death. But not his, the death of a person he couldn't be open with when that was all it would have taken.

"You are the dumbest of dumb people. The Shadows are

better off without you," he declared. "Dumblemore, the wizard of stupidity. That is so Tc'aarlat. The universal failure."

"You're not," Wo'Fek mumbled.

Tc'aarlat stared. "How are you not dead? You were dead."

"I assure you, I'm not, but I *am* in a great deal of pain," she explained, finally opening her eyes.

"You had no pulse," Tc'aarlat argued.

"You can't feel an Enkelite's pulse," she replied, relaxing into his arms as well as she could as her body trembled with spasms and mini-seizures.

"Here, this will help. It is the only thing I can do." Tc'aarlat pulled out his small knife and sliced his arm until the blood ran freely, then dripped it into Wo'Fek's head wound. She closed her eyes against the splatters. He continued speaking softly. "I guess there *is* something else I can do. I can tell you that I think I love you. I don't know what that is, though. I've never loved anyone before."

"I know, Tc'aarlat," she murmured.

The flapping of wings signaled the arrival of an over-sized bird.

"Mist! I have missed you," he said. "I love Mist. She's a good bird."

The Raal hawk landed on Tc'aarlat's shoulder and looked the Enkelite over before turning her attention to the Yollin. She squawked and flapped her wings.

"Everything is going to be all right," he cooed to her. "Can you get help? Does this mean *Fortitude* has landed nearby?"

The bird didn't respond. She leapt from his shoulder and flew through the broken shuttle's open side.

Tc'aarlat used his knife to dig into his arm again since his nanos had already stopped the bleeding. Tc'aarlat wasn't finished helping Wo'Fek, not while he was still conscious.

Renasta, the Woods Beyond New Fruling

Mist flew above the trees, but once she spotted Adina, she circled down to harass the engineer, darting away and then returning when Adina and Imis didn't follow.

"She's trying to tell us something." Adina looked at the distraught bird. "Tc'aarlat. You found Tc'aarlat."

Mist flew away again, but this time Adina ran after her, nearly dragging Imis, who still had her by the hand. They raced a short distance to find the crashed shuttle. Mist landed on top of it and screeched to shatter the woods' calm. Again and again, she let out the Raal hawk's terrible cry.

Adina picked her way inside to find Tc'aarlat and Wo'Fek.

Imis cried, "Mother!" and tried to get past Adina, but she caught him before he hurt himself on the sharp edges of the torn metal. She carried him to his mother.

"My son," Wo'Fek muttered, eyes fluttering until they stayed open as the Yollin's nanocytes worked to repair the damage to her body. She tried to sit up. Tc'aarlat and Imis both helped.

Imis dabbed at the wound on her head, and the blood

cleared away. "Whose blood is this?" Imis looked at Tc'aarlat's arm, still healing from his last cut.

Wo'Fek smiled at the men in her life.

It wasn't Nee'pkan or any other Elder there to help her. It was Tc'aarlat, the one she was forbidden to see, and her son Imis. Neither had given up the search for her. "Where are the others?"

Imis shrugged and hugged his mother tighter.

"Aliporta thinks she knows a way to stabilize the Onbir into our time," Adina offered. "But she has to use Bon Noh's ship."

"Fuck that guy!" Tc'aarlat blurted.

"I punched him right in his lady bits," Imis said proudly. He looked Tc'aarlat in the eye. "You look like ass."

"I feel like ass," the Yollin replied.

"You smell like ass," Imis countered.

"Is this what my life has become?" Wo'Fek shook her head.

"You're the adult here. You tell us." Tc'aarlat winked at Imis.

"Stop saying 'ass,'" Wo'Fek stated.

"I think that's bullshit," Imis replied.

"The most bullshit that bulls have ever shit."

Wo'Fek closed her eyes. "Stop saying 'bullshit.' Imis, those are Tc'aarlat words, and they are not to be repeated."

"Mom! Taccyrat is cool. I want to be cool."

"Taccyrat is not cool," Tc'aarlat said. "He's an ass, a bullshit-spewing ass, but your mom makes me want to be better, so I will be, for you and especially for her. Let's find *Fortitude* and see what's going on."

Wo'Fek was able to stand, and she checked herself

where she'd hurt before to find that her injuries were mostly gone.

"You saved me," she said, diving in for a hug that Tc'aarlat was ill-prepared to receive. His mandible jabbed her in the forehead. "On second thought…"

She held out her arms, and Tc'aarlat enveloped her in his.

Adina smiled from near the hatch.

"Time to go, people," she said once the two unclinched.

ICS *Fortitude*, New Fruling Town Square

The Enkelites drifted away. With the imminent danger behind them, they would return to their fields and crops, where the serenity of the land would embrace them and give them the peace they sought.

They deplored wars, even ones fought on their behalf. No one thanked Tc'aarlat, Solo, or Benjamin for their work in defeating the Onbir forces. The Elders had a different take.

Nee'pkan was first at the hatch when it opened to discharge one figure, a person the Elder had not yet met.

"Are you responsible?" Nee'pkan demanded.

"Yes. I'm responsible for defeating the Onbir, mostly. I had lots of help."

"I saw no threat except the one you created with your weapons and your alien ways."

Benjamin raised one eyebrow. The short walk to the hatch had worn him out. The damage to his shoulder needed to be repaired before it could heal. He wasn't enhanced like the others. He should have been in a doctor's care, convalescing.

"No threat?" Aliporta said as she bumped past him on the way inside *Fortitude* to move the terraformer to Bon Noh's ship. "Did your fifty people slaughter themselves? Must suck going through life as a dumbass."

She disappeared inside the ship.

Tc'aarlat, Adina, Wo'Fek, and Imis appeared. "Did someone say the terraformer needed to be moved?" Tc'aarlat asked.

Wo'Fek glared at the Elder as they entered the ship one by one. Adina waited outside.

"You might want to rethink the future of the Enkelite people. Xenophobia is an ugly look that leaves deep scars. Recognize who is helping you and who isn't. Know that your future is in the hands of others. Denying that only reflects on you and your ignorance. Please take a moment to answer this question. What are you doing to guarantee the Enkelites' future?"

Adina left him standing there in silence, threw Benjamin's arm over her shoulder, and guided him into the ship. "I'm angry at you, you bastard, even though shooting you has provided some relief," Adina said in a muffled voice from inside the ship.

The cargo hatch lowered, and after a few moments, Tc'aarlat walked out, struggling under the burden of the terraformer. It was balanced on a stretcher, and Adina and Aliporta lugged the other end. Imis and Wo'Fek walked behind them.

The hatch to the ship closed, nearly hitting Nee'pkan as

it went up. Solo was less than pleased with the Elder, too. He had caused the Shadows pain, and the AI didn't like it.

She closed the cargo hatch too because she didn't want to deal with any more intruders.

Renasta, City of the Onbir

"Behind me, you'll find a doorway. Go through that and down twenty flights into the bowels of the mountain. There, you'll find the stasis pods," Designation One told them.

"We need you. Thank you for not making me blast you. I would have felt bad."

"You would not have been able to revive the Onbir from stasis had you destroyed me."

"Sounds like a win-win, then. I don't shoot you and don't commit an alien genocide. Thank the hairy spider gods!" Jack gave the machine two thumbs-ups.

Zorxia stared at him. "You are a strange man."

"Thank you. And for the record, you make me feel funny."

Zorxia laughed. "After seeing you Shadows in action, my scientific findings are that you are all emotionally incapacitated in your inability to discuss your feelings like adults."

"Who's a dolt?" Jack held up his hand to stop Zorxia. He peered into the space behind the section of wall that slid inward to reveal a hidden staircase. "What's twenty flights when you're going down?"

"What goes down must come back up again."

"That's not how gravity works," Jack parried. He started down the stairs.

"Did you forget about the little incident that left you underwater?"

"That was what, two years ago?"

"Three weeks," Zorxia clarified.

"Mentally and emotionally stunted," Jack said, pursing his lips and staring at the steps while descending. "I guess I've been called worse. It's clear that you want me, though. You do, don't you?"

"Oh, yeah. Once we get back to the ship, we have business to take care of."

Jack froze, then turned to her. He couldn't see her eyes because of the goggles, but the smile on her face told him everything he wanted to know. "Then what the hell are we doing lollygagging? Designation One, bring those people out of stasis. Let's fix this. Time is wasting!"

Captain Jack Marber bolted down the stairs, taking them three at a time.

"Emotionally stunted. And such a man," Zorxia called after him.

Bon Noh's ship *Joshua*, Flying over Renasta on the Way to Onbir

"Hooking something up a second time is so much easier," Aliporta said to no one in particular. Adina watched her work while Tc'aarlat and Wo'Fek sipped the drinks that had graciously been provided by the cowed crew. Bon Noh stayed near them, not out of a desire to be helpful but because he couldn't walk. Imis kept making a fist and flashing an uppercut at him.

"You fucking suck," Tc'aarlat told the Malatian.

"You're using my ship. What else do you want from me?"

"I want you not to suck," Tc'aarlat stated simply.

"Yeah," Imis agreed. "Stop sucking."

Bon Noh pulled back from the boy.

"Imis," his mother called and gestured for him to join her. She pushed him into the seat next to her, away from Bon Noh.

"There!" Aliporta declared. "All set. Tc'aarlat, can you tell me when we've arrived?"

The Yollin kissed Wo'Fek's hand as he stood before grabbing Bon Noh and propelling him toward the cockpit. The main screen showed the mountains. Tc'aarlat moved up front and pointed.

"The city is there. Climb higher. It towers in a way you've never seen. Hover the ship in the pass. There is a bridge, then the city will spread its wings before you."

"You sound like a candy-ass," one of Bon Noh's men said.

"How many of you need to have your noses flattened against your ugly faces before you get it? No one likes you, no matter how tough you try to act. They don't respect you either." He looked over his shoulder to determine how loud he could speak without Wo'Fek hearing. "You can lick my shell, wanksplat."

The pilot started to stand.

"Just fly the ship!" Bon Noh blurted. The vessel descended to hover where Tc'aarlat told them to.

The Yollin yelled over his shoulder, "Now!"

Joshua dipped under the seizure of power by the terraformer but quickly recovered as the engines countered the outgoing magnetic surge. Wave after wave rolled from the ship, building strength with each ripple until the tidal wave splashed over the valley in which Tc'aarlat had told them the Onbir city had been built.

The pilot jerked back at the seemingly instantaneous appearance of a massive gleaming city.

"Wow," Bon Noh stated before summoning the courage to confront Tc'aarlat. "I was right. There *is* intelligent life here. The Enkelites must leave at once."

Despite Tc'aarlat's promise to Wo'Fek, he found that he couldn't hold back. He grabbed Bon Noh, slammed him into the wall, and dragged him to the side hatch. They were low enough that it opened against the air pressure.

"You wouldn't." Bon Noh's face filled with fear despite his bravado. Tc'aarlat picked him up with two hands and tossed him through. The Yollin tapped the close button and returned to the cockpit.

"Take us back to New Fruling, please," he said in his most pleasant voice.

22

Renasta, City of the Onbir

When they reached the stasis chamber, they were taken by its immensity. An entire race held in one chamber, stacked like cordwood in tiny capsules barely larger than their bodies, which were about half Jack's size.

He looked at the nearest capsules.

A voice boomed through the space.

"Your time of rest has come to an end. It is now the time of sowing, the time to challenge yourselves and join a universe that has passed your level of advancement. Rise, Onbir. Rise and earn your place as the masters of science and art."

An unseen force pummeled Jack and Zorxia from behind. They stumbled together and then went down. The chamber disappeared.

"What the hell?" Jack looked frantically for the source.

"Take off your goggles," Zorxia told him, wrapping an arm around his waist. He reciprocated, pulling off his goggles and tossing them aside.

The capsules were opening, and the first Onbir crawled from them. The nearest looked alarmed, but Jack and Zorxia smiled.

"I am an official representative of the Federation. It is my honor to welcome you to a new dawn, a new era. I have no idea how, but it appears that you are no longer out of time with the rest of the universe." Jack bowed to the first Onbir to approach.

"How is that possible? We put all our science into resolving that issue but could never succeed. We were resigned that we would always be alone."

"We've made a few advances in the past sixteen thousand years. We can travel the galaxy, reach the stars in the blink of an eye. There is much to share. Oops, almost forgot. You are sharing this world with the Enkelites, an advanced society that prefers an agrarian lifestyle."

"We like to eat," a second Onbir noted. "Where are the security forces?"

"They started a war against us and lost. But we aren't like them, willing to commit genocide."

"We never programmed them to commit genocide!" a third Onbir remarked, panic in its shrill voice.

"Then you have much to discuss with Designation One. We will leave you to reestablish yourselves in the city and will return tomorrow with information on Renasta, which is what we call this planet, the Enkelites, and the Federation. This planet is outside the Federation's sphere of control, so there's no pressure. You are free to be yourselves as long as you don't try to kill any more Enkelites."

"Any more? Oh, my!" the shrill voice exclaimed. "How many have been injured?"

"At least fifty were killed. I don't know how many more from the latest attack. We were here trying to get Designation One to call it off."

The Onbir started up the steps. Jack took Zorxia's hand and they walked up with them, answering a constant barrage of questions before Jack interrupted.

"I only have one question. As advanced as you people were, you don't have an elevator?"

ICS *Fortitude*, Bridge

The crew had gathered on the bridge before departing Renasta.

Jack draped himself across the captain's chair as if he had no bones. Adina stared at the smug look of satisfaction on his roughly shaven face.

"What's up with that look?" Adina asked.

Tc'aarlat waved a hand dismissively. "That's his 'I just got some' look. It's rare."

"Hey!" Jack straightened.

Zorxia strolled onto the bridge. "I heard that, Taccyrat!"

Imis chortled in the corridor.

"If you'll excuse me," Tc'aarlat said officiously. "I have duties to which I must attend."

"Why are you talking like that?" Jack wondered.

"Because I can't say fuck or bullshit anymore and not even dumbass, so I don't know how I'll ever be able to converse with you."

Jack gave him the finger before standing and offering the captain's chair to Zorxia. She didn't take it, opting to ease under his arm and pull him close.

Tc'aarlat tousled Imis' hair. Wo'Fek was waiting for him, and they left hand-in-hand.

"Everyone has someone but me." Adina frowned.

Aliporta shook her head. "You must come to know yourself, the same as Tc'aarlat and Jack. Can we know someone else if we aren't comfortable with who we are?"

"Biblically," Jack quipped. Zorxia poked him in the ribs.

"I'll figure out how to control my changes since the meds don't work anymore."

Aliporta smiled at her. "Ecaterina, Charumati, and a few more can help you."

Adina nodded and shrugged with a half-smile. "Maybe not having anyone is best right now."

Jack flexed his arm. "It's about time this healed."

"Thanks to the Onbir. Their medical technology rivals the Federation's. I think we'll be able to exchange a lot to help each other. I like the Onbir. Designation One, not so much," Zorxia said. "At least he's been demoted to head of city facilities and maintenance and removed from direct control of anything remotely related to security."

"Try to commit genocide on behalf of your people, and that's what you get. He's lucky he didn't get unplugged."

"Kind of. A team has gone in to reprogram him while trying to understand where their logic chains failed for him to arrive at the conclusions he did." Jack kissed the top of Zorxia's head.

Aliporta left with Adina for one last check of their cargo.

"I better get ready. We'll be on our way soon, and that means I'll be back in the lab going over the results of the terraformer. There's so much data."

"You won't consider staying on with the Shadows?" Jack wondered.

Zorxia shook her head. "You know I can't. I have a job and a life where you are always welcome. Visit me often, but not until I get a bigger bed. I miss you already, Jack."

"Captain Jack Marber, space rogue and winner of a lady's heart."

"Something like that." She kissed him and headed out, leaving Jack by himself.

He climbed back into the captain's chair. "Solo, help us find new leads, please. The Don is our next target. I owe it to Tc'aarlat to find him. It is what the Shadows must do."

"Of course, Jack. Let's review the last contact. From the information I've been able to review, I don't believe the Garbolglox Roddy Parper was being truthful, despite Tc'aarlat's threats. I think you should interrogate him. I believe you will find it enlightening."

"Solo, you are a dream. Set course for *Briccan* so we can drop off Zorxia and Aliporta as well as that scumbag Benjamin. Next stop after that is Talth. We'll revisit Mister Parper and see if he changes his story. I'm already looking forward to a conversation with a Garbolglox. What are their weaknesses?"

"You could stay," Tc'aarlat pleaded.

"Your work is dangerous. Imis needs to grow up here, learn our ways. You must return often, and once we establish trade, we can visit you."

Tc'aarlat petted Mist almost compulsively. "I never know where I'll be."

"And that's why we can't go with you. Go take care of business, Tc'aarlat, and when you are right with Don Gan'barlo, come back here. I'll have room for you in my home. You will always be welcome. The stove is only one button-press away from heating up a good meal for you."

The Yollin clicked his mandibles. "I like you for more than your cooking," he admitted. "But I love your cooking."

"Sounds like everyone gets what they need." Wo'Fek ducked under Tc'aarlat's mandibles to hug him.

Imis pulled on the Yollin's pocket. "You don't have to go," he whined.

"I do, and that means you have to be the man of the family. If anything happens to your mother, you must fix it, just like you did when she was taken by the metal creatures we couldn't see."

"We can see them now," he said softly.

"So you know how scary they were, but you weren't afraid. Go, Imis, and do great things."

The boy smiled but didn't let go. Wo'Fek peeled him off Tc'aarlat's pants leg and waved on her way off the ship. Bon Noh's ship was parked nearby. Bon Noh stood outside, staring at Tc'aarlat and *Fortitude*.

Tc'aarlat made sure Wo'Fek wasn't watching so he could give him the finger.

Imis gestured with an uppercut. Bon Noh cringed before boarding his ship, buttoning up, and taking off.

"All's secure. Adina called as she walked back to the bridge."

Benjamin waved. He had been the recipient of Onbir medical assistance, too.

"Fo guck yourself, you slimy smashed turd," Tc'aarlat snarled.

"Fo guck?" Benjamin wondered.

"He's trying to learn not to swear because he has a girl-friend and he's trying to be a better man. Unlike you. Get back in your quarters so we don't have to look at you, or do you like the idea of getting pitched out an airlock?"

"I saved the ship. I saved the Enkelites," he cried.

"You sound like Bon Noh. Now, fuck off."

Adina joined Tc'aarlat and Jack on the bridge.

"Solo has a lead for us," Jack said.

Tc'aarlat perked up. "Don Gan'barlo?"

"Seems Roddy Parper wasn't telling you the truth."

"What a shlong-faced fucknugget!" Tc'aarlat declared before straightening. "I'm a work in progress."

AUTHOR NOTES - CRAIG MARTELLE
MARCH 31, 2021

Greetings, Shadows fans! Thank you for picking up your copy of Shadow Vanguard 5 – Alien Genocide! You are contributing to the legacy of our departed friend. By buying this book, you are putting money directly onto the table of Tommy's family. They count on the income from these books to simply survive. So thank you, from the bottom of our hearts.

We tried to have this book written by a third party, thinking that we'd be able to tweak it, but alas, the writer disappeared into left field and kept going with the plot. We dithered with it until Craig lost patience and pulled it back into his control at the beginning of 2021. Three months later, the book has been completely rewritten to establish a consistent plot and reaffirm the characters you love to follow.

Tc'aarlat gets prime time in this book. I hope that I've done him proud, as well as Jack and Adina. Each member of the Shadows goes on a different journey to find them-selves. There are some serious themes in here as there were in all of Tommy's books, but presented in a way that doesn't suck the life from you. We don't do darkness. We do reality with a smile.

Tommy delivered six outlines to us in the final weeks of his life to make sure that these stories carried on. We looked at our budget and decided to have three stories written and then give the funds from the other three directly to Tommy's wife. Money now and money later. The last three stories in the series will probably be shorts that we write at some later time when we have a few moments and as a way to reenergize the series.

Shadow Vanguard. A fun and wild ride with some crazy characters.

Shadow Vanguard 6 is next in the queue. I'll rewrite that one to bring it into alignment with the rest of the series. Don Gan'barlo can standby. He's got the Shadows coming and they're bringing hell with them in Shadow Vanguard 6 – *Family Reunion*.

That's it – I'm working on Judge, Jury, & Executioner 12 – Blood Trade, another book set in the Age of Expansion. And then I have a military science fiction book to write before getting back to more Age of Expansion. Ideas for books 13 and 14 are starting to gel.

Break is over, back on my head. Lots of words to gather into a nice, trim package, known as a story.

Peace, fellow humans.

Craig

Thank you for not only reading this story but these author notes as well.

First out of the gate is a massive tip of the hat to Craig Martelle, who pulled this book together with blood, sweat, and tears. Well, probably blood and tears. He did it during a freakingly cold Alaska winter, so if he did sweat, it would have turned directly into icicles.

Not the best solution to be a walking popsicle.

Without Craig, this book wouldn't exist for you to enjoy Tommy's legacy or provide a bit more to his family. So, raising a glass of my favorite beverage in Craig's direction.

To Lynne Stiegler, who edited the work without cost to support this book. To the social marketing and marketing teams who help promote it.

(*Editor's Note: And to Michael and Craig, who are giving all proceeds to Tommy's family!*)

And to you, the readers who pay it forward by supporting this series.

Thank you from the bottom of my heart.

Ad Aeternitatem,

Michael Anderle